ABOUT THE AUTHOR

STANDARDS OF STARLIGHT BOOKS

## ITHACA'S SOLDIER

Kelly Utt-Grubb was born in Youngstown, Ohio in 1976. She grew up with a dad who would read a book on a weighty topic, ask her to read it, too, and then insist they discuss it together, igniting her passion for life's big questions.

Prior to writing fiction, Kelly told the stories of small businesses and their founders so the most positive and authentic parts could shine through. She lives in the Nashville suburb of Franklin, Tennessee with her husband and sons. *Ithaca's Soldier* is her first novel.

www.uttgrubb.com

facebook.com/kellyuttgrubb

twitter.com/kellyuttgrubb

instagram.com/kellyuttgrubb

## ALSO BY KELLY UTT-GRUBB

### Love and Transience Novels

### Coming Soon

*Heavenmost*

*Mortal Darlings*

### Love and Transience Short Stories

### Coming Soon

*Love Becomes Us*

*Blue Like Thunder*

Be the first to know when new novels and short stories are released by signing up for news and updates at www.uttgrubb.com.

# ITHACA'S SOLDIER

## A LOVE AND TRANSIENCE NOVEL

### KELLY UTT-GRUBB

STANDARDS
OF STARLIGHT
· SINCE 2018 ·

Ithaca's Soldier is a work of fiction. Any references to historical events, real people, or real places are used fictitiously. Other names, characters, places, and events are products of the author's imagination, and any resemblance to actual events or places or persons, living or dead, is entirely coincidental.

2018 Standards of Starlight Paperback Edition

Copyright © 2018 by Kelly Utt-Grubb

All rights reserved. No part of this book may be reproduced in any form or by any electronic or mechanical means, including information storage and retrieval systems, without written permission from the author, except for the use of brief quotations in a book review.

www.standardsofstarlight.com

ISBN: 978-1-7324528-1-7

Cover art by Ivan Kurylenko

*For*

*Sam, Andrew, Christopher, David, and Harold*

*my men among men*

# ITHACA'S SOLDIER

# PART I

## NEW YORKERS

## GEORGE: HOME

Only a madman would move to Upstate New York in January. But, here I am in Ithaca. It's snowing. Hard. And I have two young kiddos and a pregnant wife in tow. My life is nothing if not interesting.

The family and I have been staying in a hotel the past couple of days while we wait for the moving company to haul our stuff up from D.C. We chose the Hampton by Hilton over on Elmira Road, per my grandpa's enthusiastic recommendation. John Wendell has probably stayed at Hampton Inns in at least thirty different states back when he and Grandma were in their traveling heyday, and he has the handwritten logs to prove it. He hasn't been out of Ithaca near as often since she died, but he's plenty familiar with the local Hampton because he recommends it to everyone who visits and then goes there and hangs out with them while they're in town. I suspect the hotel's close proximity of his favorite sandwich shop is also a selling point.

It's been nice to relax a bit without anything on the schedule. I love seeing Ethan and Leo's cute, chubby little faces as they scarf down bagels and Raisin Bran in the crowded hotel breakfast area. At ages four and two, they've already been to plenty of hotels, but every single thing is still new and exciting to them. Orange juice machine? Fascinating. Warming plates for the bacon and eggs? Awe-inspiring. It's a whole world we don't have at home, so they're -- understandably-- crazy for it. Aside from the breakfast area, the indoor pool is the other big highlight of the place. Admittedly, it's pure, simple heaven for a young family like mine. I'm pretty sure I tossed those little boys into the water more times than I could count yesterday, all while eyeing my smoking hot wife Alessandra as she lay sprawled out on a chaise lounge nearby, completely enthralled in some girly novel she picked up at the Walmart next door. I get all sentimental and choked up over this type of scene more than I should probably admit. But honestly, who needs a five-star hotel in an exotic location? Instead, give me a Hampton Inn next to a Walmart in my cozy, snowy hometown where I can admire my wife's body and throw my kids around in a pool. I'm a happy man.      I start my new job at Cornell the week after next, and I'm hoping the movers come early so I can swing by and meet the other engineering professors this afternoon before they head out for the weekend. The new gig is a tenure-track faculty position in the

School of Mechanical and Aerospace Engineering, with an emphasis on space technology. It should be a lot of fun. I've always loved electronics, rockets, and things that are loud and go boom. That's what led me to the Air Force as a young man. I signed up through ROTC in college and jumped head first into being a legit rocket scientist. Well, a rocket engineer anyway.

We're not checking out of the hotel until tomorrow since we figure there won't be enough time to get beds set up before these boys conk out for the night. Ali and I will do whatever unpacking we can this evening and then pile everybody into the Tesla and head back to the Hampton by bedtime. But first, we're having lunch downtown with Mom and John Wendell. Four generations! This simple lunch date is the kind of thing Ali and I would get all mushy over when we thought about moving to Ithaca. Mom's an only child without siblings and so am I, so I imagine it's pretty special for John Wendell to have his entire family right down to the great-grandkids in one place. The big, warm smile he can't hide when he sees us walking up the sidewalk tells me I'm right.

"George!, Ali!, E-boy!, and Leo the Lion!" John Wendell calls out from where he's standing under the cheerful red and white awning in front of The Cupboard Kitchen. He could have waited inside, but I guess he's excited. The Cupboard Kitchen usually has an outdoor table and chairs in the spot where he's standing, but they've removed those for winter. We all smile back so hard it almost hurts our cheeks.

It might sound unusual for a grandson and his

family to have such a close relationship with his ninety
—five-year-old grandfather, but it's a reality for us. Ali
and I share lots of common interests with John
Wendell. We did with Grandma too, and we miss her
terribly. Back before the boys were born, the four of
us-- Ali, me, John Wendell, and Grandma-- would
travel together as often as we could. We've been
cruising in the Caribbean, sightseeing on the East
Coast, and we've enjoyed waterfront dining and
dancing to Big Band music under the stars in too
many places to count. It's a shame so many years
separate us and that we couldn't spend more time
together.

I aim to make the most of the years John Wendell
has left now that we're going to be living nearby. He's
in fantastic shape for his age. Hopefully, he'll live
another five or even ten years. He sure seems like the
perfect candidate to be one of the lucky outliers who
live past one-hundred. He's pretty sharp mentally. He
doesn't walk with a cane or walker, and up until last
summer, he was driving himself around. Mom had to
intervene when a neighbor called to report him going
fifteen miles per hour the wrong way on Green Street.
He didn't seem to realize anything was out of the
ordinary and was pretty torn up about it, both because
driving has always been so important to him and
because he would never want to put others at risk.

The Cupboard Kitchen was named by the owner's
grandfather who passed away a few years ago. He was
known for cooking amazing dishes using ingredients
from his kitchen cupboards and wanted the restaurant

to have the same homey feel. Seems only fitting that it's the first place we get together with John Wendell now that we're officially Ithaca residents. The small, dim dining room is brimming with people when we walk inside, and Frank Sinatra's voice is crooning over the speakers with *It Had to Be You.* I thought maybe people would have stayed home given all the snow, but I guess winter weather is par for the course in a place like Ithaca. I remember once during my senior year of high school when we had so much snow over the course of a few days that it brought the city to a standstill. Today, though, people seem relatively unfazed.

Ever since I was a kid, John Wendell has done this thing where he stands beside me and sort of holds my elbow for a minute while my arm is bent. I don't know if he does it with everyone, or if it's our special thing. It's sort of like a squeeze of a hand or a pat on the back, I suppose. He's doing it now while we walk to our table and he whistles along with Frank's song. Ali sees and flashes me a knowing smile. It's good to be home.

"So, George," John Wendell says as he gets situated in his chair and hangs his coat carefully over the back. "How in the world are you, son?" I wonder if the waitress who just walked by thinks I'm really his son. Hey, I'd take it if she did. John Edgar Wendell is an incredible man.

He started calling me "son" around the time my dad died. I was sixteen, and even though we never really talked about it, I'm pretty sure John Wendell consciously decided to be a key source of stability in my life. Mom and I moved from Brooklyn to Ithaca a couple of months after the funeral, and it was John Wendell who attended my basketball games, helped me tie my tie for senior prom, and did all of the miscellaneous dad things which inevitably needed to be done. I'll never forget him showing up for me like that. When I was hurting, John Wendell stood by me. I mean literally stood by me. He'd seem to appear out of nowhere and I'd notice him sitting by me or standing by me as if to physically reassure me that I wasn't alone. It brings tears to my eyes just thinking about it. Sometimes all you need in the world is one good person who will simply stand beside you.

I suppose strangers might find it odd that I call him John Wendell instead of grandpa or grandfather. Mom calls him John Wendell as well, with a "Dad" or two added in every once in awhile. That tradition got started before my time, so I'm not sure how it came about. I mean, not only do we call him by his first name, but we use his last name, too. He's a guy who has a larger than life presence about him. I don't mean that he's a big man. In fact, looking at him now in his brown Mr. Rogers sweater (as I like to call it) and his crisp, starched, button-down collared shirt with tiny blue and white checks, he looks small. He's always been strong and healthy as an ox, but with a lean build. His spirit and big, warm presence seem to take up more room than his physical body does. This man can find the positive in any situation. He was a kid during the Great Depression, and when you ask him about the poverty and difficult conditions he experienced, he'll tell you about how his mom used the tiny bits of extra money his family had to bake bread for anyone who wanted a loaf, and how he had the best parents. He doesn't focus on the negative. I'm not even sure the man holds negative memories in that little bald head of his. We'd all do well to take a page from his book.

"I'm good, John Wendell. Really good. It's a little strange to be living in Ithaca after so many years away, but it feels right," I say as the waitress drops off a bread basket and some paper and crayons for the boys. "It'll feel a lot better once we get moved into the house and settled."

"I hear that," he says with a smile. "Your mom took me out to see the place last week and it is a looker. Our magnificent Cayuga Lake is right in your backyard. The views are stunning. You are going to be very happy there."

"You think so?"

"I sure as hell do."

"It's a little showy, especially for a place like Ithaca," I say, leaning in closer so the people next to us don't overhear. "I mean, I don't want to come across as pretentious."

"Now you sound like your mother, George. Your dad worked hard all his life and earned the money he left you fair and square. You shouldn't be ashamed of that."

Mom is sitting at the other end of the table near Ali, and I see her grimace out of the corner of my eye.

Mom feels even less comfortable than I do with Dad's money.

"I know, John Wendell, but it still feels funny. I'm not sure I'm cut out to be the wealthy type."

"And why not?" he asks. I can tell he sincerely wants to know. "Nothing wrong with being wealthy so long as you're a good man and you help others when you can."

The waitress is back and wants our drink order. Ice waters all around for the adults, and milk for the boys.

"I don't know. Maybe I'd feel better if I'd earned the money myself. I know Dad worked incredibly hard for it though."

"He wanted you to have it. Everything Alec Hartmann did was for you. He was self-made in every sense of the word, and he did it all for his family. Remember now, I was around for the whole thing from start to finish. You know," he says as he leans back in his chair and puts a hand down gingerly on the edge of the table, "I remember your dad's friendly eyes. They were an awful lot like your own. I remember the first day I met him. He was a scrappy go-getter and a little rough around the edges compared to your mom. He'd survived because he had to. He didn't have a close family to come up with. But I could tell from a mile away that he and your mom belonged together. There was a synchronicity between them. Even everyday movements like washing dishes or opening a car door, when done together, had an ease and beauty which, plain and simple, transcended this world same as what you see when you go to the ballet. They had real, true love, George. And you're the living, breathing result of that love come to life. Rest sure in that, son."

And now I'm all choked up in The Cupboard Kitchen. We've been here less than ten minutes.

Ali and Mom see what's happening from the other end of the table, but they don't interrupt. They know this is how it is with me and John Wendell. We go right to the meat of meaningful discussion almost immediately. Ali gets our drinks from the waitress and orders a buffalo turkey dip for the table. Ethan looks up from his coloring long enough to flash me a big smile, and Leo's lips curl ever so slightly upwards even though he doesn't make eye contact. They must feel the love in the room even if they don't understand everything we're saying.

I was away with the Air Force so damn many days over the past twenty years-- days when I didn't have the opportunity to sit with my family and feel the positive energy bursting right out from each one of them. I know I keep saying it, but I sure do love my people. I look around the table and into their eyes, and I'm smitten. I finally have a home that feels like a home where I *belong*. It's been a long time coming.

My eyes are still moist as John Wendell reaches into the breast pocket of his coat on the back of the chair and pulls out a folded section of *The Ithaca Journal*. "Have you seen today's front page?" he asks. John Wendell is a huge lover of newspapers. He reads them every day without fail and mails us articles he thinks we'll find interesting. He even wraps Christmas and birthday presents with the comics sections. But the look on his face tells me this goes beyond his usual level of interest.

"Not yet. What is it?"

"See for yourself."

I take the paper out of John Wendell's hand and slowly open it on the table in front of me. There I am, looking important under huge letters that read "Military aerospace pioneer and Ithaca native George Hartmann joins Cornell's engineering faculty." I'm surprised, and it probably shows. That was unexpected. Where did they even get the photo? Most of my career has been spent in special ops working on top secret projects. I've never been in the spotlight like this before. In fact, I have carefully avoided drawing attention to myself so as not to jeopardize national security. Although, I must admit, I'd probably be uncomfortable drawing attention to myself even if national security wasn't an issue. John Wendell chuckles out loud. He knows exactly what I'm thinking.

"It's a new world, George. You're back in your hometown now. You're Ithaca's very own soldier. Our guy. The town has a legitimate claim to you, and we're incredibly proud."

"I was born in Brooklyn, John Wendell, you know that. And I lived there most of my childhood," I say.

"I know, but you graduated from Ithaca High School. Your mom's from Ithaca, just like Grandma and me. You have roots here. You're ours, for better or worse."

I appreciate that. I really do. But my work at Cornell is funded by the DOD and will be classified. They recruited me based on my particular knowledge and experience, and although I don't yet understand the full scope of what we'll be working on I know enough to realize that the public might not be so enthusiastic about my participation if they knew the truth. John Wendell probably gets that general idea, but even he might not be too happy to hear the details.

As I ponder that uncomfortable thought, an older lady walking behind us on her way to the door stops and taps me on the shoulder. Her small group takes up a lot of space in the tiny restaurant. Probably eight or ten folks, presumably colleagues, stand around her and listen as she speaks.

"You're him," she says with wide eyes as she points to the newspaper spread out on our table. I can't immediately tell if her wide eyes are because she disapproves, or if she's sort of starstruck and in awe because the front page newspaper guy is sitting right in front of her. A jolt goes through me as the reality that this lady might not approve settles in on me. She might know what my new group at Cornell does behind closed doors. She looks kind of like an old hippy. The type they describe as crunchy like granola. Her hair is long and gray, and it's divided with clips into two long ponytails which rest on each of her shoulders. She wears simple rimless glasses, a thin strand of pearls around her neck, and no makeup. She looks highly intelligent. I wonder if she's about to get loud and call me out. I can easily envision this lady holding nasty signs and screaming at political protests. She probably went to jail a time or two back in the day in support of her political beliefs. Civil disobedience suits her. Ithaca is certainly a bleeding-heart liberal town.

After what feels like way too long, the lady's eyes soften and a smile appears, first from her lips and then her cheeks.

"Hometown hero," she says as she pats me hard on the back, almost like she's burping a baby. I force a smile in return and mumble something about how it's not quite like that, but before I can get anything intelligible out she grabs my hand and shakes it hard.

"Wonderful to meet you, Dr. Hartmann. Welcome home, sir."

The group of colleagues nod in agreement and add a few encouraging words of their own as they walk past on their way out. John Wendell beams with pride. That was close.

The rest of the lunch is uneventful, other than my noticing a creepy guy who came in after we did and who seems to be staring at us from a table in the back corner of the restaurant. I decide to let that go. Creepy guys are everywhere. What harm could he possibly do us here? We eat, and we talk. Ali and Mom run down a list of places to find necessities: Harold's for groceries and prescriptions, Glenwood Pines for a cozy atmosphere and an amazing burger, and the Cornell Lab of Ornithology for an educational, kid-friendly afternoon on days when the weather isn't good for playing outside. Ali has been in town to visit plenty of times, but living here will be a lot different than visiting.

When our bellies are full of tasty greens and artisan sandwiches, we say our goodbyes and pile into our cars. Mom takes John Wendell back for an afternoon nap, and the rest of us head to the new house.

## GEORGE: TAKING ROOT

I'm fiddling with a loose switch plate cover in the dining room as I wait for the movers. My lovely wife is waiting in the kitchen, propped up on the kitchen island. Poor Ali has been a trooper. I'm told it's not wise to move a pregnant woman. Goes against the nesting instinct and all. She isn't due until the end of February, but she looks like she could pop any day now. Apparently, that happens once you've had a couple of babies and the ligaments are all stretched out. She says the weight of the baby is hurting her back sometimes, too.

I find my wife even more attractive when she's pregnant. Which means I find myself having to take a breath and remember that she might be uncomfortable before I try and jump her bones. Like right now, as she bends over to pick up a water bottle that rolled off the counter and she lifts her tight, muscular backside up into the air pointed in my direction. I'm not sure if she's doing it on purpose or if she just so happened to angle towards me, but in a warm rush, I'm instantly ready to unzip my trousers, peel down her curve-hugging jeans, and place my hands firmly on her hips while sliding inside her from behind. If the boys weren't awake and in the next room, that's exactly what I'd do. She'd feign protest for a minute, saying things like how it's the middle of the afternoon and the blinds haven't been hung and anyone could walk up to the window. But then I'd wrap my arms around her, and slowly move my hands along the surface of her skin upwards under her blouse until they found her soft breasts and firm nipples. She'd melt into me and moan with delight. I could have Alessandra Davies every single day and never get enough. For now, though, I'll have to wait.

Ethan and Leo are playing on the living room floor with tiny trucks from their toy bags. "Vrooom, vrooooom," I hear cheerfully echo against the empty walls. Those toy bags are the ticket. Ever the practical one in our relationship, I had the idea when Ethan was a baby. We used to bring a toy or two with us when we left the house, but he'd always get tired of the same old same old pretty quickly. While problem-solving, I thought about the different kinds of gear required when conducting a military operation. I figured we should take the same approach to mobile entertainment for our little one: plan way ahead for every imaginable possibility. Ali was skeptical at first, and she laughed while watching me pack the little bag with what she considered way too many unnecessary options. Rolling toys, chewy toys, building toys, and colorful toys all got a spot. The very first time we used the bag at a restaurant, it worked like a charm. Ethan was about ten-months old and we'd gone out to a waterfront place on the Potomac to celebrate Uncle Liam's birthday. We knew it would be loud and busy and full of adults who wouldn't want to hear a baby fussing, so we came prepared. When Ethan got tired of a toy, we'd simply switch it out for a different type. If he was tired of the rolling car, we'd put it back in the bag and pull out a colorful board book instead. When that got boring, we'd hand him a few connecting beads to work with. He stayed occupied, and quiet, for the entire four-course meal with the exception of a little happy babbling which won the hearts of the restaurant staff. Good baby. And good daddy, if I do say so myself. We all need something to occupy ourselves with. I get it.     Our custom home on a hill with unobstructed views of Cayuga Lake has been built from scratch and fitted with a cozy, craftsman-style door I really dig. The kind made out of solid wood with three rectangular windows at the top. Ali's idea. Gooseneck lanterns sit dutifully on either side, ready to light the way home. There's a wreath in the back of our SUV she wants me to hang. It's a looker -- golden magnolia, lush cedar, vivid blue thistle, and tender eucalyptus, according to the item description-- handmade by a company out of San Francisco. She had the company make and ship a fancy wreath to us in D.C. ahead of time so we could immediately hang it on our new door. I'm not kidding when I tell people she must have been some sort of designer in another life.

We bought the house a couple of months ago when I first accepted the new position and we decided to make the move north. Even though the place had already been partially completed at that point, I couldn't imagine how we were going to whip the rest of it into shape from a distance. The first builder had gone out of business last summer due to a death in his immediate family, and the house had been sitting partially completed for several months. The hardwood flooring wasn't installed yet, a defect in the fireplace made it unsafe, and it looked like there might have been a water drainage problem in the front yard. Luckily, Mom jumped in and has been great overseeing the necessary construction projects for us. I suppose that's one major bonus that comes along with living near your mother. She found a builder with a specialty in mimicking original historic details from the local area, and boy, those folks are worth their weight in gold. The work was done on time and the place looks fabulous. I can't wait to get everything in and unpacked.

The house is big at more than seven thousand square feet, and luxurious. It's by far the nicest home we've ever lived in. There are six bedrooms and three and a half bathrooms. There's a large area in the finished basement that we've made into a game and media room, and an amazing screened porch on the back that looks out over the lake and surrounding woods. There are three total fireplaces: one in the great room, one on the screened porch, and one in our master bedroom which shares a wall with the master bathroom and can be accessed from either side. Ali can't wait to get into the clawfoot tub with a glass of Moscato and listen to cinders crack and pop in the fireplace. It's not like I've ever really been poor, but this is a whole new level. Even our street name, East Shore Drive, sounds rich.

My wife grew up wealthy in Manhattan. I doubt this house feels out of the ordinary for her. Her dad, Roderick Davies, is a famous playwright from London. Roddy has had more hit Broadway shows than I can count. On top of writing and directing plays, he somehow finds time to teach drama at NYU Tisch School of the Arts. Ali's mom is no slouch either. Marjorie Dyer plays a mean viola in the New York Philharmonic. She has proudly sat first chair as Principal Viola for the better part of two decades, and she doesn't show any signs of slowing down. Marjorie studied at Juilliard, where she met and married Roddy when he was a young visiting professor in the seventies. Together, those two provided Ali and her brother Nicky with the best New York City had to offer. To their credit, though, the kids are grounded in a way that doesn't always happen for rich kids in the city. They're good people.

My dad, on the other hand, grew up dirt poor in a little village called Bannersville in the Pocono Mountains of Pennsylvania. His parents got pregnant with him at their high school prom and tried to make a go of it. Uncle Liam came along not even eighteen-months later, but by that time the young family was already falling apart. Their dad took off for a stint in the Army, but never returned to the kids' lives when he returned to American soil. Their mom was often strung out on prescription meds she stole from the understaffed hospital where she worked as a pharmacy clerk, and she wasn't caring for my dad and his brother properly.

When Dad was three and Liam was two, their mom fell completely apart and abandoned them in heartbreaking fashion. Would you believe she left those boys alone in their upstairs apartment while she mailed a letter to an older couple she knew? She later said she felt certain they'd take the boys in, but still. What if they hadn't? What if the letter had been lost in the mail? It's hard to not be angry with her, but I assume she wasn't even in touch with reality at that point. Dad and Liam were left wearing nothing but pajama bottoms in the winter, and they spent nearly three days alone before Grandad and Grandmother, as I called them, came to the rescue. Thank God it was mid-week when the letter was in transit. If it had been over a weekend, I'm not sure the boys would have made it. And thank God they didn't figure out how to unlock the door because they could have wandered downstairs and into the busy downtown street outside. Dad was found with peanut butter crusted on his face and shirt. He had somehow opened the jar, or maybe his mom had opened it before she left. It looked like he had tried to feed some peanut butter to Liam as well, but no one knows for sure what the boys ate or drank during their three days alone. Both were dazed and withdrawn when they were rescued. They had, of course, soiled their pants multiple times, and because the wood furnace used to heat the apartment had burned out long before help arrived they showed early signs of hypothermia. EMTs who responded to the scene said it was one of the most upsetting things they'd ever seen.

Grandad and Grandmother Marks raised Dad and Liam as their own. They were some of the kindest, most forgiving people I've ever met. They even allowed Dad and Liam's biological mom to visit every now and then when she got up the money to travel north from her sister's house in Maryland. But they were urgently, painfully poor. Both were in their late fifties when they took the boys in, and they were barely getting by themselves. They'd had one biological son, Benny, who was a young adult at that point, and they'd never imagined having to support and care for two toddlers during what would have otherwise been their retirement years. They scraped together what money they could to make it work, mostly relying on social security disability benefits for a logging injury Grandad had sustained, and then later social security retirement benefits. They raised their own livestock and grew their own food, but there were times when it didn't stretch and they all went hungry. Other times, they couldn't pay the electric bill and were cold. They were too proud to ask for help.

I sometimes think about them and what it must have been like, especially because Ethan and Leo are

about the same age now as Dad and Liam were when
their mom left. What a completely different world that
must have been. Liam's the only one around to tell the
stories anymore, and he was so young when it
happened that he doesn't really remember the three
days spent alone in the apartment with Dad. What he
does remember is how close he and Dad always were.
They bonded tightly. Because no one else understood
what they'd been through. And because they were the
only blood relatives each other knew.

The minute Dad was old enough to get out and
get busy on his own, he did. When he was seventeen,
he saved up money from his part-time job at the
service station in Bannersville and bought a train
ticket to Brooklyn. He loved Grandad and
Grandmother dearly and hated to leave them and
Liam, but he had work to do. He made it his life's
mission to earn a fortune he could pass on to his
family so that none of his people would ever have to
suffer in poverty again. His determination must have
shown because as soon as he stepped off the train he
walked into the Food Center next to the elevated train
tracks on Bushwick Avenue and secured a full-time
job. He made a friend right away, too, in the owner's
son. Tommy Macca agreed to let Dad stay on the
couch at his apartment until he could find a place of
his own, and the two of them ended up long-time
buddies. When Dad opened his own store in the
borough five years later, Tommy was one of his first
employees, followed by none other than Liam
Hartmann himself. By the time Mom and Dad got

together and I came along, Dad was a successful businessman with a chain of thriving local department stores called Hartmart. He was careful with money and we lived frugally. I never had to worry about having the basics taken care of, but I'm pretty sure my childhood was very different than what my wife was living on the other side of the East River. No matter how successful Dad was, I think he held onto the fear that it could all be taken away at any moment. It's hard to completely shake the kind of extreme poverty he experienced as a kid. I think Dad's childhood also made him hyperaware of everything happening around him. He had to be in order to survive. And I think he somehow passed that on to me. I've always scanned every environment I've stepped into. I notice all the fine details. It's a skill which served me well in the Air Force.

Mom grew up comfortable enough in Ithaca, but for some reason, she seems to be morally opposed to being wealthy. I can't quite figure it out. John Wendell was a salesman for the New York, Auburn and Lansing Railroad, the only line to operate in Tompkins County. He was a careful saver and did more than okay for his family through smart investments over the years. He and Grandma were able to pay for Mom to attend nursing school up in Syracuse, no problem. And Mom makes a respectable living as a R.N. all on her own. She has for years. Dad left her a lot of money, too, but you wouldn't know it. She lives in a simple little house and chooses cars based on what looks least ostentatious. Her latest pick:

an older model Buick Century. I won't get started on her social justice warrior activities. Her heart's in the right place, but I think she goes overboard in sympathizing with the oppressed and demonizing the military and those in power. We agree to disagree on a lot of things.

The movers are here. Finally. I'm not going to make it over to Cornell today, but at least our things have arrived. I can see eight or ten guys huddling outside on the front stoop wearing nothing but t-shirts and jeans with long sleeved thermal shirts underneath. No coats. They look freezing cold now as the snow falls hard around them and their breath fogs up the afternoon air, but I'll bet they're anticipating the physical work ahead and know coats would just get in the way. I, for one, sweat my ass off when physically exerting myself if I'm bundled up too heavy. Then I get a chill from being all wet and sweaty in the cold air, and it ends up worse than if I had suffered through being cold in the beginning. These are practical guys, apparently. I can respect that.

"Come in, folks! Can I offer you some hot chocolate or coffee?" I hear Ali say as the group of them streams through the front door and the guys begin to take off their hats and gloves. It's probably good we haven't hung that wreath yet anyway. It would get bumped and banged around. And I know what you must be thinking. Yes, Ali had me haul our espresso machine with us in the Tesla, along with some handmade mugs featuring snowflake lace detailing, I might add, in order to make warm drinks for our guests. I mean, hey, these people are carrying our worldly possessions through the cold and snow and over the slick ground. She says it's the least we can do. They smile and seem to appreciate the gesture. Who wouldn't smile at a beautiful woman handing them a warm beverage on a snowy day? I have that wife. She is a treasure. They sip and make small talk before getting down to business.

It's remarkable, to reflect on the fourteen years me and Ali have spent together. We'll be celebrating another wedding anniversary this summer. Sometimes it feels like just yesterday that we met and like the world is whizzing by too fast. Other times, I'm convinced we've known each other forever and that there's no real hurry.

Our story began with good old Uncle Liam who happened to know Ali from a French cooking class he and his wife Estella took together in Arlington. Ali was a participant in the class, too, and they all got to know each other over the course of the three-month curriculum and then stayed friends afterward. As Ali recounts it, Liam once told her that she absolutely had to meet his nephew, big George Hartmann. "You're both knuckleheads," Liam told her with a grin. Looking back, I think that meant neither one of us much liked to follow directions or the beaten path. Which is a good thing, in my book.    Liam and I served together in Germany and then again in D.C. around the time Ali was also in our nation's capital attending law school. It was all very patriotic. As the story goes, Liam had told Ali just a few sparse details about me, but they were enough to pique her interest. He told her how I was so tall I parted a crowd as I walked, how I was from New York like her, and how I must have lived near her apartment building because there was a donut shop down the street and I often brought in a box of their warm, gooey goodies for my colleagues when I was running late. Guilty as charged. Uncle Liam told her I was smart, and that the Air Force trusted me with important jobs. He, of course, wasn't at liberty to go into any more detail about what those important jobs involved. Ali said she'd love it if Liam would arrange a meeting.    Fast forward two years. Yes, two whole years. Uncle Liam dropped the ball. Ali hadn't met me and still wanted to. Liam hadn't even mentioned her to me at all. I know, right?

Ali bumped into Liam in a grocery store parking lot one day and he explained how I was up for reenlistment and had to make a decision which might send me overseas for the next few years, effective pretty much immediately. "Come on, Liam," Ali said. "At least connect us before George leaves town so he and I can have lunch together." This was before the days of easy social media access to everyone you wanted to look up, and besides, I kept a low profile online due to the top-secret nature of my work in the Air Force. Liam assured her he'd make the connection.

Two weeks later, Ali was sitting at a table alone, studying for law school exams at the food court in Patriot Park mall. Odd choice, as I pointed out, but it was Christmas time and she had always loved the festive environment at the mall that time of year. Kids were all smiles riding the big, pretty carousel nearby, and the smell of freshly baked cookies filled the air. The music coming over the loudspeakers had Ali humming *Have a Holly Jolly Christmas* when she noticed me. I eased down at the table next to hers and our eyes met. As she tells it, I was a cool drink of water. I don't know about all that, but she says she loved my lush head of dark hair and friendly blue eyes. She remembers thinking right away that I had a family-man vibe about me and that I was surely already married. She was radiant. Like a beam of light. Her golden-brown hair fell just below her shoulders and framed her elegant long neck and her jawline. I thought she was out of my league. I was smiling. A lot. And I'm pretty sure it was a goofy smile, too. I couldn't seem to stop myself, even though I was trying hard to play it cool. I had zero game. Ali jokes with me now about how I was trained by the United States government to withstand torture in a prisoner of war situation, yet I came completely undone when I first saw her. She always asks how that even makes sense, and I don't have a good answer.

"Hey," I managed, nodding in her direction while grinning from ear to ear.

"Hey, how are you doing?" she said back, warmly.

"Good, um, good. Good," I stammered, wishing I'd been able to keep it to just one 'good.' Ali chuckled. She turned and looked down at her textbook, but definitely wasn't reading anything.

Neither of us had been planning to meet anyone that night. In fact, I was wearing one of my least favorite sweaters and felt self-conscious about it. The sweater was the kind I'd set aside and intend to get rid of, but for some reason would pull it out of the closet when I wanted variety. I think Mom gave it to me. It was a black turtleneck, and it had a snowflake design woven in small, straight rows. Let me just say, that snowflake design was a far cry from the sophisticated snowflake lace design on the handcrafted mugs Ali set out for the movers. And besides, I'm not sure how many grown men even wear sweaters with turtlenecks or snowflake designs on them these days. Over the years styles have, thankfully, changed.

Ugly Christmas sweater or not, I'm pretty sure I saw Ali's face flush with excitement as my gaze rested back on her and my huge smile returned. I don't think the smile ever left; maybe for a couple of seconds as I assessed the 'goods.' I must have seemed pretty enamored, so she figured she'd give me an in.

"Are you from around here?" she asked. "Need any directions, or restaurant recommendations, or anything?"

"Nope. I'm good," I said. Another good. Damnit. She laughed heartily out loud this time and covered her mouth with her left hand. No ring.

I looked down, so she looked back down, until about ten seconds later when I guess she could feel me staring at her again. I couldn't help it. I could not take my eyes off of her. She was magnificent. She'd given me a chance to talk to her in more depth, but I was too flustered to take it. I was embarrassed at my own dorkiness but seemed powerless to do anything about it.

"So what brings you to the mall tonight?" she asked, smiling her most sincere smile.

"Just looking around," I mumbled, then looked down again. I hadn't even taken the first bite of my General Tzo's Chicken.

And here's where it gets really interesting. Ali looked down again at her book, and she swears to everything holy that something magical settled over her. She claims that in that instant, she knew like she knew her own name that she was sitting right next to that big George Hartmann Liam had told her about. She doesn't know how she knew, but she knew. She remembers her body feeling almost numb as she opened her mouth to speak.

"Are you in the Air Force?" she asked.

"Yep," I answered.

It wasn't a stretch to assume I was military, what with the short haircut and the muscles and the close proximity to a plethora of military duty stations. I figured she might have known me from somewhere. But there was much more at work.

"Is your name George?" she asked.

"Yes," I said.

"George Hartmann?" she continued.

"Why, yes," I said, a little perplexed but having no real idea of the gravity of the situation at hand.

"Well, Liam Hartmann is your uncle, right?" I nodded eagerly as she explained. "I know Liam and Estella, and for the past two years, he's been telling me that you and I should meet because we'd be good for each other. He says we're both knuckleheads."

"Liam never once mentioned you to me," I said, smiling big, "but if you want to go out, we can certainly go out."

We talked for a while in the mall that evening and went on our first date to good old Outback Steakhouse two days later. The rest is beautiful history. We were engaged within six weeks and married six months after that. Needless to say, I passed on the overseas assignment.

Can you believe Liam? He finds the perfect woman for me, and then for two whole years never mentions her. We still give him a hard time about it. I always say Dad had to give an assist from the great beyond since his little brother fell down on the job. I mean, really, what are the odds that Ali and I would sit down beside each other at the mall, of all places? And that she'd almost instantly know she was, in fact, looking right at that big George Hartmann she'd been hearing about? It's not like she had that much to go on. She hadn't even seen a picture. Serendipity, plain and simple.

The movers are finished with their warm beverages now and are ready to get down to work. A tall, slender Asian man with a buzz haircut who seems to be some sort of supervisor or manager speaks for the group and outlines their plan of attack. They'll begin by hanging padded blankets on the interior doorways and walls in high traffic areas so they don't accidentally gouge up the place. Next, they'll bring large items in, starting with the upstairs rooms, then the basement, and lastly the main level so as not to have to step over a lot of things sitting around. Once that's done, they'll move on to the shit-ton of boxes located in the interior-most section of the truck back towards the cab. Each piece is tagged with a sticker bearing a unique item number. They'll check each one off their master list as it enters the house. I've heard horror stories about bad movers, but these folks seem pretty good so far. I guess we'll rule on that once everything is inside and in one piece.

The guys have spread out within the house and are prepping the doorways when our friends Duke and Jen pull up out front. Ethan recognizes their blue Subaru and squeals excitedly. They've been keeping Lady for us over the past few days since the Hampton Inn didn't allow dogs. Ali has Leo on her hip and is smiling happily as she walks to the door to greet them and to welcome Lady into our new home. German Shepards are notoriously territorial, so we know it will be important to help Lady get properly oriented.

Lady is such a good girl. She's big, even for a German Shepard, so to the boys, she must look huge. She's pushing ninety pounds. They ride her like a horse. We got her as a puppy when Ali was pregnant with Ethan, and it ranks right up there as one of the best decisions we've ever made. Lady is wicked smart and fiercely protective of the family. Having her around always made me feel better when I'd be gone TDY and Ali and the boys were home alone. I'd pity the person who had the nerve to physically threaten us. Lady would tear them up. She's dark as compared to the breed standard, with solid black on her face and back and only a smattering of brown in a ring around her neck and on the bottoms of her legs and tail. She looks kind of like a big black wolf, actually. I imagine she'd look damn menacing in attack mode, especially at night.

"Jennie!" Ali says warmly as she opens the door and reaches out her free arm to hug her friend tight. Leo lowers his head and flashes a shy smile. Ali and Jen are exactly the same height and even though Jen has dark hair and an olive complexion thanks to her mom's Korean descent, they look like a matched set. Maybe it's like how old married couples end up looking alike. These two clearly go together.

"Come in, come in, you guys!" Ali continues, standing on her tiptoes to wave in Duke as well. I pick up Ethan and walk over near my wife to greet our guests.

We're seriously stoked to have friends in Ithaca even though we just got here. What a bonus. Ali and Jen have been close friends all the way back to first grade in Manhattan, and Jen just so happens to be a Sociology professor at Ithaca College. Well, I say that, but the truth is Ali and Jen have been scheming about how to live in the same area together for most of their adult lives. This is a dream come true for them both.

Jen's husband Duke is a veteran officer with the Tompkins County Sheriff's Department and an all-around great guy. He and Jen have been dating for a couple of years and just got engaged over the holidays.

Duke is African American and his tall, muscular physique and impeccable sense of style are a perfect match for Jen. Together, they look like they're straight out of a GQ photo shoot. Duke and I have mostly bonded over basketball so far, but I look forward to getting to know him better.

"Hey, man," I say, as I do the masculine bro-hug thing. "We'll set that hoop up around the side of the house just as soon as this weather clears. Can I count on you to come over and help me break it in?"

"You know it, brother," Duke says with a smile. "You gonna let me see the entertainment situation while we're here? This big house is causing visions of Super Bowl parties and summer cookouts to dance in my head."

"Absolutely. You're speaking my language now. What good is a new house if it doesn't work for parties, right? Come on, I'll show you around," I say as we head down the long hall towards the kitchen. Ethan is still on my hip and going along for the ride. I turn to look at Ali on my way and we give each other a subtle nod. Without having to say any words, we have agreed that Ethan's with me and Leo's with her right now. We have to keep close track of them while the movers are in the house. Jen is still holding Lady on a lead, and it looks like she and Ali will work on getting the fur baby settled in.

Duke and I excuse ourselves as we step around a couple of movers and walk into the kitchen. "Check it out, man," I say. "Sub-Zero and Wolf appliances. Top of the line. Red knobs on the range and everything."

"Nice, man, real nice. The good life." Duke says. I feel a little self-conscious talking about things that clearly cost a lot of money, but I do it anyway because I've got to get more comfortable. Even though Duke earns a police officer's salary, Jen comes from a wealthy family just like Ali does. A nice big house is no doubt in his future by virtue of who he has chosen to marry. I'm pretty sure it's all good. Maybe they'll even get a place nearby.

"Did I hear that you guys are house hunting?" I ask. "It would be great if you end up with a home near us. We could be friends and neighbors."

"Right, right. We are house hunting. And wedding planning. And honeymoon planning. Jen has specifics in mind. I'm sort of along for that ride. She narrows down what she likes and then asks my opinion. It's a system that works. I think," he says with a laugh.

"I hear that. Ali definitely listens when I have a strong opinion, but we've sort of agreed that if I don't say anything, she's free to pick what she likes. I'm rarely disappointed in her choices. This house is case in point."

"Noted," Duke says. "I think that's what's happening with me and Jen. Hey, if we're anything like you and Ali, we must be doing something right."

Ethan jumps down from my arms and runs towards the pantry. "Daddy, Daddy, show him the food room."

"Ok, bud, good idea," I say as I raise my eyebrows and gesture Duke toward the huge walk-in pantry. A pang of guilt hits me. I mean, it's technically called a pantry and not a room, but Ethan's right. It is a room. It's not lost on me that people are starving all over the world and we have an entire room to store our food in. Food that we can easily afford to buy and stock these shelves with. Maybe I should have a talk with Ethan about how we describe the house. But how would I even communicate these types of concerns to a four-year-old? He shouldn't be taught to feel guilty about the house he lives in and the things we own.

"Look, Dukie," Ethan says as he runs around the perimeter of the pantry and traces his fingers along the built-in shelving. Ethan got the habit of shortening names and adding an "e" sound at the end from Ali. Some names don't sound right with an "e" on the end, but any that do are sure to get that sing-songy modification when Ali's around. Duke already knows and doesn't mind, but decides to play with the little guy a bit.

"Dukie, eh?" Duke says with mock skepticism. "You'll make me sound like a Blue Devils fan from North Carolina. I'll have to start wearing all blue and white and picking fights with Tarheels fans."

Ethan looks confused, but sees Duke's big smile and knows it's all in good fun. "Devils are red, Dukie. I know 'cause Connor wore a devil costume on Halloween and it was red, red, red. Dark red, and with a long, pointy tail," he says, placing his hands on his hips.

"Connor is Ethan's best friend from the neighborhood back in D.C.," I add.

"Ah, well," Duke explains, "the devils in North

Carolina are definitely blue, and they're crazy about basketball."

"Basketball?" Ethan asks. "The one with the ball that goes into the high net up on the pole?"

"That's right, basketball," Duke continues. "There's a school in North Carolina called Duke University, same as my name, Duke. Their basketball team is called the Blue Devils, and their uniforms are blue and white and inside the letter D, there's a devil who wears blue. The people who like them-- the fans-- are called Dukies as a nickname for Duke. Here, I'll find you a picture," he says as he squats down to Ethan's level and pulls out his iPhone to search. Ethan eagerly climbs onto Duke's lap, fascinated, and waits for the picture to appear. Duke is a natural with kids. It's going to be great having him around as our boys grow up. Good male role models are so important. I wonder if he and Jen plan to have kiddos of their own.

"Duke, man, you look like you were born to be a dad," I say with a sly smile. "Are you guys going to make that happen?"

"Probably so," he responds slowly, blushing. "I'd love to have some mini guys-- or girls-- of my own running around. And since you've got a good start on a basketball team, Jen and I only need to pop out a couple to round it out, right?"

"Now that's what I'm talking about," I add, to the delight of Ethan who raises his arms in the air and yells, "Basketball!" Duke and I join in and yell even louder, "Basketball!"

We're happily cheering in the food room when we hear Lady suddenly start barking upstairs. I step out into the hallway and listen for a minute thinking maybe she'll stop, but she is apparently very upset about something.

"I wonder what that's about," I say, walking back towards Duke and Ethan. "I'd better go check it out. Can you two hang out together for a few minutes while I go?"

"Yes, Daddy," Ethan says. "I like Dukie. He will keep me safe. He's a policeman."

"Right on, Ethan," Duke, says. "We're good," he adds, looking up at me with a sincere expression. "Truly, no problem at all, George. Me and Ethan are having fun together. Go see what's up with the dog. Sounds like Jen might need an assist."

I walk back down the long hall from the kitchen and see Ali opening boxes in the formal dining room while Leo naps on an ottoman brought in from the living room. He has his fuzzy blue lamb blanket and favorite stuffed puppy dog named Jimbo curled tightly to his chest. Luckily, our boys are pretty good at napping whenever and wherever they need to. Jimbo the puppy dog always helps.

"Oh, good, Georgie. Jen took her upstairs to smell around and get used to the place," Ali says in answer to my obvious concern about Lady's barking. "I'm glad you're here because I didn't want to leave Leo alone to go up myself, and I knew I'd wake him if I tried to move him."

"I've got it," I say. "You stay here with little Leo.

Ethan's in the kitchen talking basketball with Duke like one of the guys." Ali smiles and kisses me on the cheek, and even in the midst of the chaos, I break out into my goofy grin that I can't seem to keep under wraps when I'm around her. I'd do anything for that woman.

I turn the corner and begin to walk up the stairs, and I hear Jen's distant voice urging Lady to back off. Jen is great with animals and is definitely not a pushover when it comes to instruction and discipline. I'm surprised Lady isn't listening to her.

"Come on already, Lady," Jen shouts. "Down girl, down. Easy. No barking."

"Jen, where are you?" I call out. "What's happening?"

"In the boys' room, George," she hollers back, barely audible over the barking and closed bedroom door. "Come help me out, please. Lady sees something out the window that has her all worked up."

I reach the top of the stairs, excuse myself as I pass a trio of movers hoisting our bonus room sectional, and walk down the hallway to the second door on the right. We've already decided this will be the boys' shared bedroom. It's the best option out of the available bedrooms: it's across from a bathroom and within earshot of our room on the main level, yet not too close to the top of the stairs. The door is unlocked when I try it, and I go on in.

Lady's barking is incessant at this point. She's at the window looking out to the backyard down below and she is furious. The sound is loud. Jen is holding

Lady's lead and pulling hard to get her away from the window, but Lady isn't having it. I suddenly feel uneasy. Lady means business. She has been with us almost five years, and I have never seen her like this. We got her when she was a pup, so it isn't like she has some difficult history we don't know about. She came from a mild-mannered family in Virginia that has one or two litters of pups each year simply for the enjoyment of it.

"Did you get a look at what's out there?" I ask Jen.

"There were a handful of movers carrying things out to the carriage house when she started up. Two stayed behind when the others headed back to the truck. It looked like maybe they were taking a smoke break." she says.

"Huh," I mutter. "Odd."

"Yeah," she continues, "One of the smoking guys seemed to be peering hard at the back of the house. A big guy. Muscular. Looked a little like John Malkovich when he played Lennie in *Of Mice and Men* in the early nineties. Lighter hair though."

"Has Lady been out to the backyard yet?" I ask.

"No, she hasn't. That struck me as strange, too. How would she comprehend that she needs to be protective of the yard? She doesn't have any sense of where the boundary is." Jen says.

Jen and I have known each other almost as long as I've known Ali, so we're old friends at this point. When she was single, she would often travel with us if she had vacation time to spare. We've been all over the country together as a cozy little group of three. Then after Ethan was born, we traveled as a group of four. Jen used to walk up to cash registers and ticket lines with baby Ethan on her hip so she could practice for the day she has a baby of her own. She'd strap on the snuggly and wear Ethan as needed, or push him around in the jogging stroller to give us a break. I don't think it's possible to really know Ali without also knowing Jen. They're a package deal in many ways, which means Jen is like a sister to me. We haven't had as much time with her since Duke has been in the picture, but hopefully, this move to Ithaca will change that. I enjoy having her around.

As I take the lead out of Jen's hand and then step close and look out the window, Lady settles into a concerned whine rather than an all-out bark. Progress, at least. I don't see anyone in the backyard, but she seems to feel better now that I'm looking out the window. My instincts tell me we had better pay attention. Jen is thinking the same thing.

"George, how about we take Lady out back and see what she does when she gets down there?" Jen says.

"Yes, good idea. Let's see this through. If she's being territorial, maybe she'll feel better after walking the perimeter of the yard."

"And if she's barking at someone in particular," Jen says hesitantly. "Awkward or not, we should see who it is."

"I'm with you. Movers probably have run-ins with dogs all the time, like how postal carriers do, right? I doubt they'll be insulted," I add. "I once knew a mail carrier who kept milk bones in his pocket. He lived in a tiny town where he had to walk up to everyone's porch to deliver the mail, and he says those milk bones were a lifesaver more times than he could count."

We exit the bedroom and walk downstairs, this time excusing ourselves around two movers who are carrying shelves for our big armoire up to the bonus room. Lady is mostly quiet now, happy that we're giving her concerns the appropriate attention. Another pair of guys is in the foyer downstairs, ready to carry up our reclaimed wood coffee table that fits like a glove in the middle of the sectional. All Ali's picks, of course.

As Jen and I pass the dining room, we see that Leo is awake. We motion for Ali and Leo to follow us outside. Duke and Ethan have moved to the family room at the back of the house, so they follow us out, too. The entire group of us throws on coats and hats and passes through the back door onto the screened porch. Lady walks proudly at the head of the pack.

"She seemed to be upset about movers being in the yard," Jen explains to Ali, Duke, and the boys. "We figure we'll let her take a good look. Duke, come down with us?"

Duke nods in agreement. "Sure, babe."

"Yeah," I add. "Hopefully we can determine what, or who, specifically has Lady upset. I've never seen her like this. Ali, can you keep the boys here on the porch? Maybe get a fire going?" The snow has let up a little, but it's still bitter cold out. Luckily, the builder stocked the outdoor fireplace with wood for us, so it shouldn't be difficult to get it up and running.

"Of course, Georgie. You guys go do some recon," Ali replies. I love it when she uses tactical terms like recon. It's hot. My wife may look sweet and unassuming right now, what with the pregnant belly and two toddlers who hang around her most of the time, but don't let that fool you. She's tough.

Jen, Duke, and I walk with Lady down the tall set of stairs from the screened porch and deck to the lawn below. We take her around the perimeter and out to the carriage house. She sniffs around as we canvas the area, but doesn't act really concerned. No movers in sight. They've finished with the carriage house and the outdoor items and are working just in the main house now. It looks like they only have a few upstairs items to go. They were fast. And the beds are set up, so I guess we don't have to go back to Hampton Inn tonight after all. Score, big time. We weren't expecting this to be our first night in the new house, which makes it feels extra special. It's too late to cancel our reservation, so unless the front desk clerk at the Hampton feels generous when we call, we'll be paying for the night. But who cares? I can live with that. I'll make sure to tell the boys how this is a good example of a bonus, which is something good that you didn't know you were going to get.

"Well, damn," I say to Duke and Jen. "We're out here ready for some serious investigation, and Lady seems like she could care less. That was anticlimactic."

"Yeah, man," Duke adds. "I don't know. I'm here

because you two asked me to be. Were you exaggerating the urgency of the situation? You trying to get me down here in this isolated section of the property for a reason?" he says playfully, winking at Jen. She smiles back and moves to ease her arm around his waist.

"I guess that's my cue," I say, turning towards the house and lifting my shoulders and one leg up as if I'm going to make a dramatic exit. We all laugh.

"Seriously though, guys," Jen says. "That dog was sounding an alarm. George, how about you take her inside around the movers before they leave? If she was barking at one of them, it would be good to know which one."

"Agreed," I respond. "I'll do that right now."

Back through the yard and up the tall stairs Lady and I go, weaving our way past Ali and the boys and into the great room. I walk her through each room on the main level, then up the staircase and onto the second level. No reaction. The tall Asian guy who seems to be a supervisor stops what he's doing in the playroom to pat Lady's head for a minute, and she basks in the attention as if she doesn't have a care in the world. I read his nametag while we're standing there: Ringo. Seems like an odd fit for him.

I figure I should make a complete sweep while we're at it, so I take Lady down into the basement and then back up and out to the front courtyard area. Still nothing. No barking, no whining. Not even a concerned glance. I guess that's the end of that. Maybe the guys she was upset about have left already.

If so, no need to worry about it, I suppose. I make a mental note to remember the barking incident just in case, but otherwise, it's time to move on.

"Alright, Lady girl," I say. "I'm letting it go. Okay? Are we done here?" She looks at me and sits down at my feet. I guess that's my answer.

It's beginning to get dark. Jen, Duke, Ali, and the boys have come back inside and Ali is giving hugs to Jen and Duke and saying goodbye when I walk back into the foyer. Jen and I exchange a glance about Lady, and I raise my eyebrows and shrug my shoulders to let her know that nothing turned up. I wish I had something more interesting to report. She nods her understanding and walks over to pat Lady on the head.

"Leaving so soon?" I ask. "You know you're always welcome here, and you're welcome to stay as long as you like." Ali cocks her head in my direction and puts a hand over her heart to express how touched she is by my words.

"George, you're too sweet," Jen says. "We have to get home to watch our shows. *Hawaii Five-O* comes on tonight, and Duke's a sucker for a feel-good cop drama."

"True, true. I won't deny that." Duke admits. "Don't forget about *Blue Bloods*. I like to watch them back to back."

"Well, get out of here then," Ali says with a laugh. "We have plenty of things to do anyway. Like seeing these baby boys settled into their beds in their new room. Maybe we'll keep them in our bedroom tonight so they have time to get comfortable in the house. None of us are used to their room being so far away from ours."

"We'll sort it out," I add.

"Ok, then," Jen says and kisses Ali on the cheek one more time while rubbing her pregnant belly. "We'll see you five Ithaca residents again real soon."

We watch out the window as they tiptoe through the snow to their car and start it. It takes a few minutes to warm up before the windshields are clear enough to see out of. We stay at the window, waiting to wave as they pull out of the driveway. When they finally go, Ali turns and hugs me tight.

"Georgie, I'm happy we live in Ithaca. It was time for a slower pace. And time to live closer to family, Jen and Duke included. The boys needed that. Hell, you and I needed that. We made the right move."

"I'm happy, too," I say as I graze my palms back and forth across my wife's strong yet delicate shoulders. She has the body of a dancer. "I think it will be perfect for us here."

Ringo walks in through the front door just as our embrace is beginning to get a little handsy. We take a step apart and turn to face him. The boys have gone back into the living room to have another go with the little cars from their toy bags. I think they like how the sound of the wheels echo against the empty walls.

"All done?" I ask.

"Yes, sir. Many hands make light work. Most of the guys have gone home already. The few still left are loading dollies, furniture pads, and straps into the truck right now, then we'll head out of here and leave you to it," Ringo says cheerfully.

"Excellent," Ali responds. "Thanks for setting some things up as you went. That will make a huge difference for us over the next few days. We have family coming in."

"No worries, ma'am. It was our pleasure. Will one of you please sign here to confirm receipt of your household goods?" Ringo asks while handing us a clipboard with an old-school carbon copy form attached to the front. An iPad and a system with electronic signature capabilities would probably make his life easier, but hey, whatever works.

Ali looks at me to see whether or not everything looked okay when I did my walkabout with Lady. It did. I nod in her direction. "Yeah, everything looks great, sir. Thank you for a job well done." I say to Ringo as Ali picks up a pen and signs the paperwork. That was amazing, really. Those guys were in and out within a few hours, and there's no visible damage to the house or to any of our things. What a pleasant surprise.

"Yes, thank you," Ali says as she reaches into her handbag and pulls out four crisp one-hundred-dollar bills and hands them to Ringo. "Here's a little something for you and your crew. We appreciate your efforts."

"Oh, the thanks goes to you lovely folks for your business," Ringo responds, taking the cash and bowing his head in gratitude. "And for the warm drinks when we arrived. You're too kind."

Ringo grabs his knit hat out of his back pants pocket and puts it carefully on his head, then gives us a wave as he zips the weatherproof pouch around our paperwork and walks out the front door. Are people nicer when they know you're wealthy? I can't help but wonder if we would have received the same treatment if we were moving into a run-down cottage in a crowded part of town rather than this mansion on acreage overlooking the lake. Since my wealth hasn't ever been so visible before, I honestly don't know the answer to that question. This moving service sure seemed extra good. Well, whatever the reason, we're in and our new home is a dream come true. I feel like doing a little dance or something. It's beyond wonderful.

## GEORGE: WHAT BUDS MAY BLOOM

Ali offers to feed the boys supper and put them to sleep early since it's been such a long few days, so I decide to call Uncle Liam and let him know we made it okay. It's getting late, but he's probably still up. I step out the back door onto the dimly lit, screened porch, sit down on the cushioned wicker sectional, and pull a gray cable knit blanket over me. Thanks again to Ali's prior planning and great tastes in decor, the blanket is in place and ready to use on night one. Amazing. I smile just thinking about her. The fire's still going, and the Bose stereo system wired into the walls is cycling through a playlist Ali must have started earlier. Coldplay sings an acoustic version of *Fix You* as I lean close to one of the porch screens and see that the snow has finally stopped. It's nice and cozy, kind of like being in a hot tub on a winter day. I'm toasty warm, yet there's a biting cold around the edges.

Something about both extremes at once delights the senses.

"Hey, buddy," I say when I hear Liam's voice on the other end of the phone. "How's it going down in D.C.? You miss me yet?"

"George! Hey, stranger. Good to hear your voice," Liam says. He's smiling that big toothy grin of his. I can hear it. Maybe that's where I get it from, come to think of it. Dad's smile was much more subtle. Maybe the goofy grin gene skipped over Dad but came straight from Uncle Liam to me. I wonder what kind of smile their father had. I only met him a couple of times when I was little. I don't remember much. Maybe I should dig out some pictures.

"I'm good, man. I'm looking at Cayuga Lake right now. We are officially moved into the new house. Closing is done, keys are in hand, and all of our stuff has been deposited inside. Nothing like moving to make you realize how much you've accumulated over the years."

"I'm glad to hear it, George," Liam says, and I can tell he means it. He knows what a big deal this move is for me. Other than Ali, Uncle Liam is my closest confidant and best friend. I can tell him anything, and I do. It doesn't hurt that we've worked together on highly specialized, top-secret missions in the Air Force, so we know and understand things that very few other people in the world do. Plus, we know and understand my dad like very few other people in the world do.

"Is the house as drop dead gorgeous as you expected?" he asks.

"Oh, even more so. It's kind of like a palace, actually. I'm doing my best to enjoy it. Ali's happy." I say.

"Come on now, George, I know how you feel about all that money, but Alec worked so hard for it. I'd even say he paid for it with his life. He worked himself into the ground for his family. Use it and enjoy it. Estella and I do."

Dad left mom and me the bulk of his fortune, but he also left his brother a sizable sum. Liam had no idea it was coming until Dad's will was read at the attorney's office after he died. Of course, Dad died suddenly so none of us really knew it was coming. Hell, I'm not sure Dad would have told us if he had known he was dying. Ever since I was a kid he talked a lot about building a fortune so I would never have to worry about money like he did, so I knew I'd see some inheritance when he passed away. I just didn't think it would be so soon. I never really thought about whether or not Liam was getting money and I'm not sure Liam did either, but it makes sense that Dad would include his brother when it came time to share the wealth. He and Liam went through childhood horrors together, and they remained close-knit to the end. Plus, Liam worked with Dad for a few years during the early days when the department stores were brand new. I suppose in that way Liam had sweat equity invested and it made logical sense that he'd one day get a return on his efforts.

Liam is different than me in that he doesn't feel guilty or burdened about having money. He somehow keeps it all pretty organized and simple in his mind. His philosophy is basically that if you have money, then enjoy it and spread some around to others in need. If you don't, make the best of what you do have and don't waste too much energy feeling sorry for yourself. He doesn't get bogged down with the subtleties. Maybe it's because he was the younger sibling and didn't feel the pressures us only children and older siblings do to make things right and better. Or maybe he's just a different personality by default. I don't know. I'm no psychologist. I think about it, though. Especially because I'd like to shed some of the guilt I have about being wealthy. The guilt sometimes feels like just as big a burden to bear as poverty would be.

"I know we've talked about this a few times," I say.

"We have," Liam answers. "We can talk about it again."

"Yeah, well, this huge house has it all right up in my face," I continue, dabbing at the beads of sweat that are beginning to form on my brow. I sweat when I'm stressed, or for most any reason, really. "Did I make a mistake getting such an extravagant place? If not, I'm going to have to figure out how to get past this so I can live here day to day."

"Yeah," Liam says simply. He knows how to let me talk when I need to. He says enough to stay engaged without getting in the way of my flow.

"Jen's fiancé Duke was here visiting this afternoon," I go on. "And he's a police officer. He's marrying into money by choosing Jen Wright, of course, but I don't know much about his background. He's a great guy. I don't want him to feel separate or distant because of the money, you know? That would hurt my heart if he did. I want him to feel welcome with us, and welcome in our home."

"Yeah, but maybe you're projecting, George. Did Duke give you any indication he feels that way?" Liam says.

"No, he didn't."

"Yeah, so, hmmm." Uncle Liam says. "You've been hiding from this issue for a long time, George. You promised Ali-- and yourself-- you'd come to terms with it. Let's hash it out and get it over with. Jesus Christ! Remember who you're talking to. I've been there with you as you've chosen tiny condos and dilapidated houses to live in, all while you've had millions in the bank. That money isn't doing anybody any good tucked away. And hell, George, you have Ali sitting on the money her parents have given her, too. Roddy and Marjorie worked hard for it, same as Alec. Those two put their creativity out into the world, and the world has embraced them. One of the ways good karma comes back to people who put their creativity out into the world is as cold, hard cash. I mean, think about Roddy Davies. His plays are truly superb. Life changing, even. People come from all over the world to watch and be inspired by what has come from a pure place in that man's spirit, George. He's a legend. I agree with your wife that it's time to ease up a little and enjoy having money, for fuck's sake. Whatever you do, don't pass your balled up feelings onto those innocent boys."

"I know, I know," I respond. "But active duty servicemen and women are not usually wealthy, Liam. Neither are Ph.D. students, or law school students, or even attorneys at the nonprofit and government organizations where Ali has worked. Flashing our money would have seemed so out of place in all the situations we've been in."

"You sound like your mother," Liam says under his breath.

"Yeah, John Wendell made the same comment today at lunch."

"Glad I'm not the only one." Liam continues, getting more and more worked up. "George, listen to your grandfather. Listen to your wife. Listen to me, for Christ's sake. You've got to get ahold of yourself. Money is not going to make your life bad. Using it is going to make your life better. If some of the people you know can't hang with that and continue to be your friends, then they either weren't real friends in the first place or they have their own issues about money that have nothing to do with you. You are a good person, George. The very best. And Ali is just as good. Hell, she's an even better person than you, if I'm being honest," he continues with a laugh.

"I hear you, Liam. Thank you," I say.

"Ease up, buddy. Do some meditation. Deep breathing, maybe. Run it out. Do something. You guys deserve this house. You deserve the money your family members have left to you. And you deserve the money you earn from your demanding and intellectually challenging careers. Relax and enjoy it, George. Relax and enjoy it."

"And, about Mom?" I ask, knowing the answer. Uncle Liam lets out a long sigh. He's always loved Mom as a sister-in-law and has gotten along with her fine, but they are on opposite ends of the spectrum when it comes to many worldviews. He sometimes tells people I was raised by a liberal mother, as if that explains everything.

"George, buddy, I'm not sure what it is about your mom. I'd never want to say anything bad about her. She's a wonderful woman. You're surrounded by top-notch people in every area of your life, and she's no exception. My brother fell in love with her hard and fast and early. We were all kids when they got together, so you have to realize that Linette has been in my life longer than you've been alive. I wasn't even old enough to get my driver's license when I first met her. I learned a long time ago to keep quiet about her eccentricities and rigid beliefs. She and your Dad agreed to disagree about a lot of topics. And he and I didn't talk much about that sort of thing. We shared a knowing look and an occasional eye roll here and there, but together, Alec and Linette were a force to be reckoned with. They clicked. They worked. Who was I to interfere in any way?" Liam says.

"Funny," I add. "John Wendell said something along those lines today at lunch, too."

"Well, we've always known he's a wise man," Liam

says with a chuckle. "Thank him for me next time, will you, George?"

I smile and look up to the stars in the cold night sky. John Wendell and Uncle Liam have been the two most influential people in my life aside from my parents and Ali. Certainly, since I've been an adult and been left to face the world without a Dad, those two have had my back. They come from different generations and fairly different backgrounds, yet they often agree about what's right and best for me. When it happens, I pay attention. I trust them both completely.

"Liam?" I ask. "Is Estella waiting on you? You have another minute?" He knows there's more on my mind. More that I couldn't share with John Wendell, or even Ali.

"Yeah, I'm good. Go on."

"Look," I begin, clutching the blanket on my lap and then nervously smoothing the hair on the top of my head a few times. I stand up and step further away from the interior wall connected to the house, just in case Ali is listening. It's not that I don't want her to know how I feel as much as I don't want her to lose faith in me. "I've been in the military for damn near half my life. I haven't said this out loud yet, but I must admit I'm nervous about living a life where I'm not an active duty soldier." I pause and take a deep breath. "I know I have a good job lined up. I'm sure it will be great, although I have my doubts about how this liberal town would feel if they knew the true nature of my team's work. But I am a soldier. Down to the core. I protect my people. I need to protect my people. And that's the way I know how. This job at Cornell is an honor, truly, but, I'm saying a lot of buts."

"I hear them," Liam affirms.

"You remember, Dad always used to say that when you hear someone say but, to listen closely because after the 'but' they'd tell you how they really feel. I guess what I'm saying is that I'm afraid." I pause, and I hear Liam sigh gently on the other end of the phone.

"What if there's a threat to national security?" I continue. "And I'm in a stuffy office at Cornell rather than front and center to the resources that could actually help? I'm serious. My old job in the Air Force was that important. You of all people know I'm not exaggerating, Liam. I had that kind of access. Most people have no idea of the threats that present themselves. You know, it's hardcore."

"I do know, George," Liam responds, quietly.

"The public never hears about any of it, but it happens. I handled it. I was a great leader, too. I led the men and women under my command with great success. It was such a tremendous honor. Tremendous. I don't think there's another feeling in this world quite like the honor I felt when I literally saved the world with my quick reaction to an imminent threat. And it happened more than once. To be part of that, to work in tandem with my military brothers and sisters to protect our people, made my body come alive with purpose. Isn't it that way for you?"

Liam takes a minute to respond, and I can tell he's choosing his words carefully. "George, it is that way for me. And honestly, it's one of the reasons I never had kids. Don't get me wrong, I love kids and love being an uncle, but after living through my own difficult childhood, I didn't want to have children and then subject them to me being gone all the time. I didn't want to put that on their mom either. I see what military spouses go through. That's no walk in the park. And I had an intense need to make a difference and do something good with my life.

"I wanted better than the misery and drama my parents experienced, same as your Dad. Alec grew up to own a chain of department stores, and I grew up and eventually found my way to the Air Force, aerospace, and national security. Luckily, when I met Estella, she was on board with my no-kids plan. I had gotten a vasectomy years prior, so it was already pretty much a done deal. I do sometimes worry that she'll change her mind before her childbearing years have passed. That's a risk I took marrying a younger woman. I don't know. But what I do know is that your situation is different because you have Ali and the boys to think about. You don't want to be gone all the time while Ethan, Leo, and the baby are young. Those years go by so fast, and you can't get them back. You're a good husband, and a good dad, George. You did your time in the military, and it's ok to step back a little and be home safe with your family. You deserve that. You'll still be involved with and be contributing to our cause. Just, differently."

I had sort of assumed as much about Liam not having kids, but he'd never come right out and said it before. He's correct about my situation being very different from his in that regard. I know I'm meant to be a dad. Besides, Ali always knew she wanted kids, and I am most certainly meant to be with Ali. She and I have a grand, enduring love like few people get to experience. Our boys are an inherent part of that love and our story. I wouldn't have it any other way.

"You're right, Liam. As usual," I say. "You're a top-notch uncle. Best of the best. I don't know what I'd do without you, man."

"I love you, too, George. You're my boy, even though not technically my boy. You know?" Liam says warmly.

"I do. It was you who inspired me to get into the Air Force and into aerospace. Do you realize that?" I say.

"Well, that's been kind of obvious, but it's good to hear you say it out loud," Liam responds. "I'm glad you thought enough of me to follow my path. I hope Alec would be proud of the example I've set for you. I did my best to step up in your life after he was gone."

"I know you did," I say, choking back tears now. "I was a sixteen-year-old kid. I wasn't ready. You and John Wendell..."

"It's been one of the greatest honors of my life, George. Don't ever forget that." Liam says, choking back tears of his own.

Maybe everything seems worse because it's January. I am generally a content guy, but January has always been my least favorite month. Snow is really nice, but aside from that, it's just a dull gray mishmash that seems to bring out my doubts and insecurities. Ali found me staring out the hotel window into the gray nothingness just this morning. I had to give myself an extra kick to get moving and keep things in perspective.

That was a nice perk about traveling around the world like I did in the Air Force. My job meant that I was on an hour notice to fly anywhere in the world, and I got to visit a lot of beautiful places. Even when the mission was dangerous, there was a buzz and a thrill in feeling the fresh air on your face and smelling the smells of different lands. It was exhilarating to get on the plane and a few hours later step out in a totally different setting. Even if all we did was go from D.C. down to Charleston, South Carolina, as soon as the hatch opened, and I took a breath, the humid Charleston air was foreign and wonderful. I sure am going to miss Washington D.C. and the Air Force. And Uncle Liam.

"George?" Liam says.

"Yes?"

"You're dealing with a lot of changes at once. They're all good, but it will take some time to adjust. Remember, relax and enjoy. That's your new mantra. Repeat it to yourself every day. Uncle Liam's orders." he says with a hearty laugh.

Liam and I say our goodbyes with promises to talk soon and plan a visit. I turn out the porch light and head back into the house to order some Chinese takeout and make love to my beautiful wife. We have to christen the new place, after all. The food arrives just as Ali glides downstairs with news of the boys being conked out for the night. She's clearly thinking about making love, too. I can tell by the way she moves. We put a little Marvin Gaye on and flirt across the dining room table while holding hands and stuffing our bellies with lo mein and red wine. When we've had our fill, we light a fire in our bedroom fireplace and set the scene. We have to unpack some sheets and blankets and put them on the bed before we can get things going, but that extra step will no doubt make the evening more memorable. I find a couple of candles in one of the bags Ali packed to go with us in the Tesla and light them on the mantle. She probably put those there in anticipation of this very moment. I have that wife. There are no curtains or blinds covering the windows yet, but neither of us cares. In fact, that makes it all the more exciting. We're in our own bedroom, after all. It's not that I expect anyone to be outside peering in, but it feels sort of magical to be looking out at our snow-covered land and the lake right now as we make love in our beautiful new home. We stand to face each other in the candlelight and take each other's clothes off, slowly, tracing every inch of newly exposed skin with our mouths before slinking into bed and becoming completely intertwined. Relax and enjoy, right? Relax, and enjoy.

It's a beautiful Saturday morning when the sun wakes us up bright and early. The light is glistening off the snow, which makes for gorgeous ethereal beams coming in the windows from outside. This is a welcome change from yesterday's dreariness. Day two in our new home is going to be a good day. We have a slew of family members coming to see the new place.

Mom and John Wendell will be here in a few hours. Mom's going to help Ali choose some colors and fabrics with our interior designer while I take John Wendell and the boys to the farmers market over on Buffalo Street. The winter market is only open until two P.M. on Saturdays, so we have to be sure we don't miss it. I'm guessing we'll grab lunch while we're out, then head to Icy Scoops for some old-fashioned ice cream on the way home. Who cares if there's snow on the ground? John Wendell is always in the mood for ice cream. The mint chocolate chip in a waffle cone, made from scratch by the folks at Icy Scoops, is to die for, although their strawberry chunk is a close second. We'll keep our coats on while we chow down if necessary. I want to hit all of John Wendell's favorite places as soon as possible.

Roddy and Marjorie are coming in from New York City this afternoon to see the house and spend a few nights. They're going to help us unpack. Ali's brother Nicky is coming, too, along with his husband Luis and their eight-year-old daughter Sara. They have to head back tomorrow so Sara can be at school Monday, but we're glad they're making the trip. We're all meeting up with Jen and Duke at Yellow Cob this evening for a celebratory dinner. Party of thirteen. Yellow Cob has delicious food and big, long tables with plenty of room for us, and they're right on the lake with pretty water views. In the summer, they have live music on the deck. Ali and I love to sit in their Adirondack chairs which surround the outdoor fire pit on summer evenings and look at the boats in the marina. Sometimes you can even see one of the college rowing teams scooting by. I imagine all the Yellow Cob action will be inside this time of year, but it's still nice to see lights twinkling off the water in the background. We love living near water. I'm not sure how people live without it.

You might think we'd want the house completely set up and decorated before we have anyone over. Luckily, we don't have to be like that with our friends and family members. We keep things real and casual. Mom is the only one who might be judging anyway, and that's only due to her own insecurities. We try to let her comments pass by without upsetting us when she gets going on a rant. Besides, we've hired a company to help us unpack the big things and set up the house similar to our old place. They'll be here on Monday.

It was kind of sad to leave our old home, especially for the boys. We'd lived in the same house in D.C. for years, which translated to the entirety of Ethan and Leo's short lives. Leo took it especially hard. I'm sure that's because at two-years-old, he was just too young to understand what was happening. The day the movers came and took things off the walls was the worst. Leo cried until he was completely exhausted, and he went around trying to pick things up and put them back on the walls where he thought they should go. I'll never forget the poor little guy desperately working to lift heavy picture frames and pointing up to the spots where they belonged. It was as if he thought our whole world was coming apart, and he was the only one who realized the gravity of the situation. Poor little buddy. We tried our best to console him, but I don't think we were successful. Thankfully, he seemed relieved to see our familiar things being brought into the new house yesterday. I want nothing more than for Ali and our little guys to be happy.

Ali's still dozing, so I nudge her a little and nuzzle the back of her neck as I slide my hand just below her waist and pregnant belly. We were both naked when we fell asleep last night. She's wearing a sleep shirt now, so she must have been up during the night to check on the boys. Or to go to the bathroom for the millionth time. Or both. Fortunately for me, she never sleeps in panties. I stop to listen closely, and it's quiet in the house.

"Ali, babe, did you check on the boys yet this morning?" I ask as I pull her closer and the blood begins to rush. "We have a while before anyone is scheduled to be here. If the boys are still sleeping, I know how I'd like to start the morning."

She stretches in response to my touch, arching her body and moving that tight backside up against me in one fluid motion. If she wasn't pregnant, she might not be interested after having just made love last night. Pregnancy gets her in the mood more often though, and I take advantage of that fact every chance I get.

We're young and in love and eager to do what lovers do.

"I was in their room less than an hour ago. They were still sleeping hard," she says in a sexy whisper. "I think I might know how you'd like to start the morning." And we're at it again.

"Did you lock our bedroom door when you came back in?" I ask while lowering my hand down between her thighs. She's already wet.

"No, Dr. Hartmann, but we'd hear them on the baby monitor. We're good," Ali says seductively as she turns my way and then uses one long, magnificent leg of hers to hoist herself on top of me and sit upright. She only calls me Dr. Hartmann when she's in the mood for love making. It's an instant turn on. Once we're pieced together and she's situated snugly, my wife pulls her sleep shirt over her head with both hands and then tosses it onto the floor. And there she is, in all her glory. I love it when I get to look at her like this. The curve of her supple breasts, the lines of her back, and the enticing way she moves are almost too much.

"Congratulations on your new house, Dr. Hartmann," Ali says playfully as she grinds. "I don't think you should stop until you've made love to your wife in every single room of the place. And maybe even outdoors." She giggles and leans down for a long, slow kiss.

"Is that right, Ms. Davies?" I return. "Every single room and maybe even outdoors? That will take a while. But I think we're off to a good start." She slides off of me slowly and walks around to the cushioned bench at the foot of the bed. I sit up in anticipation and see her bend herself over it, gracefully. That's my cue. Without saying another word, I walk around and position myself squarely behind her. She knows this is my favorite. I don't put myself inside of her right away though. First, I place one hand on her shoulder and use the other one to run my fingers down the small of her back and underneath. She's dripping wet and throbbing for me. I massage her there a couple of minutes until she's squirming with pleasure. I move my free hand from her shoulder around to her breast and gently squeeze while I continue to rub down below. I love seeing her respond to my touch. When I think she's near peak excitement, I bend her over further and allow myself to push hard inside. She squeezes me tight from within and moans in total ecstasy. It doesn't take me long to release. My God, how did I get this lucky?

We're stepping into the bathroom to get cleaned up when we hear little footsteps, and then Ethan's giggle from the living room. Perfect timing. Good sex is all about timing when you have little ones around. At least he's in a happy mood this morning. Here we were worried about them sleeping so far away from us. It sounds like they did just fine.

"I'll get them, babe," Ali says. "You go ahead and shower then we'll swap places. You'll be in and out of there quicker than me anyway. Want me to start the Cream of Wheat?" The boys love Cream of Wheat, and we promised them we'd make it for our first morning in the new house.

"Oh, I'll make it once I'm dressed. We have a big weekend. You need to relax as much as possible," I tell her as she grabs her plush, floral print robe from the hook on the back of the door and wraps herself up in it. "Go sit down with those baby boys and don't worry about doing a thing."

"That's sweet," she says. "But it's going to be hard for me to completely relax until this house is unpacked."

"All in good time," I reassure as I pick up a bar of soap and a bottle of shampoo out of a canvas bag brought in last night from the car, then turn on the warm water and step into the shower. "We have help." Our new shower has herringbone tile on two walls and clear glass on the other two. I kind of love the idea of showering while on display for my wife. The deep soaker bathtub sits right beside the shower and has four gorgeous, tall windows above it, all overlooking the sparkling lake. This house has a ton of natural light. I know Ali is going to get good use out of that tub. We've talked about home birth and water birth for little Will. Maybe he'll come into the world right here, in our bathroom tub. We'll see what the midwives think when we meet with them next week. Midwives delivered both Ethan and Leo and we wouldn't have it any other way for Will, assuming no complications, of course.

"I know we have plenty of help with the house, and I'm so glad," Ali says. "Hey, are you going to wear a flannel shirt today? You know how I love you in a nice flannel. And we have company coming. Your thick red, blue and tan one, maybe? Oh, and it's going to be cold again today. How about one of your pullover sweaters on top? The gray one with the v-neck?"

"I thought you were heading to the living room to be with the boys, but instead you're still here, and you're giving me fashion advice?" I tease. "I've been dressing myself a long time, Ms. Davies. I think I can handle it."

"Oh, you've been dressing yourself, alright," she says with a smile. "Dressing yourself in t-shirts and jeans. It's hard to even keep you in jeans when it's more than 40 degrees outside. I'll never understand how you go out in the cold wearing shorts. It doesn't even seem to bother you."

"And?" I ask, wiping the steam off a section of glass and pressing my nose up against it while opening my eyes really wide. We laugh together. My goofiness is not an act. I'm that way by default. But I think it's exactly what Ali needs. From what I can tell, laughter is a big part of a happy relationship. It's certainly a big part of ours. Time passes, kids grow up, circumstances change, and looks fade. If you can laugh together though, I'm pretty sure that part endures.

Ali slides out the bathroom door, still chuckling, and I finish my shower. Then I dry myself off with a towel, apply some deodorant, and head to the bedroom where my suitcase sits unopened in the closet. Might as well take everything out and hang it up. Not surprisingly, my red, blue, and tan flannel shirt is folded neatly on top along with my gray v-neck sweater and some khaki pants. Ali didn't mention the khaki pants specifically, but I can take a hint. I'll wear them for her. She must have packed them this way so I'd have the right outfit at the right time. Part of me wants desperately to throw on some old gym shorts and any t-shirt I can get my hands on. I mean, Mom and John Wendell aren't here yet and I'm steaming hot. It feels like a million degrees inside my body, pretty much all the time. Isn't every guy like that? Besides, as crazy as it sounds, I don't think I've ever really gotten used to having more than a few items of clothing to choose from.

Before I was born, Mom was a secretary. She worked the main reception desk at the local hospital where she handled all sorts of important matters like informing media about the status of patients brought in for emergency care and coordinating with family members so they knew what was happening with their loved ones. She didn't earn much, but she was proud. It was honest, rewarding work. When I was born, she left her job and took time off to raise me. I don't think I've ever told her just how much it meant to me, but I appreciate that selfless act more than I can adequately express. I'm a better man because of it. I know I am. I have all kinds of great memories of me and Mom together during the years before I was old enough to go to Kindergarten. She took me to parks for playgrounds and shared picnic lunches, to libraries for story times, and to beaches for swimming in the summer when it got hot and sticky outside. We did the classic mom and little boy stuff that good childhoods are made of. It brings a tear to my eye thinking about it even now. I know our family had financial problems because I heard about them when I got older, but I didn't know about them then. Life was easy in those days. I remember all kinds of simple pleasures, like listening to the sound of Mom's voice as she talked on the phone and absentmindedly stroked my hair. I could lay my head in her lap and doze off without a care in the world. I remember thunderstorms in the City and the smell of falling rain. I remember birthday cakes and balloons. I remember ice cream trucks broadcasting their familiar jingles in the neighborhood and the thrill of getting in line in time to score an orange push pop before they ran out. I remember the sweet breath and tentative mews of pet kittens, and I remember Mom nursing one particular little guy named Socks back to health after he was hit by a neighbor kid's bicycle. She was a natural nurturer. I remember her sewing Halloween costumes for me, always honoring my requests no matter how complicated the pattern. She sewed me pillows and stuffed animals, too. I remember being lulled to sleep many afternoons by the sound of her sewing machine and the rhythmic motion of her foot on the pedal. I remember Mom bundling me up warm and safe when it was cold outside, and taking me out in the sled to play when the first snow of the season arrived. I remember the smell of homemade spaghetti and meatballs at supper time, and the jingle of Dad's keys in the door on evenings when he made it home in time to eat with us. I remember my parents being happy together. I remember them dancing in the living room and kissing each other on the lips. And I remember the sheer bliss of staying up late to watch TV with them in their big bed, one of my arms around each of their necks. Dad was gone working a lot, but the time he was home always seemed good. I remember knowing that I was thoroughly loved by both of my parents, right down to the core.

Things got a little more complicated when I went to school. I was carefree at first. But little by little, I became aware that not having a lot of money carried a stigma and might be an issue. A brat named Johnny Triff took it upon himself to enlighten me about the ways and means of the wealthier set. I didn't realize rich families had cars until Johnny asked me why we didn't have one. Imagine my surprise when I learned that rich families lived in entire brownstones by themselves rather than sharing the inside space like we did with other residents of tiny subdivided apartments. I'm sure Johnny was unhappy and just lashing out to make himself feel better, but his comments stung. Sometimes I didn't have the right shoes, or the right designer clothes to suit him.

Johnny grew bolder as I grew more uncomfortable. Once he found out my dad was the owner of Hartsmart, the harassment escalated even more. Apparently owning a chain of busy department stores meant we should have had plenty of money and the fact that we didn't was hilarious in Johnny's diabolical mind. I was too young to understand the realities of running a business and how revenue is very different than profit. I knew Johnny had a point. The stores were busy. And yet we didn't have nice things like the people who shopped at my dad's stores were buying. I thought maybe my dad was somehow doing it wrong. Or maybe it was something about me. Maybe he didn't want to spend his money on me and Mom. That sounds crazy, I know. Kids take everything so personally. It was hard to sort out in my mind, but I came home crying more than once thanks to Johnny Triff. Mom had started working part-time by then. She was usually there when I got home after school to help me with homework and cook supper, but not always. A neighbor checked in on me when Mom wasn't there. I kept that interaction to a minimum and said just enough to be left alone. I remember bawling my eyes out one lonely September afternoon when Johnny had told the kids at our lunch table I was adopted and that's why my dad didn't want to share his money with me. Mom and Dad were both at work. It was horrible. I knew what Johnny said wasn't true. But I was in agony. A million thoughts raced through my young mind, most prominently, thoughts of how unfair it all was and how when I grew up I'd find a way to get enough money for all the things I wanted.

I was deep in an emotional tailspin when I heard a knock at the door and a friendly voice. It was Uncle Liam, stopping by to make me dinner and hang out for awhile. Mom was running late, so Dad had called him. Liam was young himself, in his early 20s at this point, but he was good with me. He dried my tears and we talked about privilege and wealth over tuna noodle casserole at the little kitchen table in my family's tiny apartment. He told me about how he and Dad had grown up poor with Grandad and Grandmother Marks and Benny, but how they were truly and deeply loved. He told me how that love had overflowed right on down to Mom and me because Dad had so much to give, and he explained how love is worth so much more than money. We decided together that Johnny Triff must not have the kind of love I did, or else he wouldn't treat other people so poorly. On that day, sitting there with Liam, something set deep inside me and I decided I didn't need a bunch of money or material things. Those traumatic experiences had seared into my mind, into my bones, but it felt like Liam was showing me a way to tuck that all away and measure my wealth in love. From then on, I guess I got used to not having enough, and not having the right stuff. A set point had solidified, and I haven't moved much from it. That's probably why I'm having trouble moving from it now. I got the message loud and clear that love and people are more important than things. That's the absolute truth in life and the world. It's funny how it's easier to understand and rationalize it all when you don't have any money. Once you've experienced poverty and come to that understanding though, how do you go about coming to terms with the flip side of having material wealth and financial prosperity? I've got a ways to go.

I often think about all Mom and Dad did so I

could have a good life. Every day. Every walk to work. Every trip to the bottom floor of our building to wash and dry laundry. Every mended button. Every pot of spaghetti. They paved the way. They poured their best into our family. For me. So that I could lead a fulfilling life and so I wouldn't have the same worries they did. What a gift they gave me. We've come a long way in just a couple of generations.

Lady and the boys are rolling around on the leather sofa happily when I walk into the living room. I still can't get over these views of the lake from almost every room in the house. It feels like we're on vacation. I can hardly believe this is our home. "Good morning, buddies!" I say to my kiddos. I plop down between them and squeeze each of them tight before planting kisses on the tops of their little heads. I love the smell of those little heads. I'll kiss them as long as they'll let me. They smell especially nice right now, like fruity-scented detangler. Ali must have combed their hair with it as she got them dressed for the day. I'm not sure how she even had time to get them dressed during the few minutes when I was finishing up in the shower and contemplating my childhood, but she did. "And good morning, Lady girl," I add. Lady looks at me approvingly as Leo pats one of her front paws. She's in heaven when she's with these boys. Hey, I get it. She's a dog who wants to feel useful. With them, she does. In many ways, she's like a canine babysitter. Ali and I know we have a little more leeway when she's around. We can step a little farther away, and we can take a little longer to check in. If they're in any danger,

Lady will let us know. That is if she hasn't already intervened and taken care of the problem. In fact, that's a big reason we're comfortable with the boys sleeping upstairs in this big house. I'm not sure we'd be ok with it if Lady weren't around.

Ali is unpacking books and placing them on a set of low bookshelves at the other end of the room. "Get out of here, Mommy," I tease. "You need a shower."

"Yeah, Mommy," Ethan chimes in. "Daddy's gonna make us creama eat. You go get clean and dressed up like a pretty princess." I can't help but laugh every time he says 'creama eat.' Ethan's been calling Cream of Wheat that for as long as I can remember. I think it started back when he was littler and couldn't say it right, but then the new name sort of stuck. It makes perfect sense when you think about it from a little kid's perspective. Of course, Leo believes the sun rises and sets with his big brother, so he's happy to call it 'creama eat,' too. "Creama eat, creama eat," they both chant in unison. I tickle Leo's belly as I hoist him onto one hip, then I grab Ethan and sling him around my other side so he can hang onto my neck and ride on my back like a little monkey. Ali flashes us her megawatt smile as she claps her hands together to dust them off on the way to the bathroom.

"Let's do it, boys. Creama eat happens to be one of my specialties. Coming right up," I say. "What should we have in our creama eat this morning? Bananas? Raisins? Ohhhh, I know. How about cinnamon?"

"Yeah!" Ethan says. "I want all of those things."

"Me, Daddy, too," Leo says. He's not usually a fan of bananas, but we'll try them. I'll add a slice or two and see if he eats those before I cut up an entire banana for him. You never know with a two-year-old. Tastes are always changing. I sit Leo in his booster seat and pull the chair it's attached to towards the stove so he can get in on the action. Ethan climbs up onto one of the barstools at the kitchen island to get a good vantage point as I take out a small saucer and the Cream of Wheat box to get things cooking while we chat. This room has a view of the lake, too, and it's magical.

"This is a very special morning, because it's the very first morning in our new house," I say. "We're going to live here a long time. We'll eat breakfast right here in this kitchen many, many times. So many times it will be hard to count. We'll sit right over at that table, or maybe some days we'll sit here at the island. Some days we might even stand up to eat our breakfast if we're in a really big hurry. But there will never be another first time after this one. Isn't that special?"

"Wow, Daddy," Ethan says. "That is special."

"Wow, wow, wow," Leo parrots.

"Should we do something extra special when Mommy comes out of the shower to celebrate?" I ask. "Can you think of a way to make our special first breakfast in the new house extra special?" Never one to be short on ideas, Ethan takes less than a minute before he jumps up onto his knees, ready to tell us his plan.

"I know, Daddy," Ethan says as Leo's eyes grow wide with anticipation. "We can make up a breakfast song and sing it together."

"Okay," I respond. "Good idea, son. Do you have a song in mind?"

"Not yet, Daddy," Ethan says as if I'm asking a completely silly question. "That's why I said we have to make it up. You know, from our imaginations."

"Oh, I see. Right." I say. "How should we start?"

Leo's gears are turning now and he's ready to add to the discussion. "And clapping!" he says gleefully, smashing his chubby little hands together and bouncing up and down in his seat.

"You've got it, Leo. There will definitely be clapping!" I reply. Both boys are thinking hard, but I know I had better step up and pull things together for our extra special made up song. One good thing about toddlers is that they're a captive audience. I'm pretty sure I could make up a terrible song and then sing it out of tune, and they'd still like it because I'm their daddy. With that boost of confidence, I'm ready to begin.

"Okay, I think I have an idea," I tell them. "How about we pick a song we already know and then we change the words to make it our own?" They both look at me like they think they understand, but also maybe not. "I'll show you," I say. "Like, if we use a tune from a song we know and add different words. How about *Wheels on the Bus*? We all know that one, right?" I ask. They nod eagerly and we sing through it together to get a baseline.

"Now, what if we changed the words to something like The Hartmanns in the kitchen go cook cook cook, cook cook cook, cook cook cook, the Hartmanns in the kitchen go cook cook cook, on their special first breakfast morning," I sing, to instant rave reviews. "How about that?" I ask. Leo giggles uncontrollably and Ethan is so excited he has to climb down to the floor so he can dance along. Lady sits up and then prances around a bit, happy because the rest of us are.

"I know, Daddy," Ethan chimes in as he lifts up his elbows to march along. "Next can be eat, because we eat after we cook." I put Leo back onto my hip and we all sing together: "The Hartmanns in the kitchen go eat eat eat, eat eat eat, eat eat eat, the Hartmanns in the kitchen go eat eat eat, on their special first breakfast morning."

"Excellent job, Ethan! Now again with clapping like Leo suggested," I say as we launch into a repeat, this time louder and with lots of enthusiastic clapping. We try out variations on what the Hartmanns in the kitchen do, including drink, sing, play, and dance. Soon Ali hears the commotion and comes to join in the fun. She dances around the kitchen gracefully while her wavy hair dries in a sea of delicate wisps. I stop to pick up Lady's front paws, so she can walk upright like a person and the boys can barely contain their delight. When the 'creama eat' is ready, we add our bananas, raisins, and cinnamon, and we gobble it down. We share a pitcher of smooth chocolate milk, and we wipe our chins with soft napkins. Mission accomplished. This is a morning we won't soon forget. The most important people in my entire world are right here, and I'm finally going to get to spend plenty of time with them now that I've moved over into the civilian world. I am a happy man.

## GEORGE: A GLOW

The rest of our Saturday unfolds just as nicely as the morning did. Mom and John Wendell arrive on time and we split up to accomplish our tasks as planned. Ali, Mom, and Leo stay at the house to meet with our interior designer, while John Wendell and Ethan go along with me to run errands. I realize I had better pick up more groceries than just fruits and vegetables if I want to feed everyone coming into town, so after the farmer's market, we add a stop at Harold's Food Market over on South Meadow Street. It's another one of John Wendell's favorite places. Of course, he doesn't complain. Harold's is a grocery store which also has a cafeteria-style eatery popular with the retired set. I find the food in the eatery a bit bland, like I do most other cafeteria-style food, but John Wendell doesn't seem to mind. The three of us talk it over and decide to eat lunch right here at Harold's. We figure we're already here, so we might as well. I had thought about trying out a new pizza restaurant called Pepperoni Parlor, but we can hit The Parlor, as it's affectionately becoming known, one day next week. We have time. I don't report to Cornell for another nine days. And even after I start work, I expect to be able to get away for lunches with the family. When we're done shopping and eating lunch, we head to Icy Scoops for what is arguably the main event. As usual, their frozen treats do not disappoint. I'm not sure whether it's Ethan or John Wendell who is more excited to get their hands on a sweet, cool waffle cone with creamy goodness inside. Ice cream is timeless. It unites generations, and it certainly unites ours. We're grateful for the simple pleasure.

We arrive back home just in time for the boys to get a quick nap in before our New York City family arrives and we head to Yellow Cob for dinner. John Wendell parks himself on the living room sofa with today's newspaper then doses off and snores lightly while Lady lays dutifully on the floor near his feet. She knows it's her job to protect the whole gang. When Mom sees that John Wendell is sleeping, she gently slides the newspaper out of his hands and covers him up with another cable knit blanket Ali has right where it's needed. This one is a soft turquoise blue. We bought it a couple of months ago at a Nordstrom store located in the same mall where Ali and I first met. We picked up quite a few items in preparation for the move so we'd have things for the new house that came from our special places in D.C. John Wendell balls the blanket up tight under his chin and snuggles in like a sleepy child. It's nice to see Mom taking such good care of him.

"You're a good caretaker, Mom," I say, patting her on the back as she settles down on the loveseat beside me and pulls her legs up to cross them Indian style underneath her. "Your kind help is allowing John Wendell to stay out of those depressing senior living facilities so many of his friends have moved into."

"Yeah, a number of his friends moved into a facility across town and right on out of this world because they were so miserable there," she adds, absentmindedly smoothing her shoulder-length red hair to one side around the back of her head.

"Oh, I know it, Linette," Ali says, joining the conversation. "Over the years, John Wendell has told us about several of his friends going downhill once they opted for that route. It's really sad. He tells us his friends Val and Horton even had to separate when Val needed skilled nursing care because they weren't married and Val's kids moved her out of state."

"Terrible," I say.

"It is downright heartbreaking," Mom says. "I see it more often than I'd like with not only John Wendell's friends, but with my own patients in the hospital. Aging is not necessarily graceful or gentle. A myriad of circumstances can present themselves which decrease a senior's quality of life in a big way. I just want to mitigate those things as much as possible for my dad. I'm doing the best I can for him, and for now, we're okay."

"It sounds like you're both doing pretty well," I

add. "Is John Wendell still managing alright alone while you're at work?"

"For the time being, yes," Mom answers. "He's frustrated about not being able to drive anymore though. He keeps telling me how careful and diligent he is, and how he even knows how to fly a plane. I think in his mind, he just needs to convince the powers that be he's qualified. He doesn't always seem to realize that I'm the one who made the decision, with his best interests in mind, of course. And he doesn't seem to realize the extent of the danger he poses on the road."

"I completely understand his position," Ali says. "He's probably the most careful and diligent man I know."

"I agree, dear," Mom says. "He's the best."

We sit for a moment in silence, watching John Wendell nap and contemplating the fragility that is his health and life at age ninety-five. Anything could happen at any time, to anyone. But we all know the odds start to stack up against a person when they're as old as our John Wendell.

"I see seniors at the hospital, many who are years younger than him," Mom says, in a quieter voice now. "And sometimes, they are taken down quickly. A bad case of the flu turns into pneumonia, a fall causes a broken bone. Even an accident resulting from something like leaving a stove on at home can be devastating, and potentially deadly. One day they're functioning well and are seemingly healthy, and then life takes them by surprise and it's a quick decline."

"I'm hoping John Wendell will join the centenarian club, Mom," I say, probably sounding somewhat in denial. "He's going pretty strong. I'm thinking he could make it to one-hundred-five even, or one-hundred-ten. People do it. You've seen them on the Smucker's jars during Willard Scott's TODAY Show segment, right?"

"George, honey, we'll see," she answers. "He might. But there's a reality here that you'll become more and more aware of now that you're living nearby. He musters all of his energy when people visit and he seems really good during those times, but then he crashes and ends up exhausted for days afterward. You guys will be around for that part now. Did you know for the past year or so, when he first wakes up he has no idea where he is, what time of day it is, or what's happening? It's a jolt for him every single time."

Ali and I both shake our heads to indicate we had no idea. We're too busy trying to process that information to say any words.

"I think it's important for John Wendell to know we all accept him just as he is," Mom continues. "He can't help that his body will fail him any more than little Will will be able to help that his body isn't developed enough to walk or talk when he first arrives. It's the inescapable nature of being human. We all go through it. It's sad, but it's also beautiful."

"Linette, you're an inspiration," Ali says, placing her hand over her heart like she does when she's deeply moved. "You have such a way with people, and with the most vulnerable parts of life. You're an amazing nurse."

"I like to think I am," Mom replies. "It comes naturally to me. I appreciate the compliment." And then after a long pause, "I have thought about retiring."

"Really?" Ali and I both ask in unison, eyebrows raised. I wasn't expecting that. Mom has always said she wanted to continue to work as long as she possibly could. She's still in good shape physically, and her mind is good aside from her inherent craziness. Ali's right that Mom has a knack for working with people who are staring down life's hardest times. She remains calm and steady as if she's the eye of a hurricane while things are swirling out of control around her. Ironically, when things aren't swirling out of control around her, she often dreams up an imagined crisis and her anxiety gets out of whack. It's almost like she needs to handle emergencies and difficult situations for her own mental health. Her patients are the lucky beneficiaries of that need to be useful. It works, but hopefully she can find something else that works during retirement.

"Mom, retiring would be great!" I say. "You could be more available to John Wendell, and you could spend more time with us and the boys. If you want to, that is." I for one would be really happy to have more time with my mom. It's one of the reasons I moved home to Ithaca. Mom and Ali get along well so I bet they'd have a lot of fun together, especially with Ali being a stay-at-home parent for awhile. I know the boys would absolutely love having their grandma around as much as possible. Maybe she'd sew Halloween costumes for them like she did for me. And take them to the library and swimming in the summer. We could have a round two for all the fun things Mom and I did when I was little, this time with John Wendell in tow as a nice bonus. When I was a kid in Brooklyn he and Grandma lived here in Ithaca, which is several hours away by car. They came to visit us in the City and we made regular trips Upstate to see them, but it wasn't like living right in the same city together would have been.

"Georgie, don't forget to include time for Linette to enjoy herself. I'm sure she'd like some lazy afternoons. Or spa days. Or maybe she's ready to start dating again," Ali adds. I didn't mention any of those things because I know my mom. She doesn't do things for herself, really. I literally cannot imagine her at a spa. And I certainly can't imagine her dating. It's been more than twenty years since Dad died, and Mom hasn't really dated since, save for a few early crash and burn romances kindled in AOL chat rooms. Ali knows these things about Mom, too. I wonder why she said what she did. I give my wife a puzzled look. She sees me out of the corner of her eye but isn't going to make eye contact and acknowledge me.

"Goodness, Ali, dear," Mom says, blushing a little. "I don't know about any of that. Being more available to John Wendell would definitely be good though. And I'd love to spend as much time as possible with you two and the boys. This cavernous house needs to be filled with lots of activity in order to make proper use of it." And there it is. That's the kind of dig Mom throws in when she thinks you aren't expecting it. Calling the house cavernous is her not-so-subtle way of expressing discomfort with our luxury home. Ali and I ignore the comment and carry on.

"Well, I know you like to feel useful, Mom," I say. "Maybe you could volunteer part time to keep your skills sharp and put your training to good use in a more relaxed setting."

"Oh, very good idea, Georgie," Ali adds. "That makes the transition easier. I might do some volunteering myself up until I open my law practice. When you're used to working and being needed, it's unsettling to stop it all of a sudden."

"That might not be a bad plan," Mom says, and then takes a long deep breath. "I'd need to look at my budget. Right now, I get social security retirement from your dad on top of my own income. I'd be giving up a lot each month if my income went away. And I donate regularly to nonprofits that count on my payment every month. They'd come up short." Ali and I glance at each other, but neither of us says anything in response. Dad left Mom millions that she has tucked away in mutual funds. This isn't the first time I've gotten the impression that she doesn't touch that money at all. It's like she doesn't want to admit that she even has it. I'm not sure what's going on with that. It's strange, for sure. I mean, why is she okay with using Dad's retirement benefit paid through social security, but not the money he left her? He worked hard for both. And besides, John Wendell has a nice nest egg saved up as well. If money were needed for his care, or for Mom to make herself available for his care, John Wendell wouldn't hesitate to use it. He wouldn't feel the least bit bad about using it either. When he dies, it will be passed down to Mom. I swear, something must have happened to her that I don't know about. Her issues surrounding money are bizarre.

"I guess we're all going through pretty significant life changes right now," Ali says, successfully steering the conversation back to a more sane one without making Mom feel bad or like she can't be open with us.

"I know I'm facing a big change," I offer. "I'm sure my new job at Cornell will be great. It's going to be different though. I keep feeling like I'm just on leave and should be reporting back to my squadron soon."

"And every time the phone rings, I think for a split second it's my office calling to ask about a case I've worked on, or to tell me what's coming up," Ali says. "Like Georgie said, I'm sure our lives here in Ithaca will be great, but it's going to be so strange being home with the boys and not working."

"I wondered about that, Ali," Mom says. "How long do you think you'll take off?"

"I'm not really sure, Linette," Ali replies. "I know I need a slower pace so I can spend more time with the boys, especially since little Will is on the way. I've been lucky enough to have worked quite a bit from home since Ethan was born, but it was still a lot to keep up with given the way Georgie and I choose to raise our boys. We don't want them in daycare if we can help it. In D.C., we juggled between the two of us and a couple of dear friends who could stay with them at our house during daytime hours. It was better than daycare, but I decided I wanted to take the leap and devote myself to our little guys completely. After all, it will be a relatively short period of time that they're this little and need us this much. I don't want to miss a thing. When I'm ready, I'll open up my own immigration law practice here in Ithaca."

"I admire your dedication," Mom says. "You know, I was home with George before he went to school. I don't regret a single minute of it. It was time very well spent." I smile at Mom, and she reaches up to give the hair on the back of my head a quick tussle. "When you're ready to go back to work, you'll know," she continues, giving Ali a look of knowing approval. "Trust yourself, dear." The three of us are on the same page when it comes to what we believe about rearing young children. Ali puts her hand over her heart again and smiles broadly at Mom and me. My people are so good.

We spend what feels like a nice, long time talking more while John Wendell and the little guys snooze. Ali and Mom tell me about the arrangements they made with our interior designer and I make mental note of all the interesting things we plan to do together in the coming months. Then in a synchronicity that's almost comical, John Wendell begins to stir at the exact moment we hear Ethan and

Leo open their bedroom door and scoot out. Less than a minute after that, we see Marjorie and Roddy's Land Rover turn slowly into our driveway. Marjorie is driving, and Roddy is waving wildly from the passenger seat. They look excited.

"Mama Marjorie and Papa Roddy are here," I say cheerfully, getting up from my seat to greet the boys and usher them towards the front door. John Wendell takes a minute to orient himself, then sits up and continues reading the newspaper as if he wasn't sleeping. Mom moves over next to him to make room on the loveseat for our newest arrivals.

"Hey, hey, hey, Mom and Dad," Ali yells as she throws open the front door and rushes toward her parents. She's in a thin cotton shirt without a coat and it's cold, but she isn't going to let that slow her down. Marjorie jerks the vehicle into park and jumps out to hug her daughter. Roddy leaps out the other side without bothering to put his coat on either and runs around to join in. The three of them hop up and down as they embrace and squeal like school girls. Mom and I are close in a subdued way, but the Dyer-Davies family is next level. I know the boys feel the excitement and want to get out there, too, so I bundle them up in their coats and hats and carry them out into the front courtyard. No need for shoes. I hold them, one on each hip. I run a little so we can get to Marjorie and Roddy faster, and Leo giggles as he's jostled up and down. He's a giggler, that boy.

"Hello, babies," Marjorie says as she puts an arm around each boy in front of me, bracelets clanking, and kisses their cheeks. They squeal, too, and they bounce up and down. They can barely contain themselves. "You've grown since I saw you at Christmas, big guys. That was only a few weeks ago. How are you growing so fast? Are Mommy and Daddy feeding you special grow-up-fast food?"

"Noooooo," Ethan replies with a laugh. "We're growing regular because we're strong and healthy. You know it, Mama Marjorie. We're strong boys." Ethan pops up one of his biceps and makes a muscle as Leo shakes his head emphatically in agreement.

"Ah, yes, I do know that. You're very strong, and very healthy," Marjorie says as she stands on her toes to reach around the boys and kiss me on the cheek. I smile and lean in hard against her forehead, then she steps back and gives me a happy wink. "But I think you're going to be tall like your Daddy and your uncles and your grandpas. We have many tall, handsome men in this family." Marjorie is dressed beautifully, as usual, and her long red hair is perfectly positioned under her charcoal gray winter hat. Her style could be described as elegant hippie if there is such a thing. It's distinctive, and it suits her.

Roddy walks around from behind us and the boys nearly fly out of my arms to get to him. They know they can be somewhat rough with him like they can with me. Roddy's a strong man who is in fantastic shape. He has naturally broad shoulders and a muscular build, and he keeps his physique up by boxing. He and Marjorie are younger than Mom, roughly the same age as Uncle Liam, and the same as

Dad would be if he were still around. Mom's in good shape, too, but the combination of the few extra years she has on the rest of them and her more serious demeanor makes the younger crowd seem a lot more lively.

"Let me at these boys, George. I want to hold them right away," Roddy says in his deep, gravelly voice as he grins from ear to ear and his eyes beam with pride. Maybe that's why Ali likes my big grin. Her dad certainly has a big grin of his own. Mine is admittedly goofier.

"Papa Roddy!" Ethan says, as he slings his arms around Roddy's neck then pats both of his cheeks gleefully. Roddy shimmies Ethan around to one side to make room for Leo, too.

"Here are my grandsons," Roddy says as he tilts downward and pulls their little heads in towards his face. "Mama Marjorie, how did we get so lucky to have the best grandsons in the whole wide world?" he asks, looking at the boys with what seems like an even bigger smile if that's possible. "It doesn't get any better than these guys right here. Of course, little Will will be one of the best, too," he adds, nodding towards Ali's pregnant belly.

I'm about to suggest we get inside the warm house when we see Nicky and Luis' silver Tesla sedan pulling into the driveway. Sara has her window down and is pretending one of her dolls is waving to us from the backseat.

"Look, it's Nicky and Luis and Sara! Perfect timing," Ali says as Ethan and Leo begin to cheer and clap. "Did you guys travel together along the way?" she asks her parents.

"Sort of," Marjorie replies. "We had lunch together in Jersey after we left the city, but we lost each other somewhere around the Pennsylvania State line while your dad was driving. I think Nicky drives faster than Roddy does. They must have stopped again in order that they're getting here after us. Or else I made up the time once I got behind the wheel. Either way, it worked out nicely."

"Yeah, Mom, I think most people drive faster than Daddy does," Ali says, giving her father a stern, but playful look.

"Hey now, it isn't a problem in the city, because I have people to drive for me," Roddy responds. "I just sit in the back seat and read or work. Typically, there's nothing to see but other slow-moving cars anyway. When I do leave the city, who can blame me for wanting to enjoy the view?" He sure sounds like a typical city guy. I'm reminded of the Aesop Fable about the city mouse and the country mouse, and I chuckle to myself. I should read that one to the boys some time. They'd probably get a kick out of it.

We all walk towards Nicky and Luis as Sara comes bounding forward and makes a beeline for Ali. The two of them have a special relationship. Nicky and Luis met and got married when Sara was three. She's the product of a previous relationship where Luis was married to a woman who tragically passed away in a freak horseback riding accident. I think Ali reminds Sara of her mom. When Sara reaches her destination, she puts her arms around Ali's waist and hugs her tight.

"Hello, sweetheart," Ali says to Sara. "How's my smart girl?"

"Good, Aunt Ali! I'm good," Sara says enthusiastically, turning to give a high five to each of the boys then coming back to pat Ali's belly. "Little Will is getting so big."

"I know he is, and you are, too," Ali responds. Your grandma was just saying how she thinks the boys have grown since she saw them at Christmas, and that was only a few weeks ago. I think you've all grown."

Nicky and Luis grab a couple of suitcases out of the trunk and then catch up with our group on the lawn. We make the rounds hugging and chatting a bit as we greet each other. It's so good to have everybody here at our new home. It's almost exactly the same distance from Manhattan to Ithaca as it was from Manhattan to D.C., but for some reason, Ithaca feels closer. Probably because we're all New Yorkers now. Maybe the traffic will be a little easier to navigate.

Ali's family is like mine but without the emotional baggage. It's strange sometimes that they all get along so well and are so unabashedly excited about life. I've known them long enough to know they're sincere, but it's weird. It's as if they've cracked some mysterious code. They don't hold onto hurts and disappointments like most people do. They still have hurts and disappointments, but it's like they're more evolved. They work through their feelings in a healthy way and let things go. I could learn a thing or two from this crowd. Mom could as well. Speaking of Mom, we really had better head inside so she and John Wendell can say hello to everyone.

"Let's go inside, folks. It's starting to get dark," I say when there's a break in the conversation. "It's nice and warm in the house. And I know my mom and John Wendell want to see you. They're waiting in the living room."

"And Lady, Daddy," Ethan interjects. "Don't forget about Lady."

"You're right, Ethan," I reply. "Lady wants to see everybody, too."

I lead our group through the front courtyard area and into our beautiful home. I feel proud. No one on Ali's side of the family has money issues, so they're not the least bit uncomfortable with our move up to this level of luxury. To the contrary, they are used to beautiful homes and fine living. It probably feels natural to them. I'm sure Roddy and Marjorie are happy to see us finally using the money we have. I know Ali's made no secret of the fact that over the years it was me who wanted to live in a low-key way which didn't draw attention to us. I don't remember ever discussing it directly with Roddy and Marjorie, but I'm sure they knew it was my issue. They had to have known. They passed money down to both Ali and Nicky, and Nicky has felt free to use and enjoy his while Ali has mostly kept hers tucked away until now. Surely, they noticed that one of their kids was responding to wealth differently than the other. Nicky is a well-respected architect in Manhattan and he owns his own firm. He does plenty well for himself financially, but I doubt he'd be able to afford the brownstone he owns on the Upper West Side without money from his parents. I mean, maybe, but it seems like a stretch. Luis is a public school teacher. Nicky already owned the brownstone when they got together, so Luis and Sara moved into luxury as part of the new relationship. Obviously, Luis couldn't afford the place on a school teacher's salary. They all seem content with their financial situations though. Nobody seems to have unrealistic expectations. Nobody seems to resent anything.

"Kids, your new home is stunning," Roddy says thoughtfully, pausing to look around and take in all the little details as we walk through the front door. "It's modern and has a gorgeous contemporary aesthetic, yet it still feels warm and inviting. Nice wreath, too." Ali and I glance at each other and smile. She knew the wreath would be a hit.

"Thanks, Daddy," Ali replies. "We really love the place. We're going to make a lot of good memories here."

"We've already made a few," I chime in, gazing at Ali and thinking about last night. And our wake-up romp this morning. She lowers one eyebrow as a warning and looks back at me sternly. She doesn't like me talking about our sex lives when other people are around. She knows exactly what recently-made memories I'm referring to, but I decide to keep it PG so she doesn't get embarrassed. "We had an extra special breakfast with the boys this morning," I continue with an innocent smile. "It was great. We sang together and danced around the kitchen with Lady while making creama eat, as Ethan calls it."

"It was very fun," Ethan adds.

We close the door tightly and are taking our winter outerwear off as Lady trots in to greet everyone. Mom and John Wendell follow closely behind. My family and Ali's family all know and love each other. They've spent a lot of time together in our company, and they genuinely like to do so. Ali and I have hosted a number of big get-togethers over the years. Family parties are our very favorite kinds. Roddy, Marjorie, Nicky, Luis, Sara, Mom, and John Wendell greet each other warmly now.

We chat for awhile, moving in small groups throughout the house as Ali, Mom, and I give the others a tour. Mom knows her way around since she periodically checked in on the builders over the past few months while the house was being finished. Our dinner reservations are at six o'clock, so we don't waste much time. Once they've seen the new place, Luis and Roddy get the rest of the luggage from the vehicles and Ali shows them to their guest rooms. We put Roddy and Marjorie upstairs in a room across the hall from the boys. It can't hurt that Marjorie is next to a bathroom. I think she gets up to use it in the night almost as often as Ali. We give Nicky and Luis a room in the finished basement. We offer Sara her choice of spots thinking she might like to be in a sleeping bag with Ethan and Leo in their room, but she decides to take a guest room downstairs next to her dads. She is only eight after all, and this is a big house. I don't blame her for wanting to stay close to them. Truth be told, I'm a little surprised Ethan and Leo were so comfortable upstairs last night while Ali and I were on the main level. We'll see if that lasts. We did the family bed thing when they were younger and it worked well for us. Leo was the one who initiated the move to his own bedroom, and once he went Ethan wanted to join him. That was a few months ago. If they end up returning to our bed for a time, no big deal. They'll leave when they're ready. And if they go back and forth before they settle in completely, then so be it. It's a little more logistically challenging for me and Ali to make love, but we have a routine down which involves a generous amount of extended bathroom time.

We all pile into three vehicles to make the trip down the hill and across town to Yellow Cob. Mom hops into the Land Rover with Marjorie and Nicky. Luis drives his car with Roddy and Sara in tow. And John Wendell sits in the passenger seat of our SUV while Ali drives and the boys and I squeeze into the back. Ethan gets the third row because I don't think my legs would fit back there unless I folded myself up like a pretzel, and it would be equally difficult to get Leo in and out of his car seat from that spot. Ethan can climb in and out and buckle himself. He's pretty happy with the arrangement. I imagine he thinks it's fun to have a little section of his own back there. He has his toy bag on his lap and is evaluating the contents in preparation for what he knows will be a long dinner. Leo is still sleepy from all of the excitement of the past few days, so he nods off as we drive.

It's completely dark outside when we arrive at the restaurant, and it's bitter cold. I lower my head below the roofline of the vehicle and gaze out in anticipation. The dining room looks especially cozy and inviting. The parking lot is full. Must be a packed house. It is Saturday evening, after all. If Yellow Cob isn't the most popular restaurant in Ithaca, it is certainly one of the most popular. It's kind of fancy and is definitely higher-end than the local sandwich and bagel shops, so the place is often booked for celebrations. Ali pulls up to the door to let John Wendell out. I get out, too, in case he needs some help. The rest of the crew goes to find parking spots. The way the parking lot is situated next to the marina means it's long and narrow and not very many cars fit without having to use an overflow lot next door. Ali and gang are going to have a bit of a walk.

John Wendell makes his way inside and to the hostess stand to confirm our arrival. The employees all know him, and they can tell he's excited.

"We have a big group," he proclaims. "Reservation for thirteen. Name is John Wendell. W-e-n-d…"

"Oh, we've got you. We know how to spell it," the young brunette behind the counter says with a wink. "Is your daughter with you tonight? I'm used to seeing the two of you together."

"She sure is," John Wendell replies. "She's with the group parking the cars. And this here is my grandson, George Hartmann. He and his family just moved home, so you'll be seeing them quite often from now on. They bought a place on East Shore overlooking the lake."

"That's great to hear, Mr. Wendell," she says. "I look forward to getting to know them. Your table will be ready in about five to ten minutes. They're setting everything up for you right now. We made sure to put you near the back of the building so you have the best view of the lights on the lake. We know how much you love that."

John Wendell thanks her and heads for the little boys' room, as he calls it, so he doesn't have to get up and go during dinner. I wait in the lobby. I don't think we've reached the point where I need to follow him into the bathroom. Not yet, anyway. I'll ask Mom sometime soon in order to be sure.

The lobby is fun. It's decorated in low key boathouse style which straddles the line between elegant and cheesy. The hostess stand is made to look like the front of a boat, and from head on it appears the employees standing behind it are driving. That sounds pretty cheesy, I know, but the boat is made out of a rich, gorgeous wood with a thick gloss lacquer which moves it into elegant territory. Nearby, there are a couple of canoes finished the same way which are made into shelves. The same wood is used for paneling that runs halfway up the walls, and there are framed photos on the upper half of farm fresh food items and various kinds of boats. Just as I begin to sit down on a bench near one of the canoe shelves, I see Jen and Duke walk in the front door. We greet each other with hugs and smiles and small talk about how gorgeous this place is at night. The rest of our gang arrives inside not long afterward, and John Wendell grins broadly when he exits the restroom and sees us standing together.

"Would you get a look at this fine group of people," he says proudly to the young women at the hostess stand. "We're a baker's dozen." He waits a moment for a reaction and then laughs heartily at his own cleverness. Classic John Wendell. He's in his element now. Smooth jazz is playing in the background. Lights are twinkling on the lake. Wine is being poured and shared. And everyone is dressed nice and spiffy. His words. I read somewhere that the English are especially fond of plays on words. I assume that extends to a fascination with a careful choice of words in order to be clever and funny as well. John Wendell's dad came over as a young stowaway from Liverpool, England when he was thirteen. Maybe the English sense of humor came with him.

When we arrive at our table, we're pleasantly surprised to see that the instrumental jazz music playing in the background is actually live music and we're seated very near to the musicians. They look young. Ithaca College has a well-respected music program. I wonder if that's where this group is from.

"Hey, John Wendell," I say across the table as I sit down and help Ali situate her coat on the back of her chair. "Love the music. Is this Duke Ellington?"

"Yes, son, Duke Ellington and John Coltrane. This

one's called *My Little Brown Book*. It was one of your grandma's favorites. She and I used to dance to this song, on the ballroom floor and in the living room of our home out on Ellis Hollow Road. We sure did love to dance together. Your mom remembers," he says, leaning towards Mom as she chooses one of the chairs beside him and begins to get comfortable.

"Oh, I remember," Mom says. "Who could forget. You two were magical together. Your dancing was superb. You really should have entered more competitions."

"There were competitions?" Roddy asks as he sits down on John Wendell's other side and Marjorie sits next to him.

"Yes, there certainly were," Mom replies. "They did a lot here in the Upstate, and twice they even made it to regional ballroom dancing semi-finals in Philadelphia."

"Wow, I had no idea!" Roddy exclaims, placing his hand gently on John Wendell's forearm. "Too bad we didn't know each other then. I could have written you and Eleanor in as dancers in one of my plays."

"You're very kind, Roddy" John Wendell replies. "I'm not sure we had that level of talent. We had a grand love though, that's for sure. We thoroughly enjoyed dancing together and moving in sync with our favorite songs. I like to think our love shone through and made our dancing more enjoyable for those watching."

"I know it did," Roddy affirms. "I remember you two dancing at Ali and George's wedding reception.

Guests were stopping what they were doing to watch you. And I'm pretty sure the band started playing more and more jazz covers to keep you from leaving the dance floor."

"I remember that, too," Nicky chimes in from a few seats down. "You were fantastic." He turns to Luis and Sara to provide them some backstory. "John Wendell and Eleanor did such amazing dancing that day. You see, Aunt Ali and George got married in Washington, D.C. at a place right on the Potomac River. It was beautiful. There were a bunch of guests there who were family and friends. There were more than one hundred people in attendance. The wedding ceremony took place outdoors in a wedding garden. The whole thing was special. I remember John Wendell walking up to the altar in his suit and tie and lighting a candle in honor of Alec before the ceremony began. Alec is George's dad. He passed away when George was a teenager and so couldn't be there. I always thought that was extra nice. Alec was John Wendell's son-in-law, not his own son. He didn't have to do that."

"I wanted to. It was an honor," John Wendell adds, as I feel tears growing warm and full in my eyes. Ali grabs my hand under the table and gives it a squeeze. Our waiter drops a pitcher of water and a bottle of John Wendell's favorite red wine off at the table, but sensing we're having a moment he excuses himself to go take care of something else before asking for our order.

"You could feel Alec's presence there that day,"

Marjorie says quietly, glancing at Mom to see if she's okay with the discussion taking a turn in this direction. Marjorie has always been spiritual and intuitive. Hippy doesn't just describe her style of clothing. She's into all sorts of New Age ideas. She knows we're open to them. We certainly don't look down on her or dismiss her beliefs when they differ from our own. Mom meets Marjorie's gaze and gives her a sad, half smile, indicating her approval. The two of them have talked about this before. The rest of the table is quiet now, and everyone is tuned into the story. Duke puts his arm around Jen's shoulders and they settle backward in their chairs to listen. Ethan and Leo are coloring on kids menus the waiter gave them, but you can tell they're taking the adult conversation in. Ethan cocks his head to one side and listens, remaining alert.

"There was a heaviness in the air," Marjorie continues. "Not in a negative way. The best I can describe the feeling is kind of like how you feel moisture in the air on a humid day or a foggy morning. It's the same air, and it's all normal and natural. But there's an extra component. An addition of sorts to the energy around us like fog is an addition to the air. I felt it, and it felt like Alec."

"But you never knew Alec, right?" Luis asks, to clarify.

"That's right. He died several years before Ali and George met. I've known his son George, his wife Linette, his brother Liam, and his father-in-law John Wendell," Marjorie says. "And of course, his grandsons are my grandsons. He wasn't alive long enough in his physical body to meet them in person either, but I believe he knows them. I think we're all connected in a way that goes beyond these physical bodies we live in. The bodies are temporary, but our love for each other is not."

Sara leans over to Luis sheepishly, yet seemingly not able to hold herself back, and says, "Daddy, is John Wendell my family? Because that probably means that his wife Eleanor and George's dad Alec are my family, too, right?" Luis looks at Nicky, not sure how to respond. Nicky looks at me. Sara's mom came from a small family and only one distant uncle is still alive. It's especially important for Sara to know she is accepted and loved by Nicky's extended family. John Wendell answers before I can find the right words.

"Sara, my dear, you're exactly right. We are your family," John Wendell assures. "You're Nicky's daughter. And Nicky is Ali's brother. That's why you call her Aunt Ali, yes?" Sara nods as she looks over at her aunt and smiles. "And Ali is married to George, which makes him your Uncle George. So your Uncle George's family is your family, too. That includes Linette, Alec, me, and my late wife Eleanor. You're ours, kid. If you'll have us."

"Don't forget Liam in that list," I add. "He'll want to be counted as an uncle and his wife Estella as an aunt." I sure wish he and Estella could have been here tonight. He had a prior commitment and couldn't get away. They're planning a visit soon though. Sara smiles big and leans on Luis' shoulder. It looks like she feels loved. I hope so. She's our girl, for sure.

"You guys are such a nice family," Jen says from the end of the table. "Can you adopt me?"

"I thought we already did that," Roddy says, winking at Jen.

"Yeah, didn't you receive the paperwork?" Ali jokes. "You spent so much time at our place when we were kids. I thought for sure the paperwork was signed a long, long time ago."

Ethan decides to speak up now, feeling confident. "And Jenny, that means everybody at this table is your family. Right, Mommy?"

"I'd say so, baby," Ali replies. "I like that."

"Family doesn't only come from being blood relatives," John Wendell says. "It's about much more. Family finds each other all kinds of different ways. But one thing is for sure: family always, always, always finds each other. I miss my sweet Eleanor tonight. And we miss Alec. I know Sara misses her mom, and Luis misses her, too. There should be three more chairs at this table with those folks seated here with us. It's heartbreaking when the ones we love move on without us. Like Marjorie, I, too, believe they're still around. Or at least I think they pop in from time to time to check on us and to reconnect. Who knows how all the logistics work? But I feel like they're not gone. They're just in another realm. In another form." After a pause, he looks around the table at us and continues, "I'm grateful to have each and every one of you with me right here and right now. During this beautiful, snowy January. In my beloved Ithaca. On the spectacular Cayuga Lake. At one of my favorite restaurants. You people make this old man's heart swell with happiness. There's nowhere else I'd rather be."

I don't think there's a dry eye in our group as we smile at John Wendell and each other.

"To family," Roddy says, placing a hand over his heart just like Ali does and lifting his wine glass in the air for a toast. We raise our water and wine glasses to join in. They clank together and make a happy sound.

"To family," we say in unison.

Same as the earlier part of our Saturday, this evening is shaping up to be one we won't soon forget. Ali and I envisioned this type of scene from our old house in D.C., but I don't think our visions did the reality justice. I'm so glad we moved home. My wife and boys look relaxed and content.

Roddy kicks the dinner off by ordering a sampling of egg rolls, calamari, and coconut shrimp for the table. It's kind of nice to watch Roddy spend his money because he seems to legitimately have fun doing so. Once the appetizers are eaten, we order our main courses. John Wendell's long-time favorite pick is the Georgia Peach Grilled Chicken with sweet potato mash, peach chutney, and fresh vegetables on the side. He doesn't even have to tell the waiter. I'm not sure this particular guy would have known because he seems new, but apparently, the hostesses filled him in.

"The usual, Mr. Wendell?" the server asks.

"Yes, sir."

"Wow, John Wendell, how does he know what you want to eat?" Ethan asks.

"He knows because I've been here a lot of times,

E-boy," John Wendell responds. "A whole lot of times. And I always order the exact same thing. I'm predictable." Ethan smiles, satisfied.

Roddy, Luis, Jen, and Duke all order the same Georgia Peach chicken, inspired by John Wendell. He swears you can't go wrong with the choice. Marjorie's a vegetarian, so she orders an eggplant dish. Ali, on the other hand, is usually in the mood for steak when she's pregnant. She orders a filet mignon, and Nicky and I follow her lead with similar cuts of beef. Mom chooses salad and crab cakes, and the kids pick flatbread pizzas. It's all delicious.

We're finished with our main meal and are leisurely chatting over cheesecake and crème brûlée when the band begins to play the original Frank Sinatra version of *The Way You Look Tonight*.

"Awe, Georgie, wasn't this their song?" Ali asks me as she leans in close.

Before I can answer, John Wendell is up out of his seat and heading towards the musicians. We all watch him go, surprised. No one says anything for a minute as we survey the scene. He's slow but steady on his feet. He looks down as he walks, taking care with each step as he weaves around tables and chairs filled with restaurant patrons. The crowd begins to grow curious as they watch him pass by. His body language is strong and determined.

"What's he doing?" Roddy asks. "Is he…"

"He's dancing," I say. "My grandfather is dancing." I look back at Ali and she nods in agreement.

There's a small tiled area in front of the band where I've seen couples dance in the past. I hadn't noticed anyone dancing there this evening, but I've seen John Wendell and Grandma do it before. Ali and I have even joined them a few times.

When John Wendell reaches the band members, he whispers something to the saxophone player who nods approvingly then turns to the others and motions with his hand for them to start the song over. These guys probably all know him, too, same as the restaurant staff and the majority of people in Ithaca. The keyboard player lays down a soft background rhythm as John Wendell swivels around to face the dining room and picks up a microphone. He takes his time, carefully removing the mic from the stand and breathing deeply in and out before he begins.

"Hello there, fine people. I hope you're enjoying this beautiful evening so far."

The crowd erupts into enthusiastic applause. They're a peppy bunch.

"My name is John Edgar Wendell," he continues. "People usually call me just John Wendell. I'm a long time Ithaca resident, and Yellow Cob is one of my favorite restaurants. Oh, and I'm ninety-five years old." This time the applause is thunderous. John Wendell seems to appreciate the response. He smiles broadly and waves, sort of as if he's a movie star on the red carpet. Again, he waits for quiet and then continues. "I'm here celebrating with my family tonight because my grandson and his beautiful wife and their wonderful little boys have just moved back home. You may have seen the article about my grandson in this morning's Ithaca Journal. I'm so proud of him. He's Ithaca's very own soldier, recently retired from the Air Force after a decorated military career. He's an Aerospace Engineer. A real-life rocket scientist! He'll be working over in Cornell's Engineering Department once he gets his family settled into their new house. His name is George Hartmann. He's right over there," he says, pointing towards our table. I blush at the attention and the mention of the newspaper article. So much for keeping a low profile. Ali turns and kisses me slow on the lips while the rest of the group cheers. A surge goes through my body when I feel my wife's mouth on mine. She had better not get me too wound up in here or I might have to take her out to our SUV and have my way with her. There's room in the back seat. It's happened before.

John Wendell waits for the crowd to quiet down then goes on. "My amazing daughter Linette is here tonight, too. You may have seen us together around town. She and I have taken care of each other in recent years. But George is home now. He's going to take care of his Mom." The room claps politely, unsure where this is going. I'm unsure where this is going. A quick glance at Mom's face tells me she's unsure where this is going as well. "There's more, and it's the reason I'm up here telling you all of this. My lovely wife of sixty-two years, Eleanor Wendell, isn't with us tonight. Sadly, she passed away nine years ago. I miss her every day." Several audible gasps and a few groans of pity rise above a low murmur. "I know, I know," John Wendell says, working the crowd. He is surprisingly comfortable in front of a microphone. I guess there's a lot I still don't know about him. "But what I'm about to tell you is a good and a happy thing," he says, pausing for dramatic effect. "This is our song."

The crowd goes wild as John Wendell cues the band then begins snapping the fingers on his free hand along with the beat while gently shifting his weight back and forth to sway from side to side.

"He's still holding the microphone," Roddy says. "Is he going to sing?"

"I think he is," I reply.

"Yes, he sure is," Ali says. "This is remarkable. And so John Wendell."

Right on time along with the music, John Wendell stops snapping and raises both hands up towards the heavens as if to tell Grandma this one's for her. He straightens his free arm out at an angle towards the floor, palm forward, and readies himself for the melody ahead by leaning backward.

"Someday," he begins singing with his eyes closed while turning his free hand upward and taking a deep breath. "When I'm awfully low, when the world is cold, I will feel a glow just thinking of you, and the way you look tonight." A seriousness settles over the crowd as they start to realize just how much this song means to him. I'm with them. His comment about me being here to watch over Mom takes my breath away. Has he been waiting for me to return home to take care of her so he can move on and be with Grandma?

"Yes, you're lovely, with your smile so warm," he croons. His voice is deep and rich. "And your cheeks so soft, there is nothing for me but to love you, and the way you look tonight." He snaps his fingers again during the break in lyrics while the band continues to play. He walks slowly across the floor in front of the musicians, every step precisely on the beat. The crowd lets out another round of cheers and applause when they see him move.

"With each word your tenderness grows, tearing my fear apart," he sings, eyes open now and taking it all in. The restaurant patrons love him. He's a natural performer. "And that laugh that wrinkles your nose, it touches my foolish heart. Lovely. Never, ever change. Keep that breathless charm. Won't you please arrange it? 'Cause I love you, just the way you look tonight."

Slowly and deliberately, John Wendell places the microphone back on its stand as the string bass amps up the volume for an instrumental solo. He takes another long, deep breath. He straightens himself, back arched, then raises his left arm up and to the side of his body while moving his right arm up and into a semicircle in front of him. We instantly recognize what he's doing. He's holding his position just like he would if he were dancing with a partner. Just like he did countless times when dancing with Grandma. As the music plays on, John Edgar Wendell dances with the grace and precision of an old pro. He moves forward, then turns, then forward again in a slow Foxtrot. He knows all the steps by heart. When it's time to twirl his imaginary partner, he holds his arm out and waits, then steps from side to side in time before dipping her on cue. The crowd looks on, deeply moved. Many people are in tears.

This is something of a surreal experience. John Wendell's rousing speech and his song and dance are communicating things that a regular old sit-down conversation never could. To an outside observer, John Wendell is happy, and positive, and pleasant to be around. But underneath all of that, his heart is broken. It has been ever since the day Grandma left him. Have I underestimated the depths of his pain? I was busy building my career and my own family. I know John Wendell would never have asked me to give any of that up. But he needs me now. My mind is flooded with new understanding, and I feel a little dizzy. I look around at the adults in our group, and they all seem to get it, too. Mom must have been trying to break it to me gently during our conversation this afternoon. Her eyes are filled with tears. I suddenly see the complexity of what she's facing.

"Georgie," Ali says as she leans her head onto my shoulder. "This is one of the most beautiful things I've ever seen. This is what life's all about."

"I know," I say. "I'd twirl an imaginary you if I were in his position. True love never dies." She nods and burrows into me as I wrap my arms tightly around her. Our family members are just as moved. They hug and hold and pat each other as they watch

John Wendell's routine. I'm awestruck by the man that he is. I'm incredibly proud to be his grandson.

"Hey," I say. "Let's go and join him."

"Good idea, Georgie, I'm right behind you," Ali replies.

"Anybody else?" I ask.

"Yes, sir," Duke says. "You read my mind. Shall we, Jen?"

"I'm in," Roddy says to us, then to Marjorie, "May I have this dance, my darling?" She curtsies, and they follow us towards the little dance floor.

"Us too," Nicky says, grabbing Luis' hand.

"Sara, dear," Mom says, "How about you and I each get one of these handsome little boys and go dance?"

"I'd like that," Sara replies as she helps Ethan out of his chair and towards the dance floor. Mom picks Leo up out of his booster seat and follows closely behind.

And there we are, the entire baker's dozen of us, on the little dance floor moving together to Frank Sinatra's timeless tune.

We stay at Yellow Cob dancing, talking, and drinking wine right up until they close down at eleven o'clock. We even watch the musicians pack up and leave. If it weren't so cold outside, we would probably hang around even longer talking in the parking lot. We have a tendency to stay out late when we get together to celebrate. The boys are used to it. Of course, the strategically packed toy bags help get them through the evening. Leo sleeps on my shoulder and Ethan sleeps on Roddy's. They'll catch up tomorrow. Maybe they'll take a long nap.

When we arrive home, we're tired, but positively glowing from our fun evening. Mom and John Wendell get in their car and head for their house without even coming inside ours. I'll bet John Wendell is exhausted after our big time. Ali and I wave goodbye to them, then head into the house to make sure everyone has what they need to settle in for a good night's rest. I don't think any of us will take long to conk out. Ethan and Leo again seem fine with sleeping in their own room, so we go with it. Marjorie and Roddy are right next door for the next few nights anyway.

I do a couple of miscellaneous chores while I wait for the house to be quiet. I want to be sure I'm available if anybody needs an extra pillow or blanket. Once it sounds like everyone is settled, I wash up, put on some flannel pajama pants and climb into bed with my wife. I have thoughts of lovemaking, because, well, when do I not? But Ali doesn't look like she has the energy for it right now. It's been a long day. I scoot up tight behind her and envelope her in my arms, and everything is right in our world. I fall asleep fast and hard.

# PART II

## ANCIENT HISTORY

## GEORGE: THINGS WORTH FIGHTING FOR

I'm not sure how long I sleep. It's one of those periods of sleep that's almost frighteningly deep. I dream of my dad, which is strange because there's no storyline to go along with the dream. It doesn't feel like a dream at all, really, but more like I'm actually seeing Dad in person. Except I know I'm asleep, and I know he's dead. I have no idea what to make of this. It's never happened to me before. We're in the kitchen of our old apartment in Brooklyn. Dad has his arms folded across his chest, his muscular forearms settled down on top of each other like old familiar friends. He stood like that a lot. He's in his usual spot between the stove and the refrigerator and is leaning back against the oak cabinets and the white tile countertop. We had countless talks in this kitchen when I was a kid. Dad always stood in the same spot. Sometimes he ate Cheez Whiz on Ritz Crackers while we talked. Other times, a bowl of cereal. We often waited until Mom was asleep and then met up in the kitchen for some special time together. I'd go to my bed in my room, but then I'd stay awake and listen for the sound of the cracker sleeve or a clank in the silverware drawer. Those were my cues. Dad sees me now, and a huge smile appears on his face. I always did bring a smile to his face. No matter how busy or tired or stressed he became, he was always happy to see me.

"Hey, Kid!" he says enthusiastically. He called me Kid.

It feels like no time has passed since he left us. So often I've wished I could hear that voice again, and here it is. It's deep and husky and warm. He unfolds his arms and extends them towards me, an invitation to go in for an embrace. After all these years, I still remember what it felt like to hug my dad. I was smaller and shorter then, so his arms always wrapped around me. He used to wrap me tight and hug me hard. When I was little enough to be held and carried, he held me just as tight. I remember being carried in his arms and leaning my head down softly on his big, strong shoulders. He might as well have been Superman as far as I was concerned. In those days, I thought my Daddy was invincible. I always figured he held me tight because he loved me so much that he couldn't help but squeeze me and keep me close. He would have done anything to keep me safe and happy. I know that for sure. He was a good man. A good dad.

I hesitate for a moment as I work to process what I'm experiencing. I wonder if we're really in our Brooklyn kitchen. Surely not. Maybe my mind needed to create a familiar backdrop. Deciding I have nothing to lose, I move forward towards my Dad. He places his arms around me, and he feels real. He feels warm and very much alive. He hugs me tight and his embrace feels just like it always did. I'm overwhelmed. I love my dad so much. I miss him more than I let myself acknowledge. And here he is. It sure seems like I'm really hugging him right now. I don't know how or why this is happening, but I'm incredibly grateful that it is. We hold each other for awhile. There are no words exchanged between us, but there is communication. Come to think of it, Dad didn't actually open his mouth to say hello to me. It was as if he sent me the message somehow. I received it, telepathically, I guess. I'm so flooded with emotion that I begin to weep. Wet tears stream down my cheeks. It feels like Dad understands every thought, without me having to speak. Images and feelings come in waves. Happy and sad are intertwined in a strange and beautiful mix. One minute, I remember being a little child with my dad holding my hand as I step onto a subway car. The next, I remember standing alone at the entrance to the emergency room when the ambulance transporting him pulls up and my legs fail me. I hold Dad close and give in to the flood of emotions. My thoughts advance to everything he's missed. I remember walking into the wedding garden and looking at my bride, my heart simultaneously bursting with happiness and aching because my dad isn't there with me. I remember the same when Ethan was born, then Leo. I remember ceremonies and holidays where other dads were in attendance. I remember times I've cried for him. Times I've yelled up at the cosmos in anger because it isn't fair.

As I continue to remember, an extraordinary thing happens. I begin to receive images that seem to be coming from my dad in response. In the first scene I receive, I see myself with Mom, John Wendell, Grandma, Liam, and Estella. We're at my high school graduation in Ithaca. Someone is taking pictures of us together after the ceremony. I see us from a different vantage point as if I'm an onlooker. I think Dad is showing me that he was there and saw us. A feeling of rightness washes over me, as if in answer to my question. Another scene appears. This time I'm shown our old apartment in D.C. where we lived before Ethan was born. Ali is pregnant and has just had her bloody show indicating that labor will begin soon. She comes out of the bathroom to tell me, and I jump up and down in celebration then cradle her head and kiss her forehead. Again, I'm seeing this from a vantage point outside myself. Dad is telling me he was there. He did see. He was with us. He does know Ali and my boys. And Roddy and Marjorie and everyone else he's never met in the flesh. What an amazing realization. It means everything to me. The images continue to come, faster now. Dad's showing me that he's been there for it all. I'm moved beyond words. To steady myself, I pull back from the embrace and look at Dad's face straight on. Suddenly the kitchen backdrop disappears and there's nothing but his face in front of mine.

He tells me, emphatically, "It's time to wake up, George. Be ready."

I do wake up, abruptly, and am instantly alert. My pillow is wet with tears. I wipe my eyes and shake my head as if to shake off the haze which surrounded me in my dream. That experience is going to take some reflection to fully absorb.

It's the middle of the night. All is quiet in the house other than the gentle hum of the dishwasher I started before going to sleep. I can see soft, falling snow out our large bedroom windows and around the silky blue and white draperies our designer hung when she was here yesterday afternoon. It makes for a serene scene. But something's happening. I can feel it. I instinctively reach across the bed to my wife. She's there, curled around her pregnancy pillow and sleeping soundly. A few seconds later, I find out why I was woken up.

Ethan screams. It's an agonized scream like I've never heard from him before. It reminds me of screams I heard during tense special ops missions in worn-torn countries. The kind of screams I'm not supposed to talk about. The kind of screams I'd hoped to never hear in a sleepy little town like Ithaca. I certainly never dreamed I'd hear one from my child in my family's own home.

He's upstairs and I'm down. Leo is up there too, in their shared room. My rational brain tries to make sense of things and I wonder if Ethan's having a bad dream. My body knows better. I leap out of bed, throwing the covers off in the process. I bolt through the bedroom door nearly ripping it off the hinges. I run down the hallway, gaining momentum. I clumsily slam the sides of the walls with my outstretched hands as I go, knocking down framed photographs and artwork that were just hung no more than twelve hours ago. My socked feet slide as I round the corner at the bottom of the stairs, and the banister groans as I grab it and heave myself upwards. I don't have anything on me. No gun. No knife. Not even a blunt object. There isn't time.

Ali's waking up slowly and she calls out to me from what seems like a far distance, "My God, Georgie, what are you after?"

Lady stirs from her spot on the rug beside the front door and cocks her head to one side to listen. Cautious woofs give way to full volume barks as she realizes the urgency of the situation. She scrambles up the stairs behind me.

It feels like we've all been thrust into slow motion. I'm conscious of everything around me. I hear the grandfather clock ticking downstairs. I see the light above the garage flickering at the next house down the road, and I notice the way it makes an angular shadow in the snow.

Ethan's voice is muffled now. I can tell he's sobbing. Every hair on my body stands up on end as I reach the top of the stairs and see that my little boy's bedroom door is closed. It was open when we put him to bed. As I rush to the door, I hear shuffling and banging around, and then, a grown man. A stranger. A deep, sinister voice in my child's bedroom.

Anger. It suddenly burns like an inferno inside my soul. It wasn't there, and then, as if a light switch has been flipped, it's raging at full intensity. It didn't get in me. It was in me. It was there in the background, or down deep, or pushed aside. I can't tell exactly where it was stored, but that doesn't seem to matter now that it's front and center. I feel my adrenaline rush and I know it won't fail me. I am ready and willing to be an instrument of destruction. I will destroy the animal who is threatening my little boys at any cost. I will shred him limb from limb with my bare hands when I get ahold of him. In this moment, I don't care about police or jail or laws or public opinion or even Ali's opinion. I have one singular focus.

The door is locked and locked tight. We chose top-of-the-line components for the new house, and the doors are big and heavy. I never in a million years would have dreamed that I'd need to breach one in order to save my child from an intruder. I shove it hard. It doesn't budge. I step back, then kick with all my might aiming just below the door knob. Nothing. All at once, Lady barks in anticipation, and Ethan screams in sheer terror. The noise I'm making at the door is probably scaring him even more.

"Ethan, son, I'm coming in to get you. Don't worry." I yell as I step back to steady myself and then kick again. No entry.

"Daddy, Daddy!" he screams, first at full volume and then muffled again. I suddenly realize that the muffled sound means the intruder has his hand over my child's mouth. A wave of nausea washes over me. I brace, then kick. Then again: brace, and kick. The door isn't moving. It feels like a heavy piece of furniture has been used to reinforce the door. I've got to step it up a notch, and quick.

Hearing the commotion, Roddy emerges from the guest room next door wide eyed and ready for a fight. Marjorie stands behind him in the doorway, hand over her mouth attempting to hide the look of sheer horror on her face.

"Marjorie, call 9-1-1. Right now," Roddy yells. "Go!"

She fumbles with her iPhone and makes the call. An operator answers immediately, and Marjorie begins to tell her what's happening.

I try to breach from another angle. Turning my back towards the door, I look over my shoulder, raise my dominant leg, and kick forcefully straight backwards. The door claps under the pressure but doesn't open. Seeing this, Roddy jumps into action and positions himself in front of me, poised to enter the room the second I get the door open.

"On three," I say. "One, two, three." I kick again with all my might. Another clap under the pressure. Lady barks ferociously as she readies herself for attack.

"One, two, three," and a kick.

Out of the corner of my eye, I see Ali. She has come upstairs and is terrified. She's collapsed into a ball on the floor, gripping her pregnant belly as she watches us work on the door. Marjorie sees her too and goes over to offer what little comfort she can.

"They're going to stop this," Marjorie says to her

daughter, putting the phone down and kneeling beside her. "Your babies are going to be okay."

I don't have time to shift my focus right now, so as hard as it is, I deliberately tune out that scene.

"One, two, three…" Roddy and I call out, together, as I kick backwards with every ounce of strength I can summon. Finally, the door creaks loudly and opens wide enough that we can use our hands to maneuver the dresser that's up against it and enter the bedroom. Roddy enters first and assesses the situation in a split second as Lady and I follow closely behind. Leo is sitting up on his bed, stunned and eerily silent. He appears to be unharmed. Swiftly, Roddy lifts Leo up into his arms and runs with him back out to the hallway.

I hear Roddy from a distance as he shouts instructions to Marjorie and Ali. "Take Leo to the basement. Wake the others up and get everyone into the rec room. Barricade the door and do not open it until we come for you. Go now! Hurry."

The bedroom window is open wide. Ethan… is gone. The intruder has apparently taken him out through the window. Lady and I quickly scan the room for clues as we make our way to the other side. Every move I make is measured, purposeful. I don't know how yet, but I'm going to rescue my boy. When I reach the point of entry, the cold, snowy air stings my nose. The way the yard slopes down from front to back means we're effectively on the third story. It's a long drop to the ground. I look down and see my son. My little boy is being carried by a tall, burly man who is holding him to one side like a football while fiddling with the metal ladder he used to access the bedroom. I don't recognize the guy. Why in the world is this happening to us? Ethan is in his pajamas with no coat or blanket to shield him from the elements. He continues to sob loudly. I throw myself against the sill and reach down to grab the ladder, but it's too late. The top rung is just beyond my reach. In a flash, I think about jumping out of the window in pursuit, but I quickly dismiss the idea. I'd likely break a leg and then wouldn't be mobile. I have to protect myself at least long enough to get my child to safety.

"Ethan, I'm coming for you," I shout. "Hold on."

Lady makes the turn before I do, and she's on her way downstairs in a flurry of barking and gnashing teeth. Roddy meets my gaze as I head for the stairs, and he falls in behind me. We rush past Ali, Marjorie, and Leo on their way to the basement, and, directed by where Lady has placed her attention, we charge full speed ahead out the front door.

The intruder is running with Ethan now and has made his way a good distance up our long driveway. He left the ladder behind and is moving rapidly. There's an industrial van idling by the curb. A getaway car. If we don't reach Ethan by the time they get him into the van and drive away, he may be gone forever. I'm familiar with the grim statistics on abducted children. The weight of this reality is crushing, but my determination to rescue him grows even stronger. Fueled by adrenaline, I bound forward in the darkness as fast as my legs will carry me. Lady rushes ahead, and Roddy follows closely behind. The three of us pant and heave as we propel ourselves forward in the most important athletic endeavor of our lives. We have everything to lose if we don't make it.

Lady gets there first, approaching the intruder as he's just steps away from the end of the driveway. It's hard to see exactly what's happening because the beams from the floodlight at the corner of the house are too far away to illuminate the shadows made by the wooded area next door. Roddy and I hear vicious biting and growling as we near the spot where Lady intercepted, followed by screams of pain from the intruder. Then, the unmistakable sound of a gunshot. My stomach falls to the very bottom of me as I swallow hard. My heart feels like it's going to beat right out of my chest. If Ethan has been shot, I don't know what I'll do with myself. This is surreal. I can't believe this is happening right now. I pump my arms harder to increase my running speed in the final stretch.

As I get closer and my eyes adjust, I see that Lady has knocked the intruder to the ground and clamped down on his left forearm like a real attack dog would. The arm is bloody. It's mangled and looks like it's broken. Lady has never been trained to attack as far as I know, but she's done a perfect job. Her onslaught apparently forced the intruder to let go of Ethan, who stands up and runs towards me, his face a heartbreaking mixture of horror and relief. He appears to be uninjured. I exhale heavily and say thanks to everything holy that my boy is alright. I grab my son up and give him a quick pat on the back as I pass him on to his grandpa.

"Go to Papa Roddy, Ethan. It's okay," I say.

Thank God for our family dog right now. She successfully slowed that monster down, giving me a chance to get our boy back and keep him from being driven away in the van to face all sorts of unimaginable horrors. I don't think I would have caught him in time without Lady.

As Roddy takes Ethan, I turn to assess the situation once more. A handgun lays discarded on the snowy driveway. I kick it as far away as I can to be sure it's not fired again. The intruder is on the ground writhing in pain. He's a big guy, but he doesn't look like much of a threat right now. Lady still has her mouth clamped hard around his forearm. She isn't moving much. I rush to her, kneeling beside her and stroking the fur on the sides of her body. It's wet. Bloody.

"Oh, Lady girl," I say, as I lean my cheek down near her head. "You're a true hero. You've done a great honor for your family." I don't know if she's going to survive this or not. She's losing a lot of blood. She whimpers, then slowly looks up at me and over at the disarmed intruder as if to tell me she got him. "I know, girl. You did it. Good girl, Lady. You're a good, good girl. Ethan is okay. He's safe." I say as I pat the top of her head. I sure hope she can pull through. I'll return to tend to her wound just as soon as I can.

I stand, considering my next move. Emergency

personnel haven't arrived yet. I look towards the road where the getaway van was parked, but it's no longer there. The driver must have left when he saw things going south for his partner in crime. I'm fairly certain the immediate threats to my family's safety are known and effectively neutralized. We didn't find anyone else. All indications point to this being a two-man operation. The intruder was apparently supposed to grab Ethan and return to the van where the getaway driver was waiting. If there had been more than two guys, I'm pretty sure we would have seen them by now. Especially since any extra guys would have picked Ethan back up when Lady attacked and the intruder released the grip on him. That means it's almost certainly just this one guy in front of me right here and now. I don't think I'm done with him. Anger continues to burn inside my core like a raging fire. It fueled me during the rescue. I moved and ran faster than I ever have before. And it saved my son. I'm still wearing nothing but pajama bottoms, and I can see that my bare feet are bruised and scratched. They're leaving bloody prints in the snow. I don't feel them though. I don't feel the cold. What I do feel is a blinding rage pulsing through my body. I have no idea why this monster targeted us. Or why he took Ethan and left Leo. The house is set up with a surveillance and alarm system. Surveillance cameras are in place and recording, but since we just moved in, the alarm system isn't active yet. The alarm company is scheduled to come out to do that on Tuesday. Did the intruder know? Is this because we're rich? Were they after ransom money? The thought of my innocent sons being in danger because of our socioeconomic status pushes me over the edge. How dare this man enter my home and put his hands on my child. My dad always told me not to start a fight, but that if I ever found myself in one I shouldn't let up until the aggressor was on the ground and not coming back for another go at me. Lady got him to the ground. Now it's time to pick up where she left off and make sure he won't come back.

Roddy sees the look on my face and knows what I'm thinking. He hoists Ethan up onto his shoulder and cradles his head in a grip that simultaneously consoles him and prevents him from seeing what's happening. He even covers his ears, muffling sound. One of Ethan's ears leans flush against Roddy's shoulder, and the other is covered by his large hand. Then, deliberately, Roddy turns around towards the house and scans the roofline in order to confirm the location of the security camera that has this area in its view. He doesn't have to tell me what he's doing. I get it. When he finds the camera, he turns slowly back towards me and takes a step sideways placing his body in the way so what happens next isn't recorded.

My mind is agitated, full of thoughts about how close we just came to having Ethan taken away from us. If I had stayed sleeping a few minutes longer, or if I had hesitated after hearing Ethan scream telling myself it was just a bad dream rather than listening to my instincts, or if it had taken me a few extra kicks to breach the bedroom door... A myriad of things could have gone differently, and if any single one of them had, we'd be facing a completely different situation right now.

I walk around Lady and stand directly above the intruder to get a closer look. He's a big guy. Probably a couple of inches shorter than me, but still over six feet tall. Caucasian. He has big bones. Looks like the build people sometimes refer to as corn-fed. He's about my age. He's balding, and has greasy, unkempt blonde hair on the sides and back of his head that's three or four inches long. He's wearing a black hoodie with a tan ball cap underneath that bears a corporate construction logo I don't recognize. Would this guy be dumb enough to wear his company's hat to an abduction? I'm sure his employer will love that. Hopefully, it will help us figure out who he is faster. As I look him over, I'm cataloging identifying information. I need to know everything I can. The police will investigate, but I need to know details for my own peace of mind. My sole agenda right now is preventing something like this from ever happening again. I pause and close my eyes, deciding whether or not I want to touch this man. Roddy has given me the opportunity. If I do, I may be arrested for assault. I may go to jail, and maybe even prison. The ripple effect would impact more than just me. It might take me away from Ali and the boys. We have enough money that it wouldn't hurt us if I wasn't bringing home a paycheck, but I might miss out on being with the people I love so dearly. I might miss spending time with John Wendell before he dies. I might miss the birth of little Will. I might miss seeing my boys grow up. I'm guessing it's nearly impossible to cultivate a meaningful father-child relationship from behind bars. Ali might grow tired of waiting and divorce me. Or she might be upset with me for assaulting this man and divorce me. She might find a new love and remarry. That stings to think about. I don't want to face a future without Ali. Yet, if I leave this monster intact, he may come back. He may pass the word to his degenerate associates that we're an easy mark, and they may coordinate a larger-scale effort I'm not able to thwart. I tend to believe that if someone is determined to hurt you, they'll eventually find a way. That's why they have to be stopped. In stopping them, I kill two birds with one stone by eliminating them as a threat and sending a message to would-be copycat criminals that they should move on to a different target. Look, I love my life and the people I'm spending it with. The world is interesting and fun. There are so many experiences I've yet to have and adventures that await. I want to live long and happy and safe, and free. But I've always known that if I needed to give my life to protect my family, I would do it. I guess I never quite imagined giving my life to mean signing up for a life behind bars, but here I am, faced with that very real possibility if I beat this monster like I should.

"George," Roddy says, stepping towards me and placing Ethan in my arms. "Console your son. Put one of his ears against your body and cover the other with your hand. Be sure his face is turned away. And stand in front of that camera, would you?"

Before I can respond, Roddy is in motion. He leaps on top of the intruder with a swiftness impressive for a man of any age, let alone one in his mid-sixties. Without giving the intruder time to rally a defense, Roddy narrows his eyes, raises his fists, and places three calculated blows. He doesn't hesitate. His moves are precise and effective. The intruder's body heaves forward from the impact, dislodging itself from Lady's mouth and coming to rest on the concrete driveway with a thud. The intruder lets out one final moan as blood begins to pool under his head on the ground and his body goes limp. And just like that, the most harrowing ordeal of our lives is over.

When I get to the basement where the others are waiting, it takes them a few minutes to remove all the furniture they used to barricade themselves in. I'm glad they followed Roddy's instructions. Things could have turned out a lot worse. The door opens and Ali leaps into me, throwing one arm around my neck and the other around Ethan. Her face is soaked with tears and strained with worry.

"Georgie," she says with a whimper.

"I know, baby," I say as I kiss her swollen eyes, one at a time. "It's all okay. We're safe now."

"Georgie," she tries again. "I couldn't... With Will... I heard a gunshot."

"Ali, I know. It's okay. Ethan's okay," I say. "He isn't hurt." I shift Ethan over into his mother's arms and she cries out in relief. I don't think Ethan has said a word yet, which is understandable. He's traumatized and in shock. He buries his head in Ali's embrace and tucks his shoulders in close like a little turtle. Our poor, sweet boy.

"How is Leo holding up?" I ask. I turn and see that Marjorie is rocking him on the other side of the room near Sara and Nicky. He's staring blankly in my direction but doesn't seem to be tracking.

"I've got him," Marjorie responds. And then, "George, where's Roddy?"

I pause before I answer. Roddy and I didn't discuss how we'd handle what just happened. I'm not sure the real story should go beyond the two of us. I'm not a fan of lying to loved ones. In fact, I've never lied to Ali other than omitting classified information related to my Air Force job that I absolutely couldn't share with her. This is something else though. We don't know what the police are going to do. The surveillance camera feeds will clearly show the intruder entering our home and taking our child out the window. They might chalk his death up to injuries sustained during the descent from the third-floor window and close the case without filing charges. From what I understand, officials tend to get pretty generous when it comes to measures necessary to protect little children from predators. But it could just as easily go the other way and Roddy could be charged with murder. If it comes to that, then everyone will hear the details. For now, I'm going to tread lightly.

"He's out by the road waiting for the police," I answer. "He's fine." There aren't any windows in the rec room, so our family members have no idea what happened.

"Georgie, where is the guy who…" Ali begins to ask, her voice trailing off. She can't yet find words to describe the monster who did this to us.

"He's laying at the end of the driveway right now. He was injured," I say, pausing to see how they seem to be taking it. "He did not survive." There's an audible gasp from the adults in the room. Ethan and Leo are too dazed to follow the conversation. I'm not sure Sara understood either. She looks scared and out of sorts.

"Oh my God, oh my God, oh my God," Ali mumbles, her hand covering her mouth.

"That's horrible," Nicky adds, standing up to help comfort his sister. "Are you and Dad shaken up?"

"I think we are all shaken up. We're doing okay though. Roddy and I worked as a team, along with Lady," I say.

"Oh, Lady," Ali says, the concern evident in her voice. "Why isn't Lady here with you? Georgie?"

I sigh deeply and furrow my brow as I prepare to answer. "Lady is injured. I'm pretty sure she was shot. She was hanging on when I left her, but I don't know if she's going to make it. She lost a lot of blood. Roddy is tending to her wounds as best he can." Ali bursts out into tears upon hearing this news. She bites her lip to try and hold some of the sounds in as she pulls Ethan closer and strokes his back. Nicky puts his hand on Ali's shoulder, while Sara and Luis lean into each other from where they're seated on the sectional.

Marjorie shakes her head. It's terribly sad for all of us. We're dog people, and Lady is our much-loved girl.

"Lady is a hero," I continue. "She saved the day. The intruder had Ethan and was almost to the end of our driveway where a getaway van was waiting when Lady intercepted him and attacked. It was too dark in the shadows for Roddy and I to see exactly what happened, but when we caught up, Ethan was free. He stood and ran towards us. Lady had the intruder on the ground and pretty much immobilized. She kept her jaws clamped down on his forearm, even while she lay bleeding."

"And the van?" Luis asks.

"It drove away. We think the intruder Lady took down was the only one on our property," I answer.

"Oh, Georgie, I hope Lady pulls through," Ali says. "We love her so much. She's our girl. Did you tell her she was a good girl? We'll be forever in her debt."

"I did tell her," I reply. "I told her she's done a great honor for her family. I don't know what to think about her injuries. I hope the medics who arrive will be able to help her. Roddy and I didn't want to leave the scene to take her to a vet."

The classic sound of a police siren rings out from the front yard and I hear a pair of car doors close.

"The police are here," I say. "I need to go with Roddy to give a report."

"Go," Ali says. "We're okay here."

"Good," I say, kissing her and then Ethan on the forehead. "I'm sure they'll want to talk to all of you, too. And they'll need to sweep the house to be absolutely sure no one else is on the premises."

"We'll stay put until we get the all clear," Nicky says. "We're alright down here, George. Go ahead. You've done a good job tonight, brother. You and Dad go handle the rest of your business."

I nod. I don't think I could muster a smile right now if I had to. I'm relieved that we came through this ordeal as well as we did, but holy shit. It's not smiling time just yet.

## 6

## GEORGE: IT BURNS

In the days following the break-in, life takes on a different hue. Snow continues to fall little by little, but it doesn't look magical like it did before. Temperatures don't warm up enough for what's on the ground to melt. I tell Cornell I'll need more time before I begin work and, thankfully, they're supportive. I stay around the house and close to Ali and the boys. I don't know if we'll ever be the same. The new home we loved and were so excited about now feels cold and dangerous. The room that was the scene of the crime feels heavy and ladened with negative energy. We move all of the boys' things out of there and the four of us sleep in the master bedroom together. Ali is despondent, laying in bed and crying until her eyes are bloodshot and puffy. We allow the setup company to unpack the house as planned figuring we need the comfort and familiarity of having our things out. It's little relief.

Nicky, Luis, and Sara head home to the City as scheduled. Sara has school, and they couldn't do much to help here anyway. We all agree it's best if they get right back to their usual routine. Sara is no doubt traumatized enough as it is. The healthiest thing for her to do is to be at her own home, attending her own school, and interacting with her friends. I hate that our house turned into a bad place for her. It was important for us to make a welcoming space where the family could gather. We couldn't have imagined the house would have become a place of fear and darkness.

Duke and Jen come to check on us and Duke promises to make sure the best investigators from his department handle the case. He can't work it himself since we're friends, but he assures me we will be well taken care of. He wears his badge when he visits and reassures the boys that local law enforcement is watching over us and will keep us safe. Jen cries with Ali, more than once. She tells me the description of the intruder sounds like the mover Lady barked at. I never got a look at him myself on moving day, but I had a suspicion it was the same guy. I'm tempted to take Duke aside and beg him to do more. To tell me more. To get involved in our case. I feel pretty helpless and want desperately to do something. What I really want to do is to go back to Saturday evening before our lives changed and to stop the break-in from ever happening. I want our innocence back. I want this house to feel like home. I want my sweet little boys to think the world is a kind and gentle place. I want my wife to feel good about bringing a new life into our family. I want her to smile. I want her to believe I can protect her.

When I call Liam and fill him in, he immediately gets in his car and drives up from D.C. to be with us. I try to protest, saying we're okay and that we have all the help we need. It doesn't work. He insists. He takes the rest of the week off and puts everything in his life on hold. I'm awfully glad he does. I'll take all the support I can get right now. My whole world feels turned upside down. When he arrives, I make a beeline out to the front yard to get to him. Our driveway is still blocked off by crime scene tape, so he parks his blue Toyota Tundra on the road in front of the house. I feel like a child who wants someone to make all of this go away. I hug my uncle and can't hold back the tears. I'm unsteady on my feet. Liam tells me to hold on to him and that he'll help me through this.

Liam and John Wendell are my go-tos for emotional support and John Wendell doesn't have the stamina to be there for me like he used to. In fact, Mom and John Wendell are the last ones I call to tell what happened. I know how exhausted John Wendell was after our big night out on Saturday. I don't want the stress of all this to set him back. I take very seriously what Mom said about him wearing himself out and then crashing. I can see his energy levels waning. He used a lot of his reserves Saturday night at Yellow Cob.

Mom is more than a little distressed to hear about

the incident and wishes I'd called her right away, but she understands my thinking about John Wendell. She is acutely aware of her responsibility to him. She realizes that when it comes to caring for him, it's much easier to anticipate and avoid problems than to be reckless and let things get out of hand. An ounce of prevention and all that. Like babies, elderly folks walk a precarious line when it comes to their health and wellbeing. If I had called Mom right away, she would have wanted to come right over. That would have meant John Wendell staying home alone while way too tired, or more likely, John Wendell coming over with her while way too tired. I would have loved nothing more than to have seen them both and to have John Wendell stand beside me like he did so often after Dad died. But times are changing. Our relationship is not all about me anymore. I think about the pitiful souls who have heart failure and die from anxiety or fear. When you're young, that sounds ridiculous and nearly impossible. I could have imagined it for a really nervous type in an extreme situation like a plane crash, but even then it seemed hard to picture. At some point as we all age though, such a scenario starts to enter the realm of very real possibilities. I'm pretty sure John Wendell is there. He needs to be shielded a bit from unpleasantries. Upsetting news needs to be delivered gently and when he's well rested.

*The Ithaca Journal* picks up the story and features it prominently on the front page. Here I was uncomfortable with my photo on the front page when it went along with the story about my position at Cornell. Now I wish that was the only story connected to my name. Ithaca is a small town and this is huge news. I have no idea if there's ever been another abduction attempt in the area. This is the kind of thing that puts cities on the map in a bad way. Think Boulder, Colorado after JonBenét Ramsey. Or Salt Lake City after Elizabeth Smart. Thank goodness ours was an attempt and not an actual abduction. The population of Ithaca is a mere fraction of Boulder or Salt Lake City's though. People are rattled. I've noticed an uptick in traffic on our street. I imagine people are curious and want to see the scene of the crime. Our house is one of the most expensive in all of Ithaca, which no doubt adds to the fascination. When a tragedy happens, it's human nature to find something that differentiates you from the victims. The value of our home checks that box. People probably tell themselves we were targeted because we're wealthy. Maybe they're right.

I do some of my own research on the construction company connected to the logo on the hat the intruder was wearing. It's a quasi-legitimate outfit called Orangeland Commercial Builders based in rural South Carolina. There's an outdated website that doesn't provide much useful information, but I'm able to piece together a little more from a Better Business Bureau profile and a couple of online listings in professional directories. From what I can tell, they contract with larger companies to provide skilled workers for short-term remodeling projects at hotels and resorts. They are on record as having worked for multiple hotels in the Finger Lakes region, so it's likely the company has a presence in Ithaca. I don't know if the intruder was an actual employee of the company's or not. He may have found the hat in a laundromat or picked it up at a second-hand store. If he is an employee though, it's likely he isn't from around here. So, how and why did he choose us? I mean, that's the question regardless of where he's from, but it seems especially odd that a random subcontracted construction worker from out of state would target us. Or maybe it's a good thing creeps like him aren't living right here in Ithaca permanently. Creeps tend to be drifters. The thought that this guy might be a sex offender has crossed my mind. I'm informed enough to understand it's a strong likelihood, actually. I just don't want to go there. If the man had sexually assaulted Ethan, I wouldn't have waited for Roddy to end the guy.

Roddy and Marjorie decide to stay longer than scheduled. They notify colleagues in the City about our ordeal and are both encouraged to take as much time as they need. Roddy and I still don't discuss what happened in the shadows. I have no idea what he tells the police. For my part, I describe the events of Saturday night in detail right up until the part where I took Ethan out of Roddy's arms. Beyond that, I confirm that I observed the intruder lying motionless and that at some point he stopped breathing. I don't mention Roddy's blows, and the investigators don't ask about them. I imagine they know. They have to. Roddy's hands were bruised and bloodied.

The police treat us fairly. They record our statements and question Roddy and I separately at the station, but so far haven't made an arrest. I'm sure glad we had the surveillance cameras up and running. We provide the footage for officials to review. The recordings clearly show the intruder entering our yard while clumsily carrying a huge ladder, then extending and leaning the ladder up against the back of the house and climbing up to break the boys' bedroom window and step inside. Of course, the recordings also show the intruder exiting the bedroom window a few minutes later carrying Ethan. They show me leaning out the window and trying with all my might to reach down far enough to grab the ladder. And they show the chase in the front yard where Lady, Roddy, and I make a mad dash for the guy and intercept him just before he reaches the getaway van. I'm sure it's chilling to watch, even for seasoned veterans of the force. I'm pretty sure most of these folks keep a soft spot for kids regardless of how jaded and hardened they become. One particular officer helps us get the alarm system at the house activated and set up with the heaviest monitoring available. We consider having a gate and fencing installed around the property. Ali and I don't want to wall ourselves off from other human beings, but we're shaken. We have to keep our kids safe.

Ali has a friend from college at the University of Virginia who was a high-level analyst for the FBI in

Albany before leaving to start his own security firm in Connecticut. He's coming out to personally assess our home and make additional recommendations. Ali and Taye Jackson have stayed in pretty close touch over the years. They talk on the phone and text every now and then. They don't get together in person all that often what with family and work obligations, but they're the type of friends who can go a long time without seeing each other and then pick right up as if no time has passed at all when they do. I get the idea Taye watched over Ali in college. They never dated. There's sort of a big brother and little sister vibe between them, probably because he's seven years older and a late bloomer who was back in school after spending his early twenties finding himself. He's a tall, muscular, smart as a whip African American guy. I imagine anyone who might have considered hassling Ali would move on to an easier target knowing Taye had her back. He and I have a chummy relationship. He was a groomsman in our wedding. But everyone knows he's more Ali's friend than mine. I'm okay with that. Taye has a twelve-year-old son who lives with his mom in Western Massachusetts, but who visits every other weekend and on school breaks. When Taye left the FBI and was looking to make a move within the region, he chose the New York City suburb of Fairfield County, Connecticut in order to tap into the ultra-wealthy clientele there and still be relatively close to his boy. The Gold Coast in the Southern part of the county, in particular, is a bastion of wealth. Lots of rich folks with waterfront Connecticut mansions need security services and consultations. I think it was a smart choice on Taye's part. As I'm learning from my own experiences, rich people sometimes have a hard time determining who is out to take advantage of them. When they spot someone who clearly has nothing but good intentions, they'll typically move forward without hesitation. Taye is an honest guy who loves what he does and that shines through. He sincerely cares about helping his clients. Hell, he cares about people in general. He's the boy scout type. And so smart. His clients realize almost immediately they can trust him, and they refer him to friends and neighbors. His business is booming. I know he'll do right by us and put all of his expertise to use in setting us up so we have peace of mind. Hopefully, we'll be able to breathe a little easier when Taye's done with our house. We trust him implicitly.

Local authorities don't share much about what they know. When I press them, and I do press them, they explain how they have to stay tight-lipped until their process is over so as not to compromise the investigation. On one hand, I completely understand. It's no different than me having to stay mum about classified military and national security information. There are countless risks that come into play when information gets into the wrong hands.

The Air Force sent me to a prisoner-of-war camp out in Washington State called Survival, Evasion, Resistance, and Escape (SERE) training, and during my time there I learned more than I ever wanted to know about the critical need to protect sensitive information. I was required to complete the training because my job entailed a risk of capture and exploitation. The reality is, leaks endanger lives. I probably understand the potential implications better than most. But now that we're talking about a situation related to the safety of my own family, I find myself burning with anger over the lack of information being provided to us. I want and need much more than I'm getting. I'm going to have to continue to research and seek answers on my own. How am I supposed to sleep at night when there may be relevant details available which would help me know what to watch out for? As it is, I only sleep when either Liam or Roddy is awake and has his eyes on Ali and the boys. We can't go on like this for long. We're all exhausted.

The intruder's body is taken to the Tompkins County morgue and an autopsy is performed. I don't know if they've positively identified him. That means I don't know the name of the man who entered my home and took my young son out of his bed. For some reason, it feels like I should. I ruminate on the various findings that might come back when the medical examiner finally releases a report. Was he under the influence of drugs or alcohol? Maybe he wouldn't have been so bold otherwise. Did he have something inherently wrong with his mental faculties? Was he intellectually disabled? Did he have a psychological disorder like antisocial personality disorder? Those patients have a total disregard for other people, and it's scary as hell. I guess I'd actually feel better about the guy having something like that as opposed to learning someone hired him to kidnap Ethan as a play for ransom money. Maybe those are my money issues talking. The uncertainty is making me a little crazy.

On top of everything else, the fact that a man died on our property is unsettling. Even though I feel hate and anger and disgust towards the guy, I find myself wondering about his family. Surely someone loved him. Even if not now, someone must have loved him at one point, right? Even the most horrible people are still loved by someone at some point. A mother? A grandmother? I wonder if there's someone out there searching for him. They could be watching a front door somewhere, hoping he'll walk through it any minute. Damn, what if he had kids of his own who now have to grow up without a father in their lives? The guy's own bad choices led to his death, but I feel the weight of the fact that Roddy and I played a part in it. Every choice we make has such a ripple effect.

No one says much about the getaway driver, which really unnerves me. The police don't seem to have any leads. Roddy and I were so focused on what was happening in the driveway that neither of us paid much attention to the van. It was too far away for surveillance cameras to record. I know it was a white industrial van, probably a domestic model. It seemed to run really loud, but my adrenaline-fueled senses might have perceived any engine as loud at that point. I have an impression of the van as being older and run down, but I'm not sure that's entirely accurate. We didn't get a plate number. There may not have even been a plate on the vehicle. I suspect the driver kept going all the way out of the city when he fled the scene. He never exited the vehicle while at our house, so it will be tough to identify and find him. He must be the smarter of the two. And he must not have been very loyal or dedicated to the guy in the yard. If he had been, he would have tried to assist. That makes me think maybe they were hired by someone. I don't know. I absolutely hate having the getaway driver roaming free out there. I'm afraid he'll come back. Of course, I don't want him to hurt anyone else either. I have to say, it gives me a measure of comfort to know that he must have seen the news reports to learn that his partner didn't make it out alive. He also must have seen the scuffle happening in our driveway in order that he decided to flee the scene, which means he should understand that his partner died at our hands. That gives me more comfort than I should probably admit, truth be told. I'd like to be more evolved and to wish these fellow human beings no harm. But I'm not. Not yet, anyway. I want both men to pay for what they did to us. For what they tried to do to us. I'm not religious, really, but if there is a hell, I hope our intruder is burning in it. Am I a bad person for saying so?

Ladygirl gives us quite a scare. That night, I thought for sure we'd lost her. She was unconscious when one of the responding police officers transported her to the local twenty-four-hour emergency animal hospital in the back of a patrol car. Ethan and Leo were more worried about Lady than anything else.

Her absence was a palpable loss we couldn't ignore. To everyone's surprise, Lady pulled through emergency surgery and has been recovering at the animal hospital ever since. The vet tells me they don't usually let visitors in this soon to see an animal who has been in such critical condition, but they decide to make an exception for us given the extraordinary circumstances and the fact that Lady is so dedicated to the family. When we get to her, we sob like a bunch of babies while we pet her limbs gently. She's still weak, but I've never seen an animal look more proud. She's a true hero and she knows it. Not only did she successfully thwart a kidnapping and rescue her boy, she survived to protect her family for many more years to come. What a dog. We're incredibly grateful to her and grateful she's ours. We can't wait to bring her home when she's healed a little more. Lady is the one bright spot in this whole nightmarish ordeal. Her survival and steady presence give us much-needed comfort. She is a beacon of love and hope. We need love and hope now more than ever.

Ethan has been pretty quiet ever since the break-in. We've tried to be supportive and to encourage him to talk, but mostly we're giving him his space. I don't think there's any right or wrong response to what he's been through. It's understandable he'd need some time to collect himself and heal. We're all sitting around the den in the basement when Ethan tells Marjorie he has something to say. We've felt safer down low, so we've been hanging out in the basement a lot. Ethan is building with some plastic toy blocks while sort of leaning on his grandma's knee when he looks up at her, ready to begin.

"Grandma Marjorie?" he says.

"Yes, my dear, what is it?" she replies, placing a bookmark in the collection of short stories by Tom Hanks she's reading in order to give Ethan her full attention. She's a huge Hanks fan. She always says if she hadn't met Roddy and Tom hadn't met his wife Rita, the two of them would have been perfect for each other. I kind of doubt those timelines would have matched up in reality, but we like to joke about it.

The rest of us are listening to Ethan, too, but we don't look up because we don't want to make him feel uncomfortable. Liam is seated on the floor near the door doing some work on his laptop. Roddy is holding Leo in a recliner while the little guy dozes off to sleep. Ali and I are on the longest part of the sectional browsing social media on our smartphones, but really just sort of staring absentmindedly at our screens.

"I think I used to be a different person," Ethan blurts out. I lower my eyebrows and cock my head to one side, but quick glances from both Ali and Marjorie tell me I had better hold it in and not react. Roddy smiles without making a sound, and I take it he knows exactly what kind of trouble I could be in if I don't heed the warning glances coming from these women.

"Okay," Marjorie replies nonchalantly. "What makes you think so?"

"I remember things," Ethan says simply.

"What kind of things?" she asks.

"I remember living in Greece a long time ago. Daddy was a soldier and he and Mommy had me as their baby." Marjorie nods and leaves him room to go on. "Me and Mommy lived in a little house in the country and Daddy came to visit us sometimes. He wore a shiny uniform with a big hat and he had a sword. Papa Roddy was there and he made medicine and took care of us."

"That's very interesting, Ethan," Marjorie says slowly. "Did you just remember this?"

"No, I've remembered a long time. The man who tried to take me from this house took me from our house then. Daddy and Mommy and Papa Roddy couldn't stop him. It was scary."

"That does sound scary," Marjorie responds, careful not to sound concerned. She shifts the conversation a little while working to gauge how upsetting this is for Ethan. "Was I there?"

"I don't know. I think so, that you were, but I don't remember everything. You didn't live with us," he answers. Then after a pause, "Leo was there. He was a grown-up soldier with Daddy and Daddy taught him everything about soldiering. He had a shiny uniform and a sword, too."

"Wow, that sounds really interesting," Marjorie says while gently stroking Ethan's hair. "What did you look like?"

"I was a boy. Bigger than now. I had black hair like Daddy's. I remembering walking to see the ocean near our house. It was bright blue. We lived up high and the water was down at the bottom. Sometimes

Mommy said we could only look at the water and not swim. But sometimes we walked all the way down to the water and could swim and catch fish to cook and eat. I remember swimming with Daddy one time. Daddy and Mommy loved each other."

"How do you know you were in Greece?" Marjorie asks.

"I just know," Ethan says as he shrugs his shoulders. "It's in my thinking."

"Okay, I see," she replies gently. "And how do you know it was Mommy and Daddy and Leo and Papa Roddy? Did they look the same as they do now?"

"No. They had different bodies. But I know. They're the same in the eyes."

"What else happened?" Marjorie asks, hoping to circle back to the topic of the intruder taking him once before.

"I had to die," Ethan says, matter-of-factly.

"Was that scary?"

"Being taken was scary. The dying part wasn't," Ethan responds, and with that, he seems to be done with the conversation. He stands up, then walks out of the room with a confidence and ease we haven't seen since before the break-in. He's probably going to turn on the TV and watch his PBS kids shows. It's that time of the afternoon. Once Ethan is all the way out of sight, Marjorie raises her eyebrows, opens her eyes really wide, and smiles at us broadly. Roddy chuckles a little, careful not to disturb Leo's rest.

"I realize I'm the only adult in the room who isn't

a parent, so stop me if I'm out of line," Liam says, "but what the hell was that about?"

"Don't ask me," I respond. "That was unexpected. I guess he's traumatized and coming up with stories to try and make sense of what happened to him. I have no idea though, really."

"Georgie, you don't know," Ali says. "It sounds crazy, for sure, but who are we to say what's real and what isn't just because we can't see and touch it."

"Oh, it definitely sounds crazy," Liam adds.

"Well, kids this age often have imaginary friends," Ali adds. "Ethan hasn't mentioned an imaginary friend before. I know it's common though. He's at an age where imaginations are very active. It's an important part of forming his own identity. Imagination helps kids figure out who they are in the context of the wider world. Maybe this is part of that developmental process."

Roddy doesn't say anything. We look at him to see if he is going to, but he just smiles and motions towards Marjorie. Apparently, he thinks she has the answers we need. She's certainly the most alternative and open-minded individual in our group. She probably does have some insight.

"Well," Marjorie begins, "I know a thing or two about past life memories. I've remembered a few different past lives of my own."

"Really?" Liam says. "I don't want to be disrespectful. I try to stay open to new understandings. But really, Marjorie? You're not shitting us right now?"

"I'm dead serious," she says. "No pun intended."

"Wow," Liam returns. "Okay, then."

"Tell us more, Marjorie. We want to know," I say. I haven't told anyone about the dream of Dad the night of the break-in. It's been on my mind though. I've never experienced anything like it. I can't shake the feeling I really communicated with him. How to square that up with the fact that he's been dead more than twenty years, I have no idea.

"Ali's right about kids and their imaginations at this age," Marjorie explains. "But that doesn't mean we should discount what Ethan shared with us. I firmly believe we've all lived before and will live again. These bodies are just vehicles which take us from birth to death. When we die, it's like we step out of the vehicle, having completed the journey. I was always aware of and open to the idea of reincarnation, but in my twenties, I had my first past life memory and knew without a doubt it was real."

"What did you remember, Mom?" Ali asks.

"I was a young girl in what would be considered the Wild West. My family was traveling in a covered wagon, and I died of starvation."

"You sure you weren't just thinking of John Steinbeck's *Grapes of Wrath*?" Liam asks with a tone of healthy skepticism. "Or maybe the old Oregon Trail computer game? That was around when you were in your twenties, right? I'm being serious. There are countless similar stories you might have heard. The power of suggestion is what's real."

"You're right, Liam," Marjorie replies. "The power of suggestion is absolutely real. But in my past life memories, there was a know-it-in-your-bones sense of having actually been there. There were sounds and smells and subtleties to anchor me. I'll never forget the feeling of remembering being out West and looking down at my feet on the dusty ground. I was wearing shoes with little straps which were far too fancy to be in the dirt, but they were all I had. I remember thinking how bizarre that it was me, but in another time and place. And that here were my feet on the ground out West. I've never even been to the Wild West part of the country in this lifetime. The feeling in the memory was that I was still very much myself, just in a different time and place. It's the same way I'd still be myself in California if I flew there next week. I'd be in a different time and place, as myself. Does that make sense?"

"Kind of, yeah," Ali says. "It's interesting."

"Once I landed in the memory, it was like a rush of information swept over me," Marjorie continues. "But it wasn't given or sent to me from an outside source. It was more like it was always in me and was somehow unlocked. I knew I had two sisters. Both older. My parents loved each other deeply, even though there was tremendous struggle as part of our daily existence. I was the most delicate since I was the youngest and the weakest, so I was the first to deteriorate when food and water really became scarce. By the end, it had been weeks of very little to eat or drink. We went a couple of days with nothing at all, and my body stopped being hungry and thirsty. I remember my mother holding me and rocking me and fretting over me. She knew I was dying and there wasn't anything she could do about it. It was terribly sad. I loved her and didn't want to leave her."

"Were you afraid?" Ali asks.

"Not really afraid, no. What stands out is the beauty that was my life there. I was so very connected to my family members. We were tight-knit. I was seen and appreciated and wanted. I remember watching sunsets with my dad while we cleaned our pots and pans after dinner. I remember my mom lovingly mending the lace trim on my dress with a needle and thread when it got torn. I remember playing and laughing with my sisters. It was a good and happy life."

"Do you remember actually dying?" I ask.

"I do. It wasn't painful at all," Marjorie continues. "I sort of floated up and away from the scene gently and watched from above for a while. I've read that we take stock of the lessons and happenings of a lifetime when we leave it. I have a sense of having done that. I think the biggest takeaway from that life was that even though the conditions my family experienced were harsh and even though I didn't live a long time, every day I did live was worth it because of the love we shared. And the beautiful earth. I wouldn't have given up the good stuff to avoid the bad. The good stuff is what living is all about, you know?"

"That's beautiful, Mom," Ali says, moving her hand over her heart. "Did you recognize any of the rest of us there?"

"You know, Ali," Marjorie says, "I did. But I don't

think I should tell that part of the story. At least not right now. I feel like it's up to everyone to remember for themselves if they choose to do so." Roddy shakes his head firmly in agreement.

"I get it," I say. "Beliefs and experiences like this are so personal."

"Yes, George, exactly," Marjorie replies. "And to Liam's point about the power of suggestion, I think it's most impactful and authentic if everyone remembers for themselves."

"So, Mom, what prompted you to remember all of this when you did?" Ali asks. "Did it just come out of the blue?"

"Yeah, I'd like to hear that part," Liam adds. "You have me intrigued."

"It was definitely strange," Marjorie says. "I was actually getting a massage when the memories came to me. I was laying there on the table having my back massaged when it suddenly felt like I was tipping forward out of my body and into what looked like space. It was dark and there were white specks that looked like stars. It wasn't painful or scary. Just peaceful. Then the Wild West scene flashed before me and I was pulled into it. And so, then I was there. Well, I should clarify. I was still on the massage table and aware of what was happening around this physical body, but it was almost as if my awareness split and I was in two places at once."

"Oh, that sounds like what some people describe as the third eye," Ali says.

"Yes, exactly," Marjorie responds. "It was like an

entirely new level of seeing became available to me. Like it was always part of me, but I somehow suddenly accessed it."

"And you've remembered other lives since?" Ali asks. "How come you've never told me about this. I know you believe in reincarnation, but I would have loved to have heard about your specific memories."

"Yes, I have remembered other lives since. Quite a few," Marjorie says. "I don't know why I never told you, honey. I wasn't hiding it. I guess I just wanted to let you come to me to discuss the topic if you ever wanted to. You know how I feel about allowing everyone time and space for their own discoveries."

"I do," Ali replies. "And Dad, you were aware of all this?"

"Yes, I've known all along," Roddy replies. "Your mom and I were already married when the Wild West memory emerged and she began to explore the topic. I haven't personally remembered anything yet, but I believe her. Why shouldn't I?"

"Yeah," I say, "I'm open to most anything if it makes sense and there's some reasonable evidence to point to it as a possibility. There's so much about life and the world and science which we didn't understand until an advancement was made and then all of a sudden, we did. You can go all the way back to Greek and Roman mythology to see how that has worked throughout history."

"There's some compelling research I can point you to if you're interested," Marjorie says. "There are a couple of classically trained and well-respected psychiatrists who come to mind who have focused their careers on past life memories. One is in Virginia at Ali's alma mater, and the other is from the Northeast but based in South Florida."

"So, Marjorie," I say, "Let me be sure I have this right. You're telling us you believe what Ethan said is true? That it really happened?"

"I'm telling you I think it is quite possibly true, yes," she replies. "The Virginia psychiatrist works specifically with children who report past life memories, and Ethan is at the age when kids tend to start talking about having lived before if they're going to. Not all kids do. But for the ones who have these memories, there are some consistent patterns."

"Huh," Liam says.

"Beyond that," Marjorie continues. "Quantum physics is beginning to suggest what many scientists believe is evidence that our consciousness creates physical reality rather than the old understanding of it being the other way around. If that's true, we have to accept the likelihood that our consciousness lives on outside of these bodies and after death. Why wouldn't we live here on planet Earth more than once?"

"I did hear something on the news recently," I say. "Apparently, we might be living in a simulation. The theory isn't completely unreasonable, in my opinion. I never thought about it as applied to past lives and reincarnation though. Fascinating."

"Do some research," Marjorie says. "There's a lot out there. It will give you something else to focus on."

"We definitely need that," I say.

I figure it's as good a time as any to tell them about Dad's visit in the dream. We're already on a similar topic. I know Marjorie will be receptive. And I know the others are open minded, same as me. I feel a little queasy though. I guess there's a difference between being open-minded while hearing someone else's unusual story and being open-minded and courageous enough to tell your own.

"Gang?" I query. "I had a strange experience right before the break-in I'd like to tell you about." They look at me intently, probably wondering why it took me so long to mention whatever it is I'm about to share.

"Alright, go ahead, Georgie," Ali says. "We're listening."

"I don't know exactly how to explain it," I reply, "but I'll do my best."

"Go on, George," Liam says. "There's nothing but love for you in this room. You can tell us anything."

"Oh, I know. It's not that big of a deal anyway," I say.

"You're kind of acting like it is," Liam adds. "Go ahead. It's okay."

"So," I begin, feeling subconscious about the whole thing. "As you know, we had all gone to bed Saturday night and were sleeping when the intruder came into our yard and leaned the ladder against the house and climbed up to the window."

"Right," Liam affirms.

"I was sleeping really hard that night," I continue. "I guess I was exhausted from the move and even before that from the anticipation of the move. It was a relief to have all of our belongings safely in the new place and to be ready to start the rest of our lives in our new home, you know? We had just had such a good night at Yellow Cob, too. It was nourishing to the soul to be with Mom and John Wendell and to have everybody in town from New York City. When my head hit the pillow, I was out fast and hard. I thought everything was okay."

"Same for me, Georgie," Ali says. "It had been a long week of emotional changes and complicated logistics. We were whipped at that point and happy to be getting settled in."

"Exactly. Here's where the strange part comes in. I dreamed of my dad," I say, pausing to gauge their reactions. "But it was more like I actually saw and communicated with him. Truly. I don't think the word dream accurately describes what happened. I've never experienced anything like it before." I see Marjorie's face light up and I can tell she immediately understands.

"Was it the same as we're sitting here talking to each other right now, George?" Marjorie asks.

"Yes," I reply. "Only I knew I was asleep."

"And you knew he was dead," she says.

"Exactly. It was surreal. Hard to put into words," I add. "He hugged me and it felt precisely like it used to." I notice myself beginning to tear up now. I can't help it.

"That's great, George," Roddy says.

"Yeah, Georgie," Ali says. "That's more than

great. It's wonderful. I'm so happy for you. Your dad sounds like he was an incredible man."

"He was," Liam says. "My big brother was one of a kind. I wish you folks could have known him. He would have loved you all."

"I haven't even dreamed of him in years," I say, no longer able to hold back the tears. "I miss him so much." Ali leans closer and wraps both of her arms around one of mine. I bow my head down and place it gently on top of hers as I cry. "I wasn't ready for him to leave when he did. I had more growing up to do. I wanted him to stick around to meet my wife and children."

"And your amazing in-laws," Roddy adds with a smile. "Alec would have been a welcome part of this big, happy, extended family."

"Yes," I say. "For sure. He would have played racquetball with us, Roddy. He was ultra-competitive when it came to sports. Racquetball was his favorite. Liam used to beat him sometimes and he'd get so mad. He'd want to try and go up against us, too."

"I certainly wish we could have known him while he was alive, George," Marjorie says. "But do you think maybe he's still around? Like I mentioned at dinner on Saturday, I believe your dad is in a different form and different dimension now. But that doesn't mean he isn't part of us. I believe he's watching what happens in your life."

"Yeah, that's what he seemed to be telling me," I reply. "He showed me scenes, like from our wedding for example. I saw us in the wedding garden, Ali, but it was from a vantage point outside of myself. It was as if I was an onlooker standing some distance away and watching. Same for my high school graduation and several other important milestones in my life."

"Wow," Ali says. "That's something."

"I know," I say. "I think Dad was telling me he was there and did see. It was a breathtaking experience. It feels weird to say, but I believe it was real."

"Interesting, George," Liam says. "I'd definitely like my brother to be around in some form like Marjorie suggests. He was my hero. I thought the world of him. In my eyes, he could do no wrong. The things we went through when we were kids…"

"I know, Liam," I say after a pause. "You and I are in complete agreement on this topic. The two of us know better than anyone how dedicated he was to the people he loved. He would have done anything for us."

"Sounds like maybe he's still doing what he can, right George?" Marjorie asks. "Is there more to this story?"

"Yes, there is," I say. "I think Dad warned me about the intruder. And woke me up."

"What?" Ali asks, in complete awe.

"We were hugging each other and sharing memories when suddenly Dad's face was right in front of mine and he told me it was time to wake up. He told me to be ready." Ali audibly gasps upon hearing this. Liam looks more surprised than I think I've ever seen him. Marjorie smiles as if she already knew.

"What happened next?" Marjorie prompts.

"I woke up in an instant and was alert. I could feel that something was happening. I wasn't sure what, but I waited and a few seconds later I heard Ethan scream. At that point, I leaped out of bed and got upstairs as fast as my body would move me. Can you believe I woke up a few seconds before I actually heard anything that was happening in the house? As hard as I had been sleeping, it probably would have taken several screams, at a minimum, before I would have woken up if it hadn't been for the dream."

"Georgie," Ali says slowly. "That is comforting and terrifying at the same time."

"Holy shit," Liam says.

Roddy grins and gestures toward Marjorie again.

"What?" I ask. "Do you know something I don't?"

"We didn't know for sure and didn't want to bring it up until you were ready to talk about the events of that night," Marjorie responds.

"Goodness, what is it, Mom?" Ali asks.

"Roddy and I were awake," Marjorie explains. "We had been asleep, but about half an hour or so before the intruder broke in I woke up to go to the bathroom. When I got back into bed, Roddy woke up and we, well, we made love."

"Mom!" Ali exclaims, looking a little embarrassed. "I don't necessarily need to know about my parents' love life." Liam chuckles and shakes his head.

"It's perfectly natural, dear," Marjorie continues. "Nothing to be embarrassed about. Your father and I enjoy each other."

"Okay, I get it," Ali says. "So what did you hear from the boys' room when the intruder broke in?"

"That's the thing," Roddy adds. "We didn't hear anything at all until you were upstairs, George, banging on the door and telling Ethan you were coming to get him."

"We were just laying there at that point," Marjorie adds. "We wondered how you knew something was going on. We hadn't heard even the faintest sound from the boys' bedroom."

"Wait, you didn't hear Ethan scream before I came upstairs?" I ask, bewildered by this information.

"No," Marjorie and Roddy say in unison. Ali covers her mouth, speechless.

"If we had heard something sooner," Roddy says, "I would have been there sooner."

"I... I know I heard him scream," I say. "Otherwise, how would I have known to get up there?"

"We wondered," Marjorie says.

"Did you hear the van on the road or the ladder clanking against the back of the house?" Roddy asks me. "We know the intruder entered the window without shattering it, but we thought maybe you heard some other commotion that woke you up."

"No, not at all," I say. "It was the dream, Dad telling me to wake up and be ready, and then Ethan's scream. Did you two hear a commotion outside?"

"No," Roddy replies. "The intruder must have been very quiet. I'm telling you, we didn't hear a peep until we heard you upstairs. There was no scream. I'm absolutely certain."

"Come to think of it," I say, "Lady was asleep on the rug by the front door when I blew by her on my way upstairs. She joined me when she saw the urgency of the situation. If she had heard Ethan scream, she would have been first on the scene. No way could she have stayed asleep while one of her boys screamed in distress. Which means..." Chill bumps cover my entire body.

We all sit silently for a few minutes, processing this new revelation. This may be the single most remarkable thing to happen to me in my lifetime. I'd say there was definitely something at work which was supernatural or otherworldly or however else you want to describe it. There's no logical explanation. I'm glad I told the others about my dream so we could piece everything together. There may be a whole lot I haven't been attuned to until now. It's going to take me some time to absorb what's happened, but I don't think I'll ever be the same.

Leo's still asleep draped over Roddy's lap and Ethan is still watching his shows in the next room. We can hear the familiar sounds of Sesame Street in the background. Something else has happened I'm ashamed to tell the others about, but I know I had better go ahead and get it over with. My anger is becoming an issue I shouldn't keep to myself. These people all care about me and will want to help. I could use some advice.

"There's something else I need to share," I say.

"I'm almost afraid to know what it is after that last doozy," Liam says with a chuckle.

"This is different," I reply.

"What is it, Georgie?" Ali asks.

"I'm going to just blurt it out. No good way to begin," I say. They all nod, expectantly. "The other day when I went out for groceries, I was almost arrested."

"What?" Ali asks. "You must be kidding."

"No, unfortunately, I'm not. There was a dispute with another driver at a four-way stop."

"Road rage?" Liam asks.

"I guess you could call it that, yeah," I say.

"Georgie, that doesn't sound like you," Ali says with concern in her voice. "In all the years I've known you, I've never seen you get upset about other drivers. You're one of the most laid back and easy-going people ever."

"I know," I reply. "Me and another guy ended up out of our vehicles and in each other's faces. Things got heated and someone watching called the cops."

"What were you even arguing about?" Ali asks.

"The guy thought I cut him off and so he flipped me the bird. Maybe I did cut him off. I've been distracted lately. The minute he showed aggression, anger surged through me just like it did the night of the break-in. It's odd. It's like a rage exists deep inside of me. It's as if it has always been in there, but now it's being touched upon. It leaps out with an intensity that's startling. I'm not convinced I can control it. It's like I want to pick a fight and I want to hurt someone."

"That's completely understandable after what you've been through," Liam says. I glance at Roddy, who knows better than anyone else in this room what I've been through recently. He doesn't react. If I didn't know better, I'd say my father-in-law was former special forces or some kind of international spy or similar. He acts like killing the intruder was simply a job which needed to be done. He's not rattled like I am. My experience tells me that his is not a normal civilian response. Maybe I'll ask him about it sometime.

"I guess you're right," I reply. "But this guy and I escalated to the point of being unreasonable. We shoved each other and were about to come to blows when the police car arrived. The responding officer happened to be the woman who drove Lady to the animal hospital on Saturday. She was thinking of arresting me. I know it. Her demeanor softened when she saw the name on my ID and then recognized me. She ended up letting me off with only a warning. She probably felt sorry for me and decided to cut me some slack. Can you imagine if I had been arrested? Cornell surely wouldn't want me working for them if they knew I almost fought in the street like a delinquent. Not to mention the damn newspaper headlines."

"Georgie, why didn't you tell me about this right away?" Ali asks. "We've always been open and honest with each other. We can't let what happened change us. And besides, have you forgotten your wife is an attorney? Even though my specialty is immigration law, if you have even the slightest brush with legal trouble I need to hear about it."

"I know, believe me," I reply. "I don't want to hide things from you. I was ashamed of my behavior. Ashamed of my anger. I mean, how immature is it to tussle with a stranger on a public street over such a minor issue? It's absurd. Yet, there I was." We again sit quietly for a minute, processing.

"George?" Marjorie inquires.

"Yeah?" I reply softly.

"Might you be open to going to talk with a professional?" she asks.

"Like an attorney?" I ask. "You think the guy might try and sue me?"

"No," she replies. "Like a psychologist."

"Oh," I say. An uncomfortable quiet settles in amongst us as I ponder the suggestion. I can immediately tell that the others think it's a good idea, but they're hesitant to say so. I've never been to therapy of any kind.

"George, I gotta say, I think Marjorie's idea is a good one," Liam offers. "There's a lot going on lately. We talked about this when you called me the night you moved in. You're adjusting to a new city, a new home, a new job, and to civilian life after a long career in the military. That would be a big deal for anyone. Not to mention that soon you'll be adjusting to having a new baby. And adjusting to Ali taking time off from work and staying home with the kids. Even though you're old pros by now when it comes to parenting, Will's arrival is going to change things. It has to. Every new personality added to a group changes the dynamic. When you stack what happened with the break-in on top of all of that, well, it's a hell of a lot."

"It does sound like a lot when you list it all out that way," I reply.

"George," Marjorie adds, "when I hear you talk about anger being inside you, it makes me think you may have unresolved grief left over from losing your dad. That stuff can stick with you for a long time if it isn't processed and released."

"Really?" I ask.

"You think that's it, Mom?" Ali asks.

"It might be," she continues. "It's worth exploring the possibility. You definitely don't want to let all of this fester and impact your relationships. What happens when your anger starts becoming directed at your family and friends instead of strangers?"

"I don't even want to go there," I say.

"I know you don't," Marjorie affirms. "You're a good man, George. But I think you could use a little help right now. There's no shame in it."

"I hear you," I say. "I know there's no shame in it. I just never pictured myself in therapy."

"Did you talk to anyone after your dad died?" Marjorie asks.

"I went to a few support group meetings at the local hospice with Mom, but I mostly listened. I've never talked to anyone about my feelings," I say.

"Your dad died suddenly, right?" she continues.

"Yeah, he had a massive heart attack and died within a few hours," I explain. "There was no warning. He was strong and healthy and in great shape. He played racquetball most mornings before he went into the store to work. I suppose it's possible he had symptoms he didn't tell us about, but Mom and I had no clue anything was wrong. It was shocking, to say the least."

"He was only forty-one when he died," Liam adds. "George was sixteen. It was devastating."

"Yeah, devastating is the only way to describe it," I say.

"And the two of you were close?" Marjorie asks me.

"Very," I reply. "We were very close." There's another moment of quiet as we sit with my statement. It must be sad for them to see my pain, which is in many ways still fresh even after all these years. Liam, of course, has his own pain from Dad dying. He was very close to his big brother.

"Georgie, say yes," Ali urges. "I want you to be okay. The boys and I need you to be okay. Tell me you'll do as Mom suggests and go talk to a psychologist."

I'm not sure if Ali fully realizes it or not, but I'd do anything she asked me to. That woman is the center of my entire world.

"Of course, I'll do it, Ali," I say, tears forming in my eyes again. "I'd do anything for you, my love. And it sounds like this is also what I need to do for me. I'll do it right away." I cup my hands gently around Ali's face and kiss her softly on the lips. She has tears in her eyes as well.

"Good man, George," Roddy says.

"Atta boy," Liam adds, wiping away a tear of his own. "I'm awfully proud of you, nephew."

"You'll see," Marjorie says as she smiles broadly and nods her approval. "It will be good. You'll be glad you had the courage to step out of your comfort zone and get help. Do you have a contact here in town?"

"I don't think so," I say. "I can ask Mom. She probably knows therapists from her job at the hospital."

"Actually," Ali says, "Jen went to see someone in town she really liked. Dr. Joseph Epstein is his name, if I remember correctly. She says he's great at getting to the bottom of things and that he seems to have a knack for honing in on just the right angle to facilitate real change. His Ph.D. is from Columbia, and he's a hypnotherapist, too. He used hypnotherapy to help Jen quit smoking."

"Did it work?" Liam asks.

"Yes, she's been smoke-free for almost five years. Jen is a sociologist, so I trust her assessment of Dr. Epstein's professional qualifications. She's not a practitioner herself. Her focus is teaching and research. But I consider her expertise to be generally in the same realm."

"Let's give him a try," I say. "I'll call Jen and ask for his number. I wonder if Ethan should see someone also."

"I thought about that, too," Ali says. "I may want to see someone myself."

"Dr. Epstein would probably refer Ethan to someone who specializes in child psychology," Marjorie says. "Why don't you begin by yourself, George, and then ask him for recommendations?"

"Right," I reply. "I really appreciate your input, Marjorie. Thanks for looking out for us."

"Of course, dear," she says. "I promise you're going to get through this."

Ali and I feel remarkably better with a clear direction. Something to do to move us forward. Maybe we'll be alright after all. The mood lightens, and Ali seems perkier and starts talking about decor for the house again. I never thought I'd actually be glad to talk about home decorating, but right now I most certainly am. It's a sure sign of progress.

A large item on Ali's decor to-do list is on its way right now. Last fall before we left D.C., we drove down to order a handcrafted dining table from a company that builds them from scratch on a family farmstead in rural Eastern North Carolina. We knew we had a huge space to fill and that we wanted room to host plenty of guests, so it made sense to have a table built to our specifications. A friend recommended the company after their own positive experience. We must have looked at hundreds of photos before selecting a design with a plank top and straight, clunky legs made out of rough-sawn reclaimed barn wood. We also went to great lengths to examine sample blocks with one of the owners in order to be sure we chose the perfect finish and stain color. The final product is being delivered tomorrow and I want Ali to be excited about it. Hopefully, the table's arrival will take her back to the positive memory of the trip to North Carolina, as well as allow her to look towards happy memories sure to be made in the future. I want my wife to be happy. A table seems like a good thing to latch onto. I mean, we've got to eat.

We haven't been out of the house together since the break-in, but when Liam suggests we finally try The Parlor for dinner and a drink we cheerfully agree to go. It should be fine. The alarm system is active and linked to my mobile phone. Roddy, Liam, and I will make sure to check the house thoroughly when we get home before everybody else goes inside. Pepperoni Parlor, here we come.

I call Mom and John Wendell to see if they want to meet us, but John Wendell isn't able. Mom says he's been sleeping more than usual and having trouble picking his feet up to get into bed. I sure hope he's better soon. I don't want to think about the alternative.

## 7

# GEORGE: YOU CAN OPEN YOUR EYES
# AT ANY TIME

The Odyssey Psychology Center is located in a
charming turquoise house on a hill just off East
State Street in downtown Ithaca. Ivy covers most of
the ground out front and a string of twinkling lights
frames the entryway. It hasn't snowed in a couple of
days, but the sun isn't making much of an appearance
this particular afternoon. Given the gloomy weather,
I'm especially glad for the little lights and the cheer
they offer. A bell chimes as I open the white wooden
screened door and then the heavy black metal door to
step inside. The whole place has a friendly vibe. I can
picture people lingering to chat on the porch in the
summertime while a fat, happy cat works the crowd
and offers its belly for rubs.

Dr. Epstein shares office space with six other
mental health professionals. There's no receptionist to
greet me as I enter the front room, but there is an
empty desk where I'd expect a receptionist to sit. On

top of the desk and facing outward is a clipboard and pen with a stack of forms and a sticky note bearing my initials G.H. in large print blue marker. The forms have Dr. Epstein's name featured prominently at the top, so I'll assume these are for me and that he wants me to fill them out. I take a seat in one of the plush armchairs near the front door and begin. I'm glad the doc had an opening which allowed me to get in to see him right away. I'm a little nervous, but sort of excited, too. I provided a short summary of my situation on the phone when I made the appointment and I'm adding more detail now as I fill out the intake forms. I'm curious as to what he'll find important and how the process will work. Jen assured me I'll be comfortable. When I'm finished with the forms, I look around the room while awaiting further instruction. I wonder if the name Odyssey is a nod to Homer's ancient Greek epic poem The Odyssey, which tells of the return journey to the island of Ithaca. We are in Ithaca, after all. Even though it's not Homer's Ithaca, the New York city of Ithaca was in fact named for the Greek island. And, of course, the therapy process could be called a personal odyssey. John Wendell would probably get a kick out of the play on words. I make a mental note to tell him about it.

I hear a door creak from down the hall and then the shuffling of quick, heavy footsteps on the wooden floors. An impeccably dressed, tall, African-American man emerges and greets me with a self-assured smile. He looks to be somewhere around Liam's age. Or Marjorie and Roddy's. It's hard to tell for sure. He's definitely a generation beyond me, but probably not quite as old as Mom. He has thick, curly black hair that is just beginning to turn gray and he's wearing a bright red bowtie.

"Dr. Hartmann?" he asks.

"Yes, sir," I say as I scramble to my feet in time to meet his outstretched hand. He moves fast. I quickly realize this guy isn't going to be the sleepy, uninterested therapist character I've seen in movies. His presence is front and center. Intense even.

"I'm Joseph Epstein. How do you do?"

"Great, yes," I say, a little unnerved. "Good. Good to meet you, sir." It feels like he will see right down to the very core of my being. And he's trained to make proper sense of what he finds.

"Very well then," he says as he tilts his head forward and looks me over for a minute while his blue bifocals slide slowly down his large, broad nose. He's standing square in front of me with his feet planted wide. It's a confident stance. He aims to face me head on. There's nothing aggressive or antagonizing about his demeanor. It's just open and direct. It takes me by surprise, but it's actually pretty inspiring. It's as if he's challenging me to meet him openly, honestly, and confidently. I suppose the plan would be for me to then go out and meet the difficulties in my life in the same manner.

"I finished up the forms you left," I say, lifting the clipboard up to give to him.

"Good," he says, continuing to look at me intently. He waits for what feels like a long while before raising his hand to take it from me. "Thank you," he replies. He then motions towards the back of the house with his head, swivels around, and begins plodding towards what I assume is his office. I follow. We pass several closed doors, most of which have soft light emanating through their frosted windows. Outlines of people can be seen in some. A couple of rooms are dark. I guess each therapist keeps an independent schedule. I wonder if it ever gets rowdy or if it's always this quiet.

"In here," Dr. Epstein sort of grunts when we reach his room. It's crowded, but cozy. We both sit down, full of purpose and focused on the task at hand. I feel sixteen again as he asks me to start from the beginning.

"It was a sunny November Sunday when he left us."

My heart jumps in my chest at the memory of Dad's sudden death. It probably doesn't help matters that my own age is just one year shy of his when he passed. For what it's worth, I had hoped to be over it by this point in my life.

"He was building a deck out back mid-morning when I called to talk to him about football scores. I had spent the night at a friend's house," I continue as the doc scribbles notes on a clipboard. "By supper time the same day we were carrying his clothes home from the hospital in a bag."

That got a reaction. Dr. Epstein gasps and grips the edges of his clipboard with both hands.

"I could tell a happier story," I offer. "Like the one where my wife Ali and I meet."

I have lots of happier stories, and would rather talk about those, truth be told. In addition to everything else going on, the typical winter blahs are affecting me. Even during good, uneventful winters, it seems like I can't help but dwell on the fragility that is my one precious life this time of year. Unless I'm ruminating on the precious lives of Ali, Ethan, and Leo, that is. *Safe, happy, healthy, together,* I silently repeat to myself at night in bed. Not every single night, but close. *Safe, happy, healthy, together. Safe, happy, healthy, together. Please, Powers That Be, keep the four of us safe, happy, healthy, and together.*

"Is it normal to wish, consciously, nearly every day, that your family stay safe, happy, healthy, and together?" I ask Dr. Epstein. "I mean, do normal people think about it that often?"

Dr. Epstein raises an eyebrow and pauses, then nods and allows me time to continue. He can tell I have a lot to say. I imagine he's had a lot of practice listening. Allowing his patients to unleash and unload in a safe space.

"You should know I'm a typical guy," I say, suddenly aware that I might be coming across as ultra-sensitive. "That's important, right?"

I've never been to therapy before and honestly don't know what I'm supposed to say. Although I guess I shouldn't say the word honestly to Dr. E. since that might make him wonder if all the rest I've said wasn't honest. Learned that in Airman Leadership School. I catch Liam saying the word honestly from time to time and tease him about it. He should have learned the same things during his stint in Airman Leadership School. He's not really that much older than I am, but maybe his old man version of the training was different.

I shift my approach. "I love her dearly, but my mom never really liked me being headstrong and assertive. I find myself sort of hiding those aspects of my personality around her. My Dad understood," I try. "He understood me in a way that gave me a great foundation in life. You know? A foundation of love and support."

Another nod.

"What is it about dads that allows them to accept and love their sons unconditionally?" I ask, "to really see them, like in the movies?"

Two raised eyebrows this time. He must be thinking about all the horrible fathers. Or maybe about what a bizarre reference the movies is. I should be more careful how I phrase things.

"Have you seen it in movies?" I ask, watching expectantly for his response. "Where people look each other in the eye and say things like 'I see you?' Those scenes often happen at gut-wrenching parts of the story, when it seems like the main character isn't going to make it."

A smile this time. At last. It brightens up his entire face all the way up to his temples and strong hairline. Maybe Dr. Epstein is a movie buff and we'll have something lighter to chat about. Or maybe he's amused by how much of a nervous mess I am. I'm asking so many questions he isn't answering though.

Too many? Damn, it's embarrassing how unsure of myself I feel lately. And this setting is bringing all of that right out for show. I feel like some kind of strange, cracked and shaken shell of my old self.

I take a long, deep breath. "That's it in this world. Probably. Beginning to end. Being seen."

"And are you being seen?" Dr. Epstein asks.

I fidget on the leather couch as he makes more notes on his clipboard. It suddenly strikes me that Dr. Epstein is old enough to be my dad, but still middle aged. Funny how we can both be in the same middle age category, yet could theoretically be father and son. I wonder if he has a son.

"I think so. I'm seen by my wife and kids," I reply. "And I have a great extended family: my mom, my grandfather, an uncle I'm really close to, a mother-in-law, a father-in-law, two brothers-in-law, and a niece. Each one is supportive and genuine. Mom is the most complicated." No response.

The office has stacks of things everywhere. Papers, file folders, and books are up to the armpits, as Mom would say. The walls are filled with framed newspaper clippings, certificates, and diplomas from City University of New York and Columbia University. One particular certificate catches my attention: *New York Hypnosis Society, President*, it proclaims.

"Do you hypnotize people right here?" I ask, smoothing the leather seat cushion beside me absentmindedly.

"I have a reclining chair in one of the front offices where patients sit during hypnotherapy," he replies.

His speech is as heavy and deliberate as his gait. "You passed the room on your way in. There are speakers in there which allow me to play recorded music, and I talk into a microphone here at my desk to provide hypnotic suggestion. It's all very relaxing. You can open your eyes at any time."

"Fascinating," I say.

"Are you interested in hypnotherapy?" Dr. Epstein asks.

"Well, maybe. I might be. I mean, I don't know," I say. He holds my gaze even as I flounder. Most people would look away.

"What do you know about hypnotherapy?" he asks.

"Mostly what I've heard from Jen," I answer. "Jen Wright is a good friend of ours. She and my wife Ali have been best friends since they were young... first grade, I think. Anyway, Jen said you helped her quit smoking."

"Is there something you want to quit?" Dr. Epstein inquires.

I take another deep breath before answering. "Well, nothing to quit like a person quits smoking, exactly, but I'm here because I seem to have developed a lot of anger inside and I don't want to be an angry person. I especially don't want to hurt my loved ones. I owe it to them to sort things out before things get worse."

"When I asked you to start from the beginning," the doc probes. "Why did you choose the day of your father's death?"

"Oh, wasn't that what you meant?" I ask. "Sorry. I just thought... I don't know."

"No need to apologize, George," he responds. "Can I call you George?"

"Sure," I say, feeling embarrassed. He has a good point. Why would I start with the day of Dad's death? Beginning with either the story of us having just moved or the story of the break-in would have made a lot more sense. I'm feeling like a hurt kid with raw, unbridled emotions hanging out for everyone to see. I've worked hard all of my adult life to keep that type of thing under wraps.

"George," Dr. Epstein continues, noting my discomfort. "You're doing well. Take another breath."

A few words of kindness from this very intense man mean more to me right now than I ever would have anticipated. I do take another breath, and tears flow from my eyes. I've been keeping my muscles tight ever since I walked in the front door. They're all wound and bound and I don't even know how to hold my body in this moment. I jerk a hand up and cover my eyes, one with my thumb and the other with my index finger.

In one smooth motion, Dr. Epstein takes off his glasses and places them down on his desk along with his clipboard, notepad, and pen, then leans forward towards me and settles with his elbows on his knees. "George," he begins. "This process is harder than most people realize. It's difficult to open ourselves up. To examine old wounds. And to share our most intimate feelings with a total stranger. I understand that."

"Yeah," I offer feebly.

"Within these walls, there's no right or wrong way to act. No right or wrong thing to say. You don't need to keep your guard up. In fact, things will move along more smoothly if you let your guard down completely. It may feel like I'm judging you at first, but in time I hope you'll come to realize that I'm simply doing what I do in order to help you connect the dots and make sense out of difficulties in your life. Every person on this planet is different. We have different personalities, different histories, different reactions, different experiences, and so on. But at the same time, there are some common patterns to human behavior. I've been trained to spot those, and to use my knowledge of human psychology to help my patients unhinge things when they get knotted up."

"Okay, I see," I say.

"It's a beautiful journey," Dr. Epstein explains. "It's hard, don't get me wrong. It will take work on your part. Very quickly, though, you'll get a feel for how rewarding the work is." He pauses for a minute, assessing me, then smiles and continues. "Will you take the journey with me, George? I'll be by your side the whole way. I know you can do this."

More tears come in a burst as I shake my head up and down to indicate that I will take the journey with him. Dr. Epstein hands me a tissue and I wipe my eyes as my chest heaves. "Thank you for the pep talk," I manage.

"No thanks needed," he replies. "I'm going to step out and fill my coffee mug. Can I get you something as well?"

"I'm not much of a coffee drinker, but water would be great," I say.

"How about hot tea?" Dr. Epstein asks. "We have one of those machines that mixes it up just right. A warm beverage is always good on a cold day."

"Black tea would be nice if you have a little sugar to add," I say. "Thank you." I'm reminded of Ali offering warm beverages to the movers and how her kindness was returned with an intrusion of the worst type. I'm glad Ali is a kind person, and I appreciate Dr. Epstein's kind gesture now. He isn't aware of the association. Even if he was, what, am I going to get upset every time someone offers me a warm beverage on a cold day? Do I want people to tiptoe around me, careful not to offer warm beverages? Certainly not.

"Very good," he responds. "When I get back, you can tell me a few of the happier stories you mentioned. How does that sound?"

"Yes, that sounds great," I say as I finish drying my eyes.

Dr. Epstein plods off towards the kitchen as I attempt to collect myself. I'm exhausted and drained from the emotional effort our short conversation has required. Therapy is going to be harder than I anticipated.

The doc returns and, as promised, we sip our warm drinks and talk about lighter topics. I tell him more than he probably wants to know about Ali and our boys and I show him a few pictures from my smartphone. When the session time is finished, he explains that since I'm self-pay and not dependent on insurance company approval we can schedule as many appointments as we wish and thus move the process along quickly. A slot is open tomorrow afternoon, so I agree to come back in for session number two. I guess this is an instance when being wealthy is a big help. Having the ability to pay for therapy and to speed it up as the doc and I see fit is huge. It makes me sad to think of all of the folks out there who desperately need therapy and can't afford it. There are a couple of hours left before the family at home will be wanting me for supper, so I decide to pop in at Mom and John Wendell's. I might as well. It's a short drive from Dr. Epstein's. The heated seats in my Tesla don't even have a chance to warm up before I arrive. I'm feeling the cold more than usual today, so I wrap my scarf around my neck and put my gloves on my hands before getting out of the car and walking up onto Mom's porch to ring the doorbell. I have a key, but figure I'm already arriving unannounced and don't want to startle John Wendell by appearing inside the house unexpectedly. It takes Mom what seems like a long time to answer the door. In reality, it's just a few minutes, but it's out of the ordinary.

"George, oh," she says as she steps outside onto the porch of her stone cottage and closes the caramel-colored wooden door behind her. "Good to see you, dear. How is everyone?" She isn't wearing a coat and clearly wasn't planning to spend time outdoors.

"We're doing fine, Mom. Why aren't we going inside your house?"

"Oh, well, I thought we'd talk here," she replies.

"Do you have a guest?" I ask.

"No, dear, just me and John Wendell right now," she says.

"Mom, you're acting kind of strange. What's going on?" I ask as she looks down at the faded wooden porch planks under her feet and wrings her hands as if debating whether or not to tell me something. "What is it?"

"I don't want to burden you, George. You look exhausted. You have so much going on with Ali and the boys and Lady, after what happened..." she replies sheepishly.

"Stop it. You're my mom. You could never be a burden to me," I say emphatically. "Roddy and Marjorie are still in town helping us out and Liam says he can stay a while longer, too. There's plenty of support to go around. What do you need? Is it John Wendell?"

Mom sighs heavily and nods as she turns and opens the door to allow me inside. "Prepare yourself," she instructs over her shoulder. "It isn't pretty." Upon hearing this, my heart begins beating faster and a chill goes up and down my spine. I stand up straight and tell myself I can do this. Although I'm beginning to wonder how much a person can take at once.

Mom's cottage is small. It has three bedrooms, but the whole place isn't more than about eleven hundred square feet. She could afford any home in

Ithaca if she decided to start using the money Dad left her. This place suits her though. It's on the National Register of Historic Places and has a plaque saying as much hung out front on the wall near the door. It was used as a private nursing establishment known as a cure cottage for tuberculosis patients in the early twentieth century like the ones made famous up at Saranac Lake. That's fitting since Mom is a nurse, I suppose. She keeps it up nice. The wooden trim which frames the windows and supports the roofline is always painted a fresh, crisp white. She loves flowers and has a springtime show of color in her front yard every year all the neighbors envy. The colors really pop against her warm, wooden front door. It's the kind Ali likes with the little windows at the top.

There's been enough room in the house for Mom and John Wendell, but that's about it. The remaining bedroom serves double duty as a project space for crafts and a makeshift exercise area for the treadmill when it's too cold to walk outside. There's a screened porch on the back which effectively extends the living space though. It's quaint. Mom's favorite part of the property is no doubt the garden in the backyard. I'd estimate that raised garden beds take up half of her yard. She wouldn't have it any other way. She's talked about getting chickens, too. When she first bought the place, Dad had just died and we had just moved here from Brooklyn. The house and yard were a total wreck. I helped fix things up some, but I was in high school and only had so much free time available. Mom has done the lion's share of the work since I've been gone. She's done a great job. She deserves to be proud.

I follow my mom into the front room and close the door behind me as I wipe my boots on the mat. I don't take my coat or scarf off. I don't want to waste any time getting to John Wendell.

"Can I go to him?" I ask.

"Go ahead," Mom replies as she waves me past her and towards John Wendell's bedroom. "He's been either sleeping or very drowsy the past few days. I've been home with him. I think he's delirious. And I'm speaking of the medical definition of delirious. I'm pretty sure he'll be diagnosed with delirium. I've already called Dr. Madera."

"Does she want him to come in?" I ask as I make my way down the short hall to my grandfather's bedroom door. It's open and I can hear him breathing hard and sort of mumbling.

"She's checking with the other partner in her practice and is going to call me back. One of them may be able to make a house call tomorrow," Mom says.

"I didn't know they did that anymore," I reply.

"Yeah, apparently they do when you've been a nurse at the local hospital for decades. Or maybe it's because John Wendell is so popular in this town," she offers. "Either way, we're getting him seen."

"Do you think it can wait until tomorrow?" I ask.

"Probably. He doesn't want any medical interventions. You do realize that, right? No heroic measures. No resuscitation. Not even oxygen," she explains. "And remember he had the prostate cancer a few years back? It's slow growing in elderly men and doctors don't usually recommend treatment, especially for folks like John Wendell who would refuse treatment anyway."

"I see. I do remember that. So you're telling me there may not be anything they can do," I say. "At least not anything John Wendell would want them to do."

"Yes, exactly," Mom replies.

"Wow," I say as I work to steady myself. When I round the corner of the bedroom door frame and see my grandfather under the blue and white square-patterned quilt Grandma made when I was a kid, I'm pulled towards him. He looks so frail and small. Almost like an infant. It's difficult to see him like this, but in an odd way, it's not as difficult as I expected it to be. In this moment, I know I'm prepared to see him through whatever may come. A feeling of calm settles over me. I'm sure glad I'm here in town and not hundreds of miles away in D.C. As I near the side of the bed, I gently take his hand in mine. He stirs a little but doesn't wake up. Mom gets me a rocking chair from the other side of the room and I sit down without letting go.

"Why in the world didn't you tell me, Mom?" I ask. "This looks serious."

"It does, dear. It is," she replies. "John Wendell is an old man. And he is adamant about being allowed to go peacefully when it's his time. This could be drawn out long while. Or he could recover and get back to normal. Either way, it's one of those things that is typically a marathon instead of a sprint."

"So why not tell me sooner and let me help?" I ask.

"George, even though you haven't filled me in on all the details yet, I'm pretty certain you've just had one of the worst weeks of your life. Correct?" Mom prompts.

"Well, yeah, that's a fair assessment," I say. "I haven't filled you in because I didn't want to stress you or John Wendell out. Particularly John Wendell. You shouldn't do this alone though. This is why Ali and I decided to move to Ithaca in the first place. We want to be here for you."

"I know," Mom replies.

"Besides, we've been doing a lot of sitting around and trying to absorb the shock. The worst part of that is over. I think it would be good for us to have something productive to focus on. None of this is easy, but feeling helpless is the worst. I'd rather be doing something-- anything."

"Well, I can understand that," she says.

"While talking with everyone yesterday," I continue, "Marjorie suggested I go see a therapist."

"Really?" Mom asks.

"Yes," I reply. "And I did. I was able to get in right away and I saw someone this afternoon before I came here. Ali and I both felt better almost instantly once I made the appointment and we knew we were moving in a good direction."

"George, that's such good news, dear," Mom says.

"I'm thrilled. I wouldn't have expected you to agree to that. At least not without putting up a fight."

"Maybe it's easier to take when the suggestion comes from someone other than my mother," I say with a laugh. I must have been louder than I realized because John Wendell startles and opens his eyes to look at me. I smile and squeeze his hand. When I do, his face lights up with the biggest, most genuine smile in return. He squeezes my hand back and raises his head part way off the pillow.

"Good to see you, son," he says, plain as day.

"Mom, look," I say. "I think he's waking up."

"Give it a minute," she responds as she shakes her head and sighs once more. As if on cue, John Wendell's eyelids begin to look heavy and he nods back off to sleep. "This is how it's been."

"Damn," I say.

"Yeah," Mom responds slowly. "You said it."

We sit for a while and listen to him breathe.

"What do we do now?" I ask my mom. "Do you want me to stay here tonight?"

"Goodness, no," Mom replies. "You have a family to tend to. It's been me and my daddy right here in this house for years. We're just fine on our own together. You go home. I'll keep you posted. What do you have planned for tomorrow?"

"Quite a bit, actually," I say. "We pick Lady up from the animal hospital in the morning."

"Oh, how wonderful," Mom says as she raises a hand to her mouth and tears begin to form in her eyes. "She's your girl. I'm so glad she's okay and that she's coming home. The boys are going to be so happy to see her."

"I know," I reply. "We'll have to watch over them closely so they aren't too rough with her. They may not realize she isn't up to full speed just yet. Especially little Leo."

"Right," Mom says. "They'll get it. You'll probably be surprised at how they instinctively know to be gentle."

"I hope so," I say as I lean back in my chair, more relaxed now. Talking to Mom while sitting here with John Wendell feels good. "Ali's friend Taye is coming in from Albany tomorrow to help us figure out if there's anything else we can do to make the house safer."

"Oh, yeah," Mom says. "I thought about him the other day and wondered if you two would call him for help. He started his own consulting firm, didn't he?"

"Yes. He left the FBI a few years ago and went out on his own. He's done really well for himself," I respond.

"Doesn't he work with high-end clients who have big houses like yours?" she asks. I'm a little surprised Mom didn't add a passive aggressive comment about the size of our home. Maybe she's feeling generous after all we've been through.

"He does," I say. "He's the perfect person to advise us. We can trust him. I know I'll feel better after he's taken a look at things. Ali certainly will, too."

"Good," Mom says.

"Oh, and our dining table is being delivered

tomorrow from North Carolina. Remember when we went down there to pick it out and place our order?" I ask.

"I do remember. Ali was so excited about that table," Mom replies. "I sure hope it will be a bright spot for her. I know how she loves to decorate."

"She sure does," I reply. "She was talking about it this afternoon. I take that as a good sign. We'll see how she feels when it arrives."

Mom and I sit quietly for a few more minutes, studying John Wendell and each other.

"I went ahead and signed up for another therapy session tomorrow afternoon," I say. "I can change it if need be though. Want me to stop by here? Or to go to Dr. Madera's with you if you end up needing to go in?"

"Do not change your appointment," she replies. "How about you take care of everything you need to take care of and we'll keep in touch between now and then. Maybe you can come by after your session."

"Are you sure?" I ask. "Liam and Marjorie and Roddy are all at the house and can fill in for me as needed. They've been great."

"If something changes, I'll let you know," Mom replies. "For now, go home to your family. John Wendell and I will be alright."

"Okay," I say as I give my grandfather's hand one more squeeze before letting go. I lean over and kiss him gently on the forehead. It's a meaningful gesture. One that I wouldn't offer if he were well and in good health. Now, it feels right.

I'm still exhausted from my conversation with Dr. Epstein and my eyes are sore from crying. I'm anxious to get home to Ali and the boys and veg out to take my mind off of everything going on. Maybe we can cue up a movie to watch together. I'm comforted by the thought that my in-laws and my uncle will be there waiting for me as well.

I say goodbye to Mom, then I get into my Tesla and drive home. She seems to have things under control for the time being. I'm glad. I want to be there for Mom, but it's reassuring to know she's taking the lead on this. She has a lot more experience with the elderly and with death and dying than I do. She's comfortable tending the threshold. I'm ready to see John Wendell though. But I won't pretend I don't like the thought of Mom being there to guide me.

## GEORGE: INTERTWINED

When I arrive at our house and walk in the front door, the comforting smell of a home-cooked dinner greets me. Judging by the intensity of the aroma, I got here just in time. As I enter the eat-in area of the kitchen, I see Liam and Ethan cheerfully setting the table together. I give my little man a high five and I give Liam a look that lets him know I have news to share. I'll wait until after dinner to tell everyone about John Wendell. Ali, Leo, Roddy, and Marjorie are all in the larger section of the kitchen around the island. Roddy and Marjorie have cooked a big dinner for us: spinach stuffed chicken breasts, mashed potatoes, roasted cauliflower macaroni and cheese, and Boston brown bread. It looks as good as it sounds. My in-laws are excellent cooks. I'd go as far as to say their creations are restaurant quality. I often joke with Ali about what a stroke of luck it was for her to have met Liam and Estella in a cooking class since her parents could have probably taught her anything she wanted to know about cooking. Leo is in his high chair snacking on raisins and Ali is relaxing in a chair next to him with her feet up on an ottoman brought in from the living room. It looks like her parents are taking nice care of her.

Our house feels like home. A home filled with love and happiness. Less than a week ago, I was thinking about getting more modest vehicles and moving to a smaller, less pretentious place. Today though, in this moment and in spite of everything happening, I think I want us to stay right here. I don't want to turn tail and run when things get difficult. That's not how I handled myself in the military and it's not how I want to handle myself in my personal life. It's been such a wild ride though. I might change my mind again tomorrow. We'll see. Right now, I'm grateful for the present. I feel surprisingly good.

We eat the scrumptious dinner Marjorie and Roddy made and we enjoy a bottle of white wine Liam picked up from the Seneca Lake Wine Trail today while he was out. It's a forty-five-minute drive west from Ithaca out to Watkins Glen, but he insists he enjoyed himself and appreciated the scenery. He spent a good part of the afternoon relaxing by a wood fire in an especially charming winery's tasting room while looking out over the snow-covered landscape. It sounds amazing. There is an interesting microclimate in this area which makes for great wine. The steady water temperature of the Finger Lakes regulates the air temperature so that harsh, cold weather is avoided in the winter and the grapes end up with a longer growing season. I'd like to stop into a few wineries soon myself. I wasn't interested when I was a high school kid and have only visited once as an adult. Maybe Ali and I will make a date of it one day next week while the boys hang out with their grandparents. Assuming my very pregnant wife feels up to the excursion, I think the idea sounds charming.

If someone had told me a few weeks ago that I'd be crying one minute, laughing the next, and planning trips to wineries in between, I never would have believed them. Yet, here I am. The craziness of the ups and downs is not lost on me. All I know to do is to keep moving forward. Slogging my way through as best I can.

I debate about how to break the news of John Wendell's steep decline to the others. I'm especially cognizant of the effect this will have on the boys. No one close to us has passed away since they've been alive. For that matter, no one close to me has passed away since Dad. I don't want to sound like I'm counting John Wendell as already gone. I know Mom's right when she says he could recover and be back to his old self. It's hard to guess exactly what will happen. My sense though, is that he won't ever be back to his old self. Mom didn't have to say as much out loud. I know she's sensing the same. That speech at Yellow Cob was significant. I knew it then and it's especially clear now, looking back in hindsight. I'm pretty sure that evening was John Wendell's farewell party. His last big hurrah. And to think, earlier that day I was talking about how he could live to be one-hundred. That sentiment sounds so naive now. Foolish even.

We're polishing off what's left of our wine when I share the news about John Wendell. I'm careful with my choice of words so as not to alarm the boys. Ethan is sticking around the kitchen table tuned in and hanging on my every utterance though, desperate for a chance to learn how these things work. I don't blame him. Curiosity is a good thing. I don't mind explaining. The adults are sad, but not very surprised. They'd been thinking along these lines ever since last weekend at Yellow Cob. After a few minutes of discussion, Liam decides to pack up a plate of food and take it over to Mom. She is still his sister-in-law, after all. I know Dad would appreciate him looking after her.

The rest of us retreat to our spot in the basement and cue up a random Tom Hanks movie we figure Marjorie will like. Everyone knows I've been to see Dr. Epstein and I'm sure they're interested to know how it went. They don't ask though. I'm glad because I don't feel like talking about it. We have a busy day coming up tomorrow and I want a reprieve from the heavy, emotional sludge which no doubt awaits me. I feel like I've made enough progress for today and wish to pace myself. Marjorie tells me Ethan has been talking more about having been another person in Greece, but she doesn't go into details. I don't inquire. I want to know. Just not right now.

When the movie is over and both boys are down for the count, Marjorie and Roddy offer to keep Ethan and Leo in their room overnight. They say they want to give us some time alone and a good night's rest. Ali and I are a little unnerved by the thought of the boys sleeping upstairs again, but we know Roddy will protect them. I'm sure he'd protect them with his life if need be. We agree to the arrangement and thank Marjorie and Roddy, then all head to bed.

My wife and I haven't made love since the break-in. This has to be the longest we've gone without, aside from times I've been away TDY. It's understandable given the circumstances this particular week. The boys have been sleeping in our room, although it's not like that has stopped us before. We're pretty regular about making love in spite of logistical challenges. It's time to end this streak because I want to make love to Alessandra Davies right now. Thinking about it warms me and in a rush, I'm aroused. I want to taste my wife's lips. To wrap my big hands around her delicate fingers and feel the energy surge between us. I want to take all of her clothes off and press myself against her soft, smooth skin, then slowly move my mouth down her wriggling body, over her firm nipples and around her pregnant belly until I reach her wet spot. When I get there, I want to wrap my arms tightly around her thighs as I dig in. I want to feel her glorious long legs in the air above me while I curve my tongue the way she likes. I want to immerse myself completely in her sweet, familiar scent and circle her throbbing bud until she moans with delight and my chin and cheeks get all slippery with pleasure.

"Ali, babe?" I try as I climb into bed. She finished her nighttime prep in the bathroom before I got in there. I was fast, but had to wash up and brush my teeth. She's rolled over towards the windows now and I can't tell whether or not she's still awake. "You still up?"

"I am, Georgie," she says as she looks over her shoulder to see me behind her. "Just lying here."

"How would you feel about a little lovemaking?" I ask as I gently move her long hair to one side and begin to rub her shoulders.

"Isn't that like being a little pregnant?" she replies with a laugh. "Just a little lovemaking?"

"Yeah, well, you're more than a little pregnant, so I guess neither description makes any sense," I say, slowly moving my hands down to her lower back.

"It has been a while, hasn't it? I know you must be itching for some of this good stuff, Dr. Hartmann," she teases. "Like fine wine, I only get better and better."

"I know that's right," I whisper.

She reaches for my arm and pulls it close around her so my hand lands on her exposed breast. She's wearing a sheer, sleeveless nightshirt with a deep v-neck which allows her exquisite breasts to appear when she twists just right against the bedsheets. She acts like it happens by accident, but I'm convinced she knows exactly how to maneuver to make me wild with desire. She turns around towards me and we're ravenous for each other. We kiss deeply, surrendering to the passion we feel. I prop myself up on my hands and knees above her and begin my descent down her body as she pulls her sleep shirt off over her head and tosses it onto the floor. No panties. She moves in response to my every touch, arching her back and panting in anticipation. When I reach my destination, she's dripping wet with desire. She's never had trouble with natural lubrication, but pregnancy hormones have taken it to a whole new level. I love it. I bury my face and do my duty. She moans with delight. She doesn't let me stay long though. When she's nearly at peak excitement, she tugs my hair and moves my head away, pulling me upwards and guiding me to enter her. I do as she wishes and it feels like home. We heave and thrust until we reach ecstasy in one glorious moment together. We ride the waves as far as they'll take us, moaning and gripping and pushing until the tension recedes.

I'm still inside her when she begins to sob. Large, insistent tears stream down the sides of her cheeks and into her pretty hair.

"Oh, Ali, what's wrong?" I ask. "Don't cry, babe."

"I can't help it," she says in return, her face contorting as the tears continue.

"I didn't hurt you, did I?" I ask. I gently slide out of her and roll over to put my arms around her from the side.

"Gracious, no, Georgie. You couldn't…" she says in between sobs.

"Then what, Ali, babe? What can I do?" I ask. She

swivels around in the bed and places her cheek down on my chest. Positioning is more difficult with little Will inside her belly, but we get as close as we can. Maybe she wasn't ready to make love yet. I hope I wasn't too forceful.

"I guess it's just a release," she says. "I have had so much tension built up inside. I've been angry, sad, and scared. And then grateful. It's been a rollercoaster of emotions. I know I've cried plenty of times this week, but being with you like this and having the release of orgasm is apparently something different. It has opened the floodgates."

"It's alright," I say. "You cry as long and as hard as you need to. I'm here."

"It's not a bad cry," she adds. "I'm just emotional. I sure do love you, Georgie. When we make love, I can feel how much you love me back. I feel it in your touch. I needed this tonight."

"Oh, Ali, I do love you, so very much. To the depths of my being. I'm glad you feel it. You and our sweet boys are my world. I'm right where I want to be. You know I'd do anything for you," I say. I almost wish I could cry with my wife now. Lord knows I've cried plenty of times over the course of the past week. At the moment though, I'm all cried out. Funny how it comes and goes.

"Georgie?" she queries, her tears beginning to slow.

"Yeah, babe?" I return.

"It makes me sad that we haven't talked much

about little Will's arrival," she says. "At this point in my other pregnancies, we were counting down and making final preparations. Will's due date is next month and it feels like it's sneaking up on us without the attention it deserves. Can we talk about Will now?"

"Of course," I reply. "You're right. Let's get the countdown going. Have you entered your due date into any of the online calendars that tell you what's happening with his development week by week?" I ask as I reach for my smartphone that's on the nightstand beside me and pull up the calendar.

"I did all that when I first found out I was pregnant, remember? I checked in on it a few times in my first trimester, but for the most part, this is old hat for me. I'm on my third pregnancy in five years. I know a thing or two about how it works," she says.

"You are an old pro, for sure," I say.

"We are old pros," she says, with a smile. I'm glad to see her smile.

"Right," I reply. "We are. But it's probably time to take a good look at the calendar. We want to have everything ready. What are you thinking about his room? I know what you wanted, but after what happened…"

We had planned to make Will's room the first one upstairs, on the other side of Ethan and Leo's from the guest room my in-laws have been staying in. All the stuff we have for him at this point is already unpacked and set up there. I'm not sure how I feel about that now. Will won't sleep upstairs until he's older anyway, but his room is where we'll keep all of his clothes, toys, and baby gear. We want it to be a positive place that feels good.

"It's a dilemma, Georgie," Ali says. "Part of me wants to move all the kids' rooms downstairs. To the basement even. It feels safe down there. Maybe because it's farthest away from the breach. Or maybe because it's partially buried in the Earth."

"I hear you," I say.

"But the other part of me doesn't want to cower in our own home. I want to find some way to reclaim our feeling of security. I'd prefer to keep his room upstairs as planned," she explains.

"I agree," I reply. "Taye will be here in the morning. How about we sort of figure on staying the course, but wait to hear from him before we decide?"

"Yeah, okay," she agrees.

"Did you reschedule your appointment at the birth center?" I ask.

We were supposed to meet with the midwives a few days ago to get established, but after everything that happened, we decided to push it off awhile. Both Ali and Will received clean bills of health from our midwife in D.C. a few days before we left town, so we feel okay about taking our time.

"I did. Called them earlier today, actually. We have a new appointment for Monday morning. I'm far enough along now that they want to see me once each week for the duration of my pregnancy, so I went ahead and scheduled for every Monday morning from here on out. They even penciled me in for the two Mondays after my due date," she says.

"Okay, good," I reply. "So that's taken care of."

"It is," she agrees. We lay quietly for a minute as I stroke her hair. It's wet from her tears. I hope I'm helping her feel better. It pains me to see my wife hurting.

"Babe," I begin. "How long do you figure your parents will stay?"

"I think they have the flexibility to stay for quite a while if they want to," Ali explains. "The symphony has a sub filling in for Mom and from what I understand, that person is available as long as she needs him to me. I know Mom would like to get back by mid-March when Yo-Yo Ma performs, but I assume even that's up for discussion. She's been with the group so long, they're like extended family. I'm certain they'll support whatever she decides."

"That's nice," I say. "Your parents have been great. They've really shown up for us lately."

"I know, Georgie. I don't know what I would do without them," Ali replies.

"Me neither," I say, thinking of Roddy's actions the night of the break-in. "So, what about your dad? When does he need to get back?

"I think he's good for quite a while, too. I'm less familiar with the specifics of his situation, but he has someone filling in for him as the cast rehearses the latest play he's written," Ali explains. "It premieres next season, which doesn't kick off until the end of May. Maybe he has named a director to fill in. I don't know for sure, but they both seem genuinely happy to help."

"Wow, okay," I reply. "That's awesome."

"I know," Ali says. "I appreciate them so much."

"Given the situation with John Wendell, I wonder if we should talk to Marjorie and Roddy about coming back before Will is born and then staying with us for at least a few more weeks after he gets here," I say.

"That makes sense," Ali affirms. "Your mom may have her hands full with John Wendell's care. I kind of doubt she'll be able to help as much as she planned. It sounds like we have no idea how things are going to unfold with him. Plus, you're going to be working soon, and I think I'll need someone here."

"Yeah," I add, "I'm not sure I'll be able to take off more than a couple of weeks after Will is born since I'm starting significantly later than scheduled. I assume Cornell has things they want me to get going on. I'd hate for Marjorie to miss Yo-Yo Ma though."

"Well, she might not end up missing him," Ali replies. "I guess it all depends on when Will decides to make his entrance. But I think Mom would rather be with us than with Yo-Yo Ma. She's worked with him before anyway. I'm pretty sure they're friends. Acquaintances, at least. Maybe she could invite him over for dinner one night when she's back in New York City if she misses performing with him in the Philharmonic. They could break out their instruments and play together right in Mom and Dad's brownstone."

"Yeah, I'd love to be there for that," I say. Marjorie is a marvelous musician. I love listening to her play the viola almost as much as I love listening to Ali play the cello.

"Then we'll talk to them about sticking around?" she asks.

"Let's do it," I reply.

"Look at us, Georgie, crossing things off our mental to-do list and making arrangements. It feels good to control what we can," Ali says.

"Yes, it does. There's plenty we can't control, as evidenced by recent events."

"Indeed," she adds, hugging me tight and pressing her cheek down hard onto my chest.

"Hey, wait here a minute," I say as I get out of bed.

"Okay," she responds, sounding intrigued. "Where are you going?"

"Just wait here," I say. "I have something for you."

I walk across the room to my chest of drawers and begin to search through the one on top. It takes me a minute to find what I'm looking for and to straighten it up within its velvety box. I can't help but smile as I walk back to the bed with the surprise tucked neatly into the palm of my hand. I pause along the way to light a couple of candles on the mantle.

"Georgie," Ali says with a sly smile. "What do you have for me?"

"I was going to give this to you after Will was born," I say. "But I want you to have it now."

"A push present?" she asks. "I haven't pushed yet."

"I don't know if anyone outside of the Kardashians really calls it that. Do they?" I say with a chuckle. "But yes, a push present. You did plenty of pushing against me a little while ago, so I think you qualify." She laughs. I love making her laugh.

I place the little black box in my wife's beautiful hands as she sits up in bed and her glorious body is on display once again. Her long, tousled hair falls around her perky breasts and frames them like art. She looks magnificent like this in the candlelight. "Open it up," I say.

"Oh, my," she exclaims as she squeezes the box and pulls it to her naked chest. "This is something special, isn't it?"

"It is," I reply.

"Did you get it at Louell's?"

"I did," I answer. Louell's is the manufacturing jeweler in D.C. where we had our wedding rings and a few other pieces I've given to Ali over the years made. I had this particular piece created and ready in time to be picked up before we left town. "Come on, open it. I'm excited for you to see what's inside."

She smiles at me sweetly, then opens the box to find a delicate gold chain with five large diamonds all in a row. Tears begin to flow from her eyes again, only this time, they are definitely happy tears.

"Georgie," she says. "It's stunning."

"Just like you," I add. I'm proud of myself. Proud to be making my wife happy.

"Are the five diamonds for the five of us?" she asks.

"Yes," I confirm. "One for you, one for me, one for Ethan, one for Leo, and one for little Will. There's strength in five. Look how balanced and strong five are together."

"Like our family," she says as she leaps into my arms and hugs me tight around the neck. A warm rush moves through me when I feel her body against mine again. "I love it so much, Georgie. Thank you."

"You're so welcome, babe," I say. "I'm really glad you like it."

"I do, Georgie. I absolutely love it. It's flashy, but I don't mind. Help me get it on," she replies as she pulls her wavy hair up and to the side with one hand exposing her long, elegant neck.

I remove the necklace from its velvety box slowly, taking time to appreciate my wife's beauty and the love we share. I'm such a lucky man. She's perfection. I gently place the diamonds just above her collarbone then fasten the clasp around back at the nape of her neck.

"There," I say. "When you wear this necklace, I want you to remember how the five of us belong together and how we can get through anything with each other's love and support. Now turn around and let me look at you."

"Pretty?" she asks as she turns to face me once more.

"Alessandra," I reply. "There's nothing more beautiful than you in this entire world. The necklace isn't bad either."

She laughs as she reaches up to touch the row of

diamonds with one hand. When she does, one of her breasts gets inadvertently jostled and suddenly I want her again. Badly. I lean down and take her voluptuous breast into my mouth, slowly moving her nipple from side to side with my tongue. I cradle her other breast with my hand and mimic the gentle side to side motion on the nipple with my fingers. She doesn't pull away. Instead, she reaches over to her phone on the nightstand and cues up *From Eden* by Hozier, which is one of her favorite songs to make love to. I move upwards, placing hot kisses on the top of her breasts, then her collarbone, then on the diamonds, and finally in the crevices of her neck. She arches her back in response to my touch and I suck hard on her earlobe.

The candlelight makes everything more sensual. It almost looks like a different setting than the darker one we made love in just a little while ago. I slide my hand between her legs. She exhales heavily as she presses herself against me and I know she's ready, too. We make love for what feels like hours. We move slowly, taking turns with our mouths on each other and then both at the same time. We kiss deeply and cycle through a variety of erotic positions. I enter her from behind and stroke passionately. Then she straddles me and rides for a long while as she stimulates her own nipples and I admire how the necklace looks on her luscious body. Seeing her pleasure herself makes my appetite even more ravenous. I reach my fingers in between us and quicken our climb as I rub while she grinds. We climax like that, again, together, in sheer bliss.

"Ali, babe, we're back," I say once I've caught my breath.

"You can say that again," she replies, sweaty and exhilarated as she slides off of me and plops down onto the bed. "There's nowhere else I'd rather be than completely intertwined with you, George Hartmann."

I grab her hand and look her squarely in the eye. "Ali, I need you to know that I'm here for you."

"I know you are," she replies. "I promise I do."

"No, but truly," I clarify. "I may be a mess in other areas of my life. I may not know what to do or how to handle things coming up."

"You mean with John Wendell?" she asks.

"Yeah, with John Wendell, with the aftermath of the break-in, with my new job, with Mom, with the changes Will's arrival will bring to our family, with therapy, and even with Ethan saying he used to be someone else. But what I know for sure is how to love you," I say. "I'm your rock. I'll continue to be. Don't ever think otherwise. Do you understand?"

"I do, Georgie. You're my rock," she replies. "I understand."

"Some couples would be weakened by the kind of stresses we're experiencing," I say. "Some would lose faith in each other."

"Not us," Ali says. "I didn't wait at home alone while you were globetrotting with the Air Force only to buckle under pressure now that we finally have a chance to spend more time together. You and I are for forever. We'll make it through."

We curl up and fall promptly to sleep just as we are: naked, exhausted, and bursting with love for each other and the life we've created. As long as I have Ali by my side, I can handle anything life throws my way.

# PART III

## EACH OTHER FOREVER

## 9

## GEORGE: STEADY

I wake up early, ready for the busy day ahead. It's still dark outside, but I decide to go for a quick run. Running is something I used to do regularly but haven't made time for since we arrived in Ithaca. It'll be good to get out there again and feel the ground under my feet. I should probably be running for my mental health at this point.

Uncle Liam is awake and sees me lacing up my shoes.

"Good morning, buddy," Liam says.

"Hey, Liam, good morning to you, too," I reply. "Did you sleep well?"

"I did. My room in the basement is nice and quiet and dark. Just the right kind of cold, too. It's perfect for deep, rejuvenating sleep. I haven't been this well rested in years," he explains.

"Good. I'm glad to hear it," I say. "I'm on my way

out the door for a run. Want to join me? The lake is gorgeous as the sun comes up."

"Hell, yeah, George. Now you're talking. I'll grab my shoes and be right back."

Liam and I have run alongside each other countless times, including in exotic parts of the world while deployed together. Our pacing is pretty much the same, so we make good running partners. Sometimes we talk. Other times we run in silence, but we always enjoy each other's company. I shoot Roddy a quick text to let him know the two of us are heading out so he can watch over the house. He must have already been awake upstairs because he responds immediately with "roger that."

"You were fast," I say as Liam returns to the kitchen in what feels like just a couple of minutes.

"I was thinking of doing some type of PT this morning anyway. My shoes were already set out on the end of my bed."

"Great minds think alike, eh?" I joke.

"Yeah, or more like military minds are trained alike," Liam says with a chuckle. "They know what they're doing to us. It's all part of their master plan. Can't have soldiers getting flabby and out of shape."

"I guess not," I reply.

We step outside into the front courtyard and lock the door behind us, making sure the alarm system is armed like it's supposed to be. It's freezing cold out, but Ithaca hasn't seen any significant snowfall in the past few days other than flurries. The roads are clear, thanks to county salt trucks.

It feels a little odd as Liam and I walk past the area where Lady intercepted the intruder and then where Roddy put an end to him. I haven't been out to this part of the yard on foot since the night of the break-in. Liam can tell what I'm thinking.

"So this is the spot?" he asks.

"Yeah, Lady grabbed the guy right about there," I say, pointing. "Then he ultimately landed pretty much where we're standing now."

"Are you going to tell me how he came to land where he did?" Liam asks.

"Should I?" I ask in return.

"I get the gist," he says as he motions with his head for us to get out onto the road and pick up the pace. "But you know you can trust me with the details if you ever want to share them."

"I know. I don't want to put you in a tough position if there ends up being a more thorough investigation."

"George, I can handle myself. Have you forgotten our training?" Liam says with a laugh.

"I wish I could have," I reply with a laugh of my own. "I think we're both scarred for life after everything the military put us through."

"But in a good way," Liam adds.

"Yeah, okay, we'll go with that," I say, laughing.

"Did Ethan see anything?" he asks.

"No, his head was turned and his ears were covered," I reply.

"Roddy was holding him?"

I pause the conversation and consider whether or

not to continue. Liam doesn't push me. He simply waits. We jog for a few minutes in silence. My calf muscles are stiff from the cold and lack of use, but they're beginning to loosen. Liam could unintentionally implicate Roddy if he were questioned. I can't let that happen. Then again, this is Liam we're talking about. He can certainly handle himself under pressure, and I would love to get this off my chest. I decide to go ahead.

"At first, yes, Roddy was holding Ethan. I hesitated, so Roddy stepped in. He handed Ethan to me. I was holding my boy when the deed was done," I explain.

Liam looks a little surprised, but not all that much. "So Roddy took care of the intruder," Liam muses. "By himself?"

"Yes. Lady had the guy pretty well incapacitated. She was something. You would have thought she'd had MPC training," I say.

"Huh," Liam returns.

"But yeah, Roddy finished him," I answer.

"With a weapon?" Liam asks.

"No weapon. The intruder had a gun, but I kicked it away once I saw that Lady had him pinned down," I explain.

"Wow. I get the impression Roddy isn't shaken up by what happened," Liam says. "Seems like a New York City playwright and drama professor would be shaken after killing a man with his bare hands."

"I thought the same thing," I say. "He treated it like a job that needed to be done. He didn't hesitate at all. And he hasn't shown any regret or remorse that I'm aware of. Granted, he and I haven't talked about it. I'm not sure we ever will."

"You think the police know?" Liam asks.

"I figure they have to. Roddy's hands were torn up. I stood in the way of the surveillance camera per his instruction during that part. I'm hoping the police have decided to let it slide given what the cameras did capture," I continue.

"So, Roddy told you to stand in front of the camera?"

"Yeah, and he told me how to hold Ethan so it looked like I was consoling him. I was consoling him, but you know what I mean. The stance served double duty. I leaned one of Ethan's little ears down on my chest and covered the other with the palm of my hand. All while turning his eyes away, of course."

"And Roddy gave you the opportunity to kill the guy yourself before stepping in?" Liam asks.

"He did," I reply. "I was standing over the intruder poised to do it, but my mind started racing with thoughts of spending the rest of my life in prison away from Ali and the boys. Roddy saw what I was going through and took over."

"That's quite a kindness he did for you," Liam says. "But it's an odd move for someone like him. Unless there's more to his story. Is it possible he could be ex-special forces of some sort? CIA maybe? Or British Intelligence?"

"I had the exact same suspicion. I'm not aware of any history like that, but he sure didn't look like a civilian as he was ending our intruder's life," I reply. "I've thought of asking him about it. You think I should? I definitely don't want to tell anyone else until police put the matter completely to rest. Remember, the getaway driver is still out there."

"Yeah, don't tell anyone else," Liam responds. "I am curious about Roddy's background. Maybe the three of us can go out together at some point and discuss it."

"I'd be up for that," I say. "It would be interesting to hear what Roddy has to say. If he'll tell us."

The sun is coming up and in full view over the lake just as we hit our stride. The scene is breathtaking. It feels good to run. Good to be with my uncle.

"Hey," I query. "Will you come with me to fetch Lady from the animal hospital after we get cleaned up? We can grab breakfast at the bagel place you like on the way."

"Sure thing," Liam says. "When is Taye supposed to get here?"

"I don't know," I say. "He was leaving from Connecticut early. Ali will stick around the house to welcome him when he arrives. I assume Roddy and Marjorie will hang with her."

"Good," Liam replies.

"I think Taye has his son this weekend and so will drive back East to pick him up tonight. Malcolm lives with his mom in Stockbridge, Massachusetts. I hear it's nice out there. It's in the Berkshires where the Norman Rockwell Museum is located. Probably looks like a Christmas card."

Neither of us says anything for the rest of the run. We could talk about how long he plans to stay. Or how Mom seemed when he took her the plate of food last night. Or why he has hardly mentioned Estella's name since he's been here. But we don't. We'll get to it all, in good time.

When we return to the house, we shower and dress quickly in order to go pick up Lady. Everyone is excited to see her home where she belongs. Roddy has the boys in the kitchen and is making oatmeal and scrambled eggs for breakfast. As good as it smells, Liam and I decide to hold out for the bagel place.

The boys seem to have done fine upstairs. Ali is still asleep and they are clearly comfortable with Roddy. He's great with them. He should be a teacher or coach to little kids at some point. I imagine he's great with the college-age kids at NYU, too, but what I see of his rapport with the preschool set is damn impressive. I'm glad my sons are lucky enough to have him for their grandpa. I kiss Ethan and Leo's little heads and thank Roddy, then head back out the door.

As promised, Liam and I swing by Unitown Bagel on the way to the animal hospital. I get bacon, egg, sausage, and pepper jack cheese on an everything bagel with milk to drink. My uncle chooses scrambled eggs, ham, asiago cheese, and salsa on sourdough with black coffee. He always did like things a little spicy. It's all delicious.

We arrive at the animal hospital eager to get our Ladygirl. It's fitting to have Liam here with me now because he was with me when I went down to

Chesapeake, Virginia and picked her up as a puppy. I'm smiling. Big. I don't think I could hide my emotion if I tried.

The waiting room is nearly empty when we enter. The hospital itself is staffed around the clock, but the clinic doesn't open for regular appointments except during weekday business hours. We are apparently one of their first appointments for the day. A young Asian guy in navy blue scrubs greets us as we approach the counter. His expression is somber. I imagine there is a lot of heartache involved with his job. He probably has to watch animals suffer and die all the time. Thankfully, our story has a happy ending.

"Hello," I say to the guy cheerfully, hoping some of my enthusiasm will rub off on him. "We're here to pick up Lady."

He stares at his computer for a minute before nodding, then turns around and walks through the swinging double doors into the back room. He doesn't make eye contact. Liam and I glance at each other and shrug. He must be having a bad day already. Oh, well. We'll get our Ladygirl and be on our way. At least the veterinarians we've talked to are more personable.

We're watching cable news on the TV in the corner of the waiting room when the guy returns and places a white plastic box down on the counter in front of him. He removes a folded up paper from a sleeve on top and begins entering information from the document into his computer. Still no eye contact.

"What's this?" I ask, feeling a little concerned. "Where's Lady?"

"Right here," he responds, setting a hand down on top of the box.

"What?" I ask in disbelief. "Are those… ashes?" I can hear my voice getting shaky. I can feel my body tensing and my hands curling into fists. Liam steps forward towards the counter and closer to me.

"Didn't you get our voicemail?" the guy asks.

"What voicemail?" I reply. "I didn't receive any voicemail."

"We left you a voicemail, confirming cremation and stating the remains were ready for pickup. Isn't that why you're here?"

"I'm here to pick up my dog," I say. "My living, breathing dog."

Adrenaline is pumping now and the switch has been flipped on my anger. I'm furious.

"I don't know what to tell you, sir," the guy says sheepishly.

Wrong answer. How dare he? Something about his callous demeanor sends me into a rage. Before Liam can stop me, I leap over the counter and grab the guy up by the collar. He's nearly a foot shorter than I am. Tossing him around is easy. My arms want to fling him and crush him like the little pissant he is. I throw him hard against the back wall, then lift him off the ground so his legs dangle. I grit my teeth and look him square in the eye. He's terrified. He should be.

"Please," he implores. "Let me down. I didn't hurt your dog."

A couple of employees from the back hear the

commotion and come out to see what's happening as
Liam races around the counter to reach me.

"You people told me my dog was alive," I yell at
full volume. "I saw her the other day. She was hurt,
but she was recovering. Now I show up to take her
home and you bring me a box of ashes? Do you have
any idea what this dog means to my family?"

I feel Liam's hand on my shoulder. "George, look
at me," my uncle says.

A woman from the back wearing a lab coat steps
forward and asks what's going on. Several others
follow her and a group of onlookers begins to gather.
An older man, also in a lab coat, has his phone out
and is dialing. The guy I'm holding in the air whines
and cries, begging me to let him go. Time feels like it
has slowed down again, just like the night of the
break-in. Only this time I'm not hyperaware of my
surroundings. Quite the opposite. The sounds in the
room blur together as they drone on in a whirr. My
heart is racing. I'm not processing normally. My
breathing feels funny.

"George," Liam says again, more sternly this time,
his grip tightening on my shoulder. "Look at me.
Right now."

Fury boils to the top of my being and has to be
released. I roar loudly in what feels like a primal
scream. I use every bit of the air in my lungs to sustain
it as long as I can while still holding the little man
against the wall. When I'm finally done, I drop the
man and slowly turn to face Liam.

"Good," Liam says as he stands in front of me,

extending his arms all the way and placing his hands on my shoulders. It's a steadying hold. "Okay, George, keep looking at me. And breathe. Deep breaths."

I follow his instructions. I can't quite get a whole breath. I think this is what it feels like to hyperventilate. Liam turns his head to address the others in the room.

"No need to panic, folks. We have this under control. My nephew here has been through a lot recently," Liam says. He keeps his hands firmly on my shoulders as he explains. "You may have heard about the break-in at his house last weekend. An intruder took George's four-year-old son out of his bedroom window and almost got away. Now George arrives here thinking he's picking up his dog who saved his son and is instead brought a box of ashes and told he should have received a voicemail with news of her death. Please, cut him some slack."

"Oh, no," the woman in the lab coat says quietly. "I'll be right back."

Liam guides me to a bench on the other side of the counter in the waiting area and sits me down. He secures one arm around my shoulders and tells me to put my head between my knees to catch my breath. I do as he says. What am I going to tell Ali and the boys? We need Lady. Losing her is too great a price to pay. Especially since we already thought she might have been gone and then were told she was out of the woods. I don't know if I can take this right now. It's too much at once. I think I'm failing my family.

"Dr. Hartmann?" the woman in the lab coat calls out from the double doorway.

"Yeah?" I muster.

"I have your Lady," she says.

"What the hell?" Liam exclaims.

I look up and my eyes can hardly believe what they see. There is our Ladygirl, alive and well. She's walking gingerly with the support of a large brace which wraps around her abdomen and under her shoulders. It has a handle on top. The woman in the lab coat is holding on in order to help Lady support her weight.

"What?" I ask. "She's okay?"

"She is," the woman responds. "There was a mistake. We had two girls named Lady with us this week. Your girl is right here. The other Lady didn't make it. I'm terribly sorry for the confusion."

I don't know whether to stay angry or to kiss this woman. I'm appalled by the little man's incompetence. But my relief at seeing Lady takes over and I can feel my strength returning. My body begins to relax. I can take a full breath again. I look over at Liam and he gives me a pat on the back as if to tell me to go ahead and embrace our girl. I drop to my knees on the floor of the waiting room and open my arms wide as Lady toddles over and leans into me. I pull her close and stroke the top of her head. I feel like crying, but tears won't come. I guess I'm still in the tearless portion of this emotional rollercoaster I'm riding.

"Oh, Ladygirl," I say, "I'm so happy to see you. You have no idea how happy I am to see you."

Liam takes a step towards the woman in the lab coat.

"Ma'am, are we all good here?" he asks softly. What he's really asking is whether or not they've called the police. Whether or not they intend to press charges.

"We are all good," she replies as she hands him post-op instructions for Lady's care. "I'll handle things here. We'll send an invoice for the outstanding balance, so no need to worry about that today. Take your nephew home. Call us if you have any questions."

I manage a nod at the woman as Liam helps me to my feet. He puts one arm around my shoulders and holds onto Lady's brace with the other as the three of us walk out of the animal hospital. I should say something on my way out to the guy I roughed up. But I don't. Some of his co-workers appear to be consoling him. I'll have to deal with that another time. We load Lady into the back seat gently and fasten a seatbelt around her midsection. She whimpers a little every time she changes position. Poor girl. We help her adjust until she seems comfortable enough for the ride home. I drove on the way here, but Liam knows I won't be driving right now. I've got to collect myself first. He goes directly to the driver side of the vehicle without mentioning it. I walk around to the passenger seat and get in.

"You're okay, George," he says once we're both seated. "I'm right here."

Upon hearing those few quiet words, the tears are

unlocked. I half-smile and nod at my uncle as wetness streams down my face. I sit in silence. I'm not sure what to say, but I know with Liam I don't have to say anything at all. He takes a few detours in order to give me time to compose myself before we get back to the house and I have to face the others. We ride around Ithaca for nearly an hour, out past the horse farms and John Wendell's old house on Ellis Hollow Road, over near the swimming hole at Robert H. Treman State Park, and up Trumansburg Road to Taughannock Falls. Lady dozes peacefully in the back seat. It's nice, riding like this. I have quite a day left ahead of me. I'll need all of my strength to get through it.

"Liam?" I ask.

"Yeah, buddy, what is it?" he replies.

"Will you stick with me today?" I ask.

"Of course, I will," he says. "What are we doing?"

"Well, Taye first," I begin.

"Right," Liam says.

"And our big dining table is being delivered, although Marjorie and Roddy can probably run point on that," I say. "Ali is getting so far along in her pregnancy that I don't want to assume she'll have energy."

"Okay," he affirms. "And?"

"And then I have to go to another therapy appointment with Dr. Epstein this afternoon. It was pretty intense yesterday. Would you like to meet him?" I ask.

"Sure," Liam replies. "I have a book on my e-reader that is just getting good. I'm happy to meet him and then plow through that in the waiting room while you and Dr. Epstein do your thing."

"That's really kind. Thank you," I say.

"I'm glad to do it," he returns. "No problem at all. You think Marjorie and Roddy can handle watching over Lady as well? They'll already have the boys to take care of."

"Probably. After Dr. Epstein's, I told Mom I'd stop by to check on John Wendell," I add.

"Right," Liam says. "We'll do that together, okay?"

"Good," I say. "That will be very good. Thank you, Uncle Liam."

"I told you, you don't have to thank me," he replies. I nod and ride a while longer before speaking again.

"Liam?" I ask.

"Yeah?" he answers.

"How am I going to live here in Ithaca when you're still living down there in D.C.?"

"That's not something we have to worry about today," Liam responds. "I have plenty of leave and plan to stay awhile, if you'll have me."

"I'd love that," I reply. "I know Ali and the boys would, too. As long as you don't mind Marjorie and Roddy also being around. I think they're planning to stay a while as well. They're especially good with the boys, you know?"

"I do know," Liam affirms. "I love those two. I like it when we're all together. As long as you don't feel like your house is too crowded and we're infringing on time that should be reserved for you, Ali, and the boys to be by yourselves."

"Not at all. We need you now. Being there for us like this means the world," I say. Then after a pause, "Liam, are you and Estella having trouble? You haven't talked about her like you normally do."

"Ah, George, you don't need to worry yourself about that," he replies.

"Well, I do. I can be there for you, too, you know? Just because my world is crazy and turned upside down doesn't mean I have nothing to give," I say. "I want you to tell me."

"I appreciate that," my uncle says. "If you must know, we are considering a separation. It's been a long time coming. Being up here now is good timing, really."

"I'm real sorry to hear," I offer. "I had no idea before you came into town."

"Yeah, it's a long story. There's nothing dramatic happening. No cheating. No fighting. We still love and respect each other very much. We've just sort of come to what may be a natural end to things. If that's the way it is, I'm okay with it," he explains.

"I'm glad you feel that way about it," I say. "If you and Estella do part ways, you could always move up here and go into business with me."

"Are you serious?" Liam asks.

"Yes, completely," I say. "I'm beginning to think Cornell isn't the right place for me. It's odd how things are happening to delay my start date. I'm toying with the idea of taking some significant time off from work altogether. I might like to travel some with the family and to spend time exploring business ideas."

"Wow, George," Liam says. "We've talked about going into business together, but it always seemed so far off. You think it's time?"

"I don't know," I say. "But I doubt I would have actually considered moving to Ithaca without the job offer from Cornell, so what if its purpose was just to get us here? I feel like a completely different person than I was two weeks ago and I have an inkling more changes are coming."

"I hear you," Liam affirms.

"I agree with what you said about needing to be home more while the boys are little, so the military isn't the right place for me anymore. But you know how I've been concerned about not having a large enough impact from my role at Cornell? What if I could have a big impact and be there for my family at the same time? A new business venture might check both of those boxes," I explain.

"Are you talking national security?" Liam asks.

"Maybe," I say. "Probably. Or private security. That's been weighing heavily on me since the break-in. Maybe national and private security."

"Aerospace?" he queries.

"Yeah, of course. It's what we know," I say.

"Aerospace for private security?" Liam asks, sounding skeptical but intrigued.

"I realize it's a little out there— pun intended," I say with a chuckle. "But what if we put our minds together to see what we can come up with?"

"Go on," he prompts.

"I've been thinking about that getaway driver in the van who is still on the loose. The surveillance cameras on our house were too far away to pick up a plate number, so the police don't have much to go on. He didn't get out of the vehicle at any point. They may never find him."

"Okay," Liam replies, furrowing his brow as he thinks. "More cameras can be added and they can be positioned to cover multiple angles. I'm sure Taye will go over all of those logistics with us."

"Sure," I answer. "And that will help tremendously. But what when there aren't any plates? Or when plate numbers and other identifying info are intentionally obscured? What then? It makes me sick to think about Ethan having been almost taken away. I'm motivated to solve this problem."

"Wait," Liam says. "Are you talking about utilizing satellites?"

"Maybe, yes. Or Unmanned Aerial Vehicles," I say. "What if, instead of losing track of the van, we create a way to have it followed and monitored?"

"Not bad," he replies. "Has that been done in the private sector?"

"I'm not sure, but even if it has we may be able to create a better mousetrap," I answer. "I'm not aware of UAVs being used over American soil for anything other than military and government purposes."

"What, you can't call them drones like us old geezers?" Liam jokes. Most people in the career field prefer the term Unmanned Aerial Vehicles since drones make it sound like they're robots without human pilots. UAVs have human pilots, just not in the cockpits.

"Something like that," I reply with a smile.

"Those military and government purposes you speak of are highly controversial. You know what I'm talking about," Liam says. "We've seen that firsthand."

"I do," I say. "My role at Cornell was going to put me in that hornet's nest anyway. Might as well take it on my own."

"Not on your own," Uncle Liam adds. "I couldn't stand by and let you do all of this on your own."

"Okay, hopefully not on my own then," I say.

"Huh," Liam muses.

"I think the applications and possibilities are endless," I say. "And I think it's only a matter of time before someone implements some variation on this idea if they haven't already. Might as well be us. The world is changing and aerospace technology will remain at the forefront."

"Sure, it will," he replies.

"We could even weaponize the UAVs, technically," I say.

"Over American soil?" Liam asks. "That's playing with fire, George."

"I'm aware," I respond. "But what if a UAV had been monitoring my property the night of the break-in and could have immobilized the intruder before he ever had a chance to breach the window and take Ethan out? I mean, we are talking about protection here."

"You want to tangle with the Federal Aviation Administration?" Liam asks. "And the Department of Defense? And probably Congress sooner or later? And God only knows who else? We're talking groundbreaking stuff here. Progress in terms of legalization will not come easy."

"Maybe it's something worth fighting for," I say. "I believe keeping my family safe is worth fighting for. I trust others will feel the same way."

"Wow," Liam says with a look of awe on his face. "You've really given this some thought, haven't you?"

"I know it sounds crazy, but what if it's not? What if it's exactly what we're supposed to be doing?" I ask. "I've heard people talk about how life sometimes shakes you up in order to place you where you're supposed to be. I don't know if I believe that or not, but a change is happening inside of me. I can't go back to who I was before we arrived here last week. I'm not sure I'd want to."

"This means I'd have to separate from the Air Force, too, of course," Liam says. "Retiring has been in the back of my mind for a while now, but damn. I didn't think an opportunity would materialize so soon. I'll need some time to wrap things up. And Estella..."

"Understood," I confirm. "I need time myself. I'd love to spend at least a few months after Will is born doing nothing but enjoying my family."

"I'd love to see you do that," Liam agrees.

"As for business, I figure we'll need to allow a significant amount of time for research and development," I say. "Months, for sure. Maybe a year."

"Or more," Liam adds. "You're talking about a massive undertaking. And it will be expensive."

"Right?" I say with a smile. "For a long, long time, I didn't want to use the money Dad left me. Maybe I'm finally ready."

"Holy shit, George. I've questioned whether or not you'd ever be ready," Liam says. "There are other sources of funding we can consider. But using our own money will make things far easier."

"I could approach Cornell about collaborating with us rather than employing me," I say. "We wouldn't be partners with the University per se, because that doesn't seem quite right and I doubt they'd even sign on to such an arrangement. But perhaps we could hire them for R&D. Or utilize their labs."

"Not a bad idea," Liam replies.

"I don't know," I continue. "There's a lot to consider. We can sort it all out in time. But if I tell Cornell I don't want to move forward with the position they hired me to fill, I'd like to provide an alternative which would allow us to work together in some capacity."

"And hey," Liam says, "they ought to be stoked about the bonus Aerospace Engineer they'd come to know and love."

"Absolutely," I say with a laugh as Liam nods in agreement. "What college engineering department wouldn't be stoked about getting to know a bonus

Aerospace guy?" We laugh together and shake our heads. It feels good.

"Are you sure Ithaca, New York is the right place to home base on this though?" Liam asks. "It's pretty isolated up here, far from military strongholds like D.C. and tech centers like Boston. Cornell's engineering department is a big plus, but still. We have to think not only about local support for what we'll be doing, but the ability to attract and retain top talent."

"All good points," I say. "But it's more of the fact that this feels like home to me. Mom and John Wendell are here, and I think Ali will be happy here. It's not far from our New York City family. We want to raise the boys in a place where we have roots. We're New Yorkers."

"I hear you," Liam says. "I'm the only straggler not jumping back on the New York bandwagon as of yet."

"Exactly," I reply with another laugh. "At the heart of it all is a gut instinct, Liam. I can feel it in my bones. This is the place. And I think this is the thing." Liam looks at me hard for a couple of minutes without saying a word.

"Really, George?" he asks.

"Maybe I have lost my mind," I continue. "And I know I had a man by the throat in an animal hospital little more than an hour ago. But, yes. What do you think?"

"I should probably take some time to contemplate the idea," he replies with a chuckle. "That's the mature and responsible thing to do, right? You did just have a man by the throat in an animal hospital, after all."

"I suppose," I say. "I haven't mentioned the whole business idea to Ali yet."

"You haven't?" Liam asks. "You had better do that, George. She may fall on the other side of the fence when it comes to privacy issues our business will raise. Even I know how she feels about that type of thing. The woman did work for the American Civil Liberties Union after all. Are you absolutely sure she will support you on this?"

"Well, she worked for the ACLU on immigration law. We'll probably disagree on some things, but she'll support me. I'm sure of that. When it comes to protecting Ali and the boys, I find myself caring less and less about other people's opinions-- hers included. I've always felt an overwhelming need to protect my people. That need is even stronger since the break-in. I feel compelled. Called. Driven. However you want to describe it. It's my mission. It feels good to have a mission," I say.

"Okay, then," Liam replies as he pulls into our driveway and parks our SUV. "Let me toss the idea around before I give you an official answer, but unofficially, yes. I can't believe I'm saying this, but I'll move up here and go into business with you, George. It would be an honor. I've been encouraging you to take some risks and enjoy life. I'd be a hypocrite if I didn't join you in making the leap."

"Seriously?" I say. "I didn't think I'd convince you that easy. That's amazing news. This whole thing just went from outrageous idea to reality within an hour. Incredible." I lean over inside the vehicle and give my uncle a big hug. "We have some serious planning to do. Should I wait to tell the others?"

"Give me a couple of days if you don't mind," he replies. "I understand if you need to tell Ali, but Estella deserves to know before it goes much beyond that."

"Of course," I say as I step out of the car and close the door. "We may be so busy over the next few days that there's hardly time to talk about it anyway."

"That would be convenient," Liam says.

"We'd like to have Estella around, too," I add. "I realize Ithaca isn't the best place for a fashion designer, but maybe she could travel back and forth to New York. We love her, you know?"

"I appreciate you saying that," Liam responds. "She and I will work something out. Like I mentioned before, it's good timing."

Our serious conversation ends as we take Lady out of the backseat. Taye is here, and Ali, Ethan, Leo, Roddy, and Marjorie are huddled with him in front of the living room windows waiting expectantly for Lady to come inside. Looks like she's about to receive a hero's welcome. She certainly deserves it. I consider carrying her in to speed the process up, but decide to let her walk with dignity. She's probably too proud to be carried unless absolutely necessary. The pathways are clear of snow and ice. She treads carefully, little by little as she makes her way inside, looking hard around the perimeter of the yard as she goes. I lean down, pat her on the head, and tell her I felt the same way the first time I came back home after the break-in. We understand each other as far as that goes. We're the protectors.

When we get inside, Ali and the boys kneel down close to Lady and hug her tight. She leans her head on Ethan's little shoulder and looks so relieved. Liam and I greet Taye and welcome him to Ithaca. He's never been here before, but he's in good spirits. He and Ali are already in a rhythm, laughing and chatting like the old friends they are. I'm glad to see them happy together. Ali has It's Only a Paper Moon playing over the sound system, which is another one of John Wendell's favorites. She must have been thinking about him when she picked today's music. The place feels warm and cheerful. The lake looks beautiful out back.

Roddy suggests I take Lady around the house and yard so she can see for herself everything is okay. I think that's a great idea. I do as he suggests and she seems appreciative. We walk the same path we did the day the movers were here-- out the back door onto the deck, across the deck and down the wooden stairs to the carriage house, around the perimeter of the yard, back up the wooden steps to the deck and inside, up the interior stairs to the top floor, and then finally down to the basement. She starts to get tired part way through, so I cradle her gently in my arms and carry her. No one else sees. I set her down again on the main level when we're done with the basement and she toddles lightly to the mat Ali placed in front of the

loveseat for her. Taye and Marjorie sit down on the
seat above our girl and welcome her with words of
encouragement as the rest of us settle into comfortable
spots of our own in the living room. The boys are
seated on the couch directly opposite Lady. I assume
she likes this positioning so she can keep her eyes on
them while she rests.

We sit together and talk while more of John
Wendell's favorite music cycles through the playlist Ali
set up. Nat King Cole sings *L-O-V-E* as we enjoy the
lakefront views and catch Taye up on the details of
our lives. Ali has already told him most of it, but it
seems appropriate to give him an overview in order to
be sure he's up to speed. Liam glances at me when my
job at Cornell comes up, but I don't say anything
other than what has already been established. It's been
years since Taye has seen Marjorie and Roddy, so they
tell him all about the concerts and plays they've been
involved with since. Roddy mentions to Taye that he
should bring Malcolm to the City to see one of his
plays sometime. Marjorie says she can get them tickets
to a Philharmonic concert as well. They might as well
make a weekend of it, she says. Ali suggests Taye and
Malcolm go ahead and stay at Roddy and Marjorie's
brownstone while they're in town. Her parents have
plenty of room for guests and they like to entertain.
Everyone agrees that would be lovely. There are so
many connections to be made here. So much fun to be
had. It feels good to talk about the future. Ethan and
Leo look through a stack of children's books as the
adults talk. Sometimes they like to be nearby and

listen without actively participating in the conversation. I get it.

When it's time for lunch, Marjorie and Roddy whip us up gourmet ham and turkey sandwiches with homemade chips, salads, and tomato basil soup on the side. We drink more of the wine Liam picked up from Seneca Lake and savor every sip. It's amazing how having a guest can lighten the mood and make everything feel festive and hopeful. We tell Taye he should come back again soon and bring Malcolm. We tell him we want him to see Mom and John Wendell and to meet Duke next time. He knows Jen, but hasn't been officially introduced to Duke.

After lunch, both boys go down for a nap and the rest of us sit around the kitchen table to talk business. Taye took a look around our property when he first arrived and has some preliminary suggestions for us. As it turns out, we're in pretty good shape for the short term. Taye says the local security company the police department recommended did a good job. He wants to do a more in-depth assessment before he leaves this evening and then will get back to us within a couple of weeks with options for the highest level of protection possible. He assures us we'll be safe in the meantime. We're all really glad to hear it. I can see my wife's face soften and her demeanor lighten as Taye reassures us. Roddy notices as well and gives me a wink across the table. Ali's peace of mind is so important.

With that taken care of, Liam and I decide to head out a little early in order to stop by the police department on our way to my appointment with Dr.

Epstein. I know Ali and the boys and Lady are in good hands, so I might as well see what else I can accomplish today. I want to check in with the detectives handling our case to find out whether or not they have any new leads. I have a feeling they won't, unfortunately, but I want to get in front of them as often as possible so they don't forget about us. I don't mean to harass them. I understand the limitations they have to work with. I'm not expecting any miracles. I just want their best efforts in identifying the intruder and locating the getaway driver.

When we get there, Liam goes inside the station with me and stays close. He's probably afraid I'll throw someone against a wall if I don't like what they have to say. Luckily, I'm not feeling much like tossing anyone around this afternoon. I suppose I shouldn't rule out the possibility since my anger seems to go from zero to sixty faster than a sports car these days, but so far, I haven't been angry at the police. I guess I see them for what they are. They're a bunch of well-intentioned human beings working with inadequate resources. I'd rather start the business or invent the thing that solves problems for them rather than raking them over the coals when they're doing their best.

Duke is out of the office for the afternoon, so we don't get to see him this visit. We do get the opportunity to speak to the lead detective handling the case though. Just as I suspected, there's not much new to report. They're still waiting on results from the forensics lab, but so far haven't been able to identify the deceased individual. I don't tell the detective I'm doing my own research on the side. I'll tell him about it later if I find something solid, but for now, I'll keep that bit of information to myself. The police department doesn't have any leads on the getaway driver either. They say they're working on a few solid theories which might pan out, but no news yet. I can't help but think about what a different story this would be if Liam and I had our UAV service up and running. Someday we will. We thank the detective and say our goodbyes. It's time to head over to the Odyssey Psychology Center for a little odyssey action of my own. I'm ready.

## 10

## GEORGE: WOUNDS TO BE HEALED

I've never been a big believer in fate or predetermination, but I suspect something like it may be at work in my life right now. I feel pulled towards an inevitable outcome. A purpose that's been formed beforehand. The very universe feels in flux and there's a churn just below the level of what my five senses can perceive. Maybe the churn has always been there and I haven't been tuned in. Ever since the dream where I communicated with Dad, I feel fundamentally different. Truth be told though, I was feeling a nagging and an aching to be different even before then. I had no idea how change was going to come to fruition or whether or not it even should. Whatever the mechanisms and the reasons, I think I'm changing to becoming more and more of myself. Maybe I'll get better at explaining the whole thing as I settle into my new reality.

We park the car in the back and I walk with my

uncle around the outside of the psychology center to the charming covered front porch. I tell him about the summertime fat cat I envision schmoozing with people as they enjoy the sunshine and warm weather. He tells me he agrees that the porch is especially charming. A great place to sip some of that Seneca Lake wine he's become fond of. We step through the white wooden screened door and then the heavy black metal door, appreciating the little twinkling lights and the cheer they provide on this cold winter day.

Right here and right now, something significant is happening. I know it the same as I did the night I woke up suddenly and then heard my son scream. The hair on the back of my neck stands straight up as this knowing settles over me. I feel certain Ali and the boys are okay at home for some reason, so even though it would make sense to check in with them I don't. This is about something else. Perhaps multiple somethings else. I take a deep breath and steel myself for whatever is coming as Liam and I settle into the soft chairs in Dr. Epstein's waiting room. Now that I've been inside his little office, I know the buzzer attached to the front door will alert him that someone has entered the building. I fiddle with one of the seams on the arm of the chair I'm sitting in while we wait for Dr. E to plod out and greet us.

Liam has his e-reader in hand and is happily cueing up his novel. One of his arms hangs loosely over the side of his chair and he places one ankle up on the opposite knee in a relaxed pose I find myself envying. I'm starting to feel wound and bound, unsure of how to hold my body. Liam gives me a quizzical look and I wonder how much of my discomfort he notices. I'm safe showing all of this to Liam, but it's still embarrassing. I don't want to be a mess.

"Dr. George Hartmann?" we hear Dr. Epstein bellow before we see him emerge from the long hallway in the back of the building. He doesn't know Liam is here. I hope he doesn't mind me bringing him along. I stand and prepare myself for the force of nature that is Dr. Joseph Epstein as Liam begins to move leisurely to stand. He's not feeling any urgency or sense of formality. I wonder if he's ever been to therapy before.

"Hello, yes, it's me, Dr. Epstein," I say feebly, my voice already beginning to falter.

"I see you brought someone with you," Dr. Epstein says while crossing his arms over his chest in front of him, leaning back a bit, and looking my uncle up and down with what I'm learning is his trademark intensity. Liam is unphased.

"This is my Uncle Liam," I reply. "I asked him to be here today. He's my closest friend and confidant, and it's been a rough twenty-four hours since I left here yesterday."

"Say no more," Dr. Epstein offers as he reaches out to shake Liam's hand and offers him a welcoming smile. "George, would you like your uncle to come back to my office with us for your session? Or should he remain here in the lobby?"

"Either is okay," I reply.

"It's up to you," Dr. Epstein says. "This is your process. What feels best in this moment?"

"I actually would like Liam to be with me," I say as I turn to look at my uncle. "Liam, do you mind coming back with us? Can your book wait?"

"Of course, George. Whatever you need," Liam says.

"Very well," Dr. Epstein says. "Follow me, boys."

The doc seems noticeably softer around the edges today. Maybe this is him displaying compassion since he saw what a mess I was yesterday. Or maybe he's simply more comfortable with me. Or maybe I'm more comfortable with him and already oriented such that the whole setting feels a little friendlier and less intimidating. My stomach is in knots again though. It's hard to say exactly why.

We follow Dr. Epstein down the long hall to his little office, past the closed doors along the way. Just like yesterday, some rooms are dark while others are dimly lit but with privacy glass which obscures the view of what's happening inside. I look hard at the hypnotherapy room as I go by now that I know which one it is. The lights are turned out and it's too dark to really tell anything. I am definitely curious about it. I haven't had a chance to call Jen and ask more questions yet. I'd love to compare notes now that I've met Dr. Epstein and been in his office space. I'll have to reach out to her soon.

"Come on in," Dr. E says when we arrive at his little room. "Make yourself comfortable. Sit anywhere you like."

Liam nods to thank Dr. Epstein as he walks inside and plops down on one end of the leather couch. There are a couple of other chairs, but the couch looks most inviting. I sit on the other end and do my best to appear composed as the doc gets his clipboard ready.

"Hey, George," Liam says, gesturing towards a red and white quilt folded over the back of a wingback chair. The red sections are a mix of a solid base and various floral prints together comprising a large sawtooth star pattern. "That looks a lot like the quilts your mom used to sew in the eighties when you were a kid. Do you remember?"

"I do," I reply. "She made them for family and friends. I think we all have at least one or two of her works of art. They're beautiful."

"They sure are," Liam adds. "Estella and I still use the one she made for me. Know which one I mean? It has navy blues, brown, white, and some black with a tan and pink floral design here and there. The overall pattern is big circles, but they're sort of cut in half and placed opposite where you'd expect them to be if the circles were intact."

"I recall," I reply as my mind drifts back to my childhood. Mom's quilts bring back good memories. I think sewing is therapeutic for her. I remember her sewing a lot when I was little before I went to kindergarten. Even after I went to school and she started working, she'd still sew whenever she could. She used to lay quilt squares all over the kitchen table. They usually had straight pins in them, so you had to be careful about not moving your hands around haphazardly. Those little suckers hurt.

"Beautiful quilt, Dr. Epstein," Liam says once the doc has swiveled his chair towards us and leaned forward to indicate that he's situated and prepared to begin the session.

"Thank you," he replies. "It was a gift." He pauses a moment to see if we're finished with our chit-chat. I can tell he's eager to jump right in. Liam and I stay quiet, so Dr. E. begins.

"George, I have two hours in a row available this afternoon. Would you like to utilize both? I recommend doing so if you have time in your schedule," Dr. Epstein explains. "We can cover more ground that way."

"Great!" I reply enthusiastically. Maybe too enthusiastically. "Works for me." Liam nods in agreement.

"So tell me what's going on?" the doc asks.

"How do you mean?" I ask. I made the mistake of jumping right into Dad's death yesterday. I want my responses to be more measured today if possible.

"I mean I'd like to hear what you have to tell me," Dr. Epstein replies. "You mentioned that you've had a difficult twenty-four hours."

"I have," I reply slowly. For some reason, my mouth is feeling dry like I've been gnawing on cotton balls. I can't get words out. Liam sees me struggling and raises his eyebrows to ask if he should fill in. I shake my head yes and gesture in his direction as I wipe the beads of sweat beginning to form on my brow. Why am I falling apart like this?

"George's grandfather has taken a turn for the worse," Liam explains. "George found out after he left your office yesterday. It's not looking good. He's mostly unresponsive."

"I'm very sorry to hear that," Dr. Epstein replies. "Is this your father, Liam?"

"No, I'm Alec's brother. George's dad's brother. Our parents were older when they adopted us and they've been gone a long time. The grandfather we're speaking of now is on George's mom's side. His name is John Wendell."

"I see," Dr. Epstein affirms, cocking his head to one side and scribbling notes as he listens.

"John Wendell is ninety-five and has lived a phenomenal, full, happy life. It's still unexpected though. The guy's been in great shape. Just last weekend, he was singing and dancing for the crowd at Yellow Cob." Then after a pause, "He and George are very close."

Tears begin to form in my eyes and I cover my mouth with one hand as Liam shares the story. I believe Dr. Epstein sincerely cares, which seems to make me quicker to break down. I happen to notice my bulging bicep while my arm is touching my face and can't help but feel a pang of insecurity. What would my Air Force colleagues think if they saw me crying like this? I don't have a huge male ego like a lot of military guys do, but I value my masculinity. I would never have envisioned myself in the middle of this scene.

"I know George wants to be there for his Mom," Liam continues. "But he has a lot on his own plate right now. There are a bunch of mixed feelings."

"I get that," the doc affirms. "You said John Wendell, with a W?"

"Yes, his grandfather is John Wendell," Liam responds. "Everyone calls him by his full name. His daughter, George's mom, is Linette."

"Huh," Dr. Epstein mutters, sitting back in his chair and scratching the side of his head while staring across the room at the red and white quilt before writing the name down in his notes. "So, Linette Wendell... Hartmann?"

"Yes," Liam affirms.

"Huh," the doc says again, this time while exhaling a deep breath it seems he's been holding onto. "Okay then, anything else I should know?"

"There is," Liam begins, looking at me to be sure it's okay to go on. Again, I shake my head to communicate my permission. Here comes the animal hospital story. It's truly embarrassing. The new anger switch inside of me somehow flipped and I flew into a blind rage. I don't know what came over me. It's almost like a Jekyll and Hyde type of thing when it happens. Well, it sounds like what I've heard people say about that story anyway. I don't think I've actually read it myself. Maybe I should add that to my to-do list.

"Go on," Dr. Epstein prompts.

"George and I went to pick his dog Lady up from the animal hospital this morning. She was shot during the break-in last weekend, but survived," Liam begins.

"You should know George and I haven't discussed the break-in yet other than what he told my voicemail system the day he called to make an appointment. I don't know the details," Dr. Epstein says, looking my way in case I want to add to the conversation. I don't. Not yet.

"Right," Liam replies. "I guess we'll get to all of those details soon enough. So, the folks at the animal hospital told George that Lady was good to go. When we arrived though, the guy at the desk mistakenly brought out a box of ashes instead of the live dog."

"Oh, that's unfortunate." Dr. Epstein says. "She's alright? You say she survived."

"She is and she did. But for a few minutes, we thought we were looking at her ashes and that she was gone," Liam explains. "George became very angry, to put it mildly."

"I see," the doctor says.

"He crossed the counter and grabbed the young guy working the desk, then held him up against a wall and yelled at him good," Liam says. "The guy's legs were dangling and everything. He was little."

All three of us in the room are tall. Dr. Epstein and I are both over six feet and Liam is just under that mark. I don't think any of us wants to intimidate little guys, exactly. But at the same time, I think there's a shared understanding that we can if we need to.

"I see," Dr. Epstein replies again.

"I had to work a bit to talk George down," Liam explains. "It was obvious he was seeing red. I got him to drop the guy at about the same time as one of the veterinarians pieced things together to understand the mix-up. She intervened with her staff and brought our Lady out to us. Then she let me know she would handle things there. I took my nephew to the car and we drove around awhile while he cooled off."

"I see."

"Apparently there were two dogs named Lady at the animal hospital at the same time," I add quietly.

"George was pretty shaken up. Had trouble breathing. I'm not sure if it was anxiety or what, but he seemed disoriented and had a sluggish response time," Liam continues. "After about an hour, he was back to his usual self."

"Has this happened before?" Dr. Epstein asks.

"The four-way stop," I manage to mutter.

"Sort of," Liam says. "George tells me he got into an altercation with another driver at a four-way stop earlier this week. It ended short of coming to blows."

"I see," Dr. E replies. "Any other incidents?"

"Not in my personal life," I say.

"Meaning you've had professional situations which have turned physical?" Dr. Epstein asks.

"All sanctioned," Liam responds for me.

"I see," Dr. Epstein replies with his familiar refrain. He takes off his glasses and leans forward in his chair to place his elbows on his knees, same as he did yesterday. He looks directly at me. "George, what are you feeling?" he asks.

"Tense," I offer.

Dr. Epstein continues to look hard at me without shifting his gaze.

"Okay," he says. "But tense isn't a feeling, really. What do you *feel?*" he asks emphatically, pointing towards my chest and my heart.

"Look, I'm going to get through this," I say. "Luckily, I have a healthy support system and healthy relationships in my life. My parents had their issues like everyone else, but they gave me enough good-- especially during my early formative years-- that I now have the self-esteem and ability to find the positive and the healthy. I just have some kinks to work out, that's all."

The doc slides his chair closer and leans in towards me.

"No one is judging you here," he says. "What do you feel?"

I shift my weight on the sofa cushion nervously. I try to sit still and focus, but it's difficult. I want to open up. I don't know how. I don't know the right thing to say.

"Since the break-in last weekend, I feel like I'm on a conveyor belt being moved along rather than moving forward with my own power," I say.

"Yes," Dr. Epstein says with a smile. "Now you're getting somewhere. How does being on a conveyor belt make you feel?"

"Like a failure," I say. "Like a bad husband. Like a bad father. Like I'm not a real man or a good man."

"George, you're a good man," Liam adds. He

looks like he's getting a little choked up himself. I guess it hurts him to see me in pain. I appreciate that. I truly do.

"I feel like I'm failing my boys," I say. "They depend on their parents totally during this time in their lives. They can't make decisions for themselves. They rely on me. There's a lot of pressure being the leader of the family."

"Your boys will learn to care for themselves and value themselves by the way they see you do it," Dr. Epstein says. "And you're here now, taking care of yourself."

"Also," Liam inserts, "Ali is no slouch when it comes to leading the family, George. You have a strong and capable partner."

"I know all of that. I believe it," I say. "But when I can't do what I want to do or what I need to do, or when I'm feeling stuck, I just want to lay down. Literally. On the floor almost. If I'm stuck, what can I do? Hell, my whole family is stuck right now. Part of me wants to give up and surrender to the struggle. At the same time though, giving up isn't an option. I'll always, always do anything and everything I can for Ali and our boys. Until my last breath. But then there's my anger."

"Sounds like a dilemma," the doc says.

"It is," I reply.

"Sounds like you're feeling helpless," Dr. Epstein offers.

"Yes," I say, surprised at the simplicity of the word. "Helpless about covers it."

We all sit in silence for a while as I always tend to do when things get heavy. It's as if I need time to absorb what was just said. Dr. Epstein feels it, too. He's following my lead. His elbows are still on his knees and he's still looking at me intently. He has abandoned his clipboard and notes in favor of a closer connection.

"The thing about suffering," I begin. "Is that you're waiting, but you don't know what you're waiting for. Waiting for someone to save you maybe. Or waiting for permission to save yourself."

"Are you waiting for someone to save you? Or for permission to save yourself?" Dr. Epstein asks, predictably.

"I don't know," I say. "Gosh. Interesting that I'd describe it that way, isn't it?"

The doctor leans back and shifts his weight. He maintains eye contact. But he's thinking. I wonder if I'm a hard case for him to crack or if my issues are obvious. I'm guessing they're obvious. Analyzing the minds of people like me is what Dr. Epstein has dedicated his life to. He's clearly good at it.

"George, do you have pictures of your dad hung up in your house?" he asks.

"What?" I ask in return. "What does that have to do with anything?"

"Humor me," he says.

"Well, I just moved into my new house a week ago today…"

"Have you ever had pictures of your dad hung up in your house since you've been an adult?" he clarifies.

"I don't know," I say. "I really don't understand what the significance of having photos of him hung up would be. But I guess not, now that I think about it. Why?"

"We're talking about unresolved grief here. I'm gathering information in order to best guide you. It may feel like we're jumping around, but please stay with me. Have you thought of hanging a few photos of your dad to help you remember and honor him?" Dr. E asks.

"Not really," I reply.

"So, let's shift gears," Dr. Epstein says, picking his clipboard up and scribbling something down. "I'd like to try hypnotherapy with you, George. We can begin right now. Or after a bathroom or coffee break if you need one. When you're ready, I'll ask your uncle to wait in the lobby and you to enter the hypnotherapy room down the hall. Is that alright?"

"Sure," I say. "I'm curious about being hypnotized. I'm ready when you are."

"Very well then," he responds. "Like I told you yesterday, it's all quite comfortable and safe. You'll still be aware of your surroundings and will be able to open your eyes any time you wish if you feel stressed or uncomfortable. The process bears very little resemblance to what you've probably seen on TV. I'll begin by suggesting you go to a childhood memory and remember all the details you can. I may ask you to tell me what you see. There's a microphone in the room which connects to a speaker right here at my desk, so I'll be able to hear what you say. Do you have any questions?"

"I don't think so," I answer. "I'm kind of excited to see what it's like. I'm feeling much better about the therapy process today than I was yesterday. Maybe I'm starting to get the hang of it."

"Excellent," Dr. Epstein says with a smile as he quickly stands straight up then leads us out of the office and down the hall. Every move he makes is powerful and deliberate. He could have been a highly effective leader in the military with his physical size and presence. I wonder if he's a veteran. That might make some sense now that I think about it. I don't know how many other veterans are in Ithaca, but surely there are some. Liam and I follow behind like good soldiers. We're in step. We can't help but fall in. It's been drilled into us.

When we reach the hypnotherapy room, Dr. Epstein pauses and waves me inside while pointing Liam towards the waiting area with his other arm. I chuckle because he looks a little like a school crossing guard with all of the arm motions.

"Remember what it's like so you can tell me all about it," Liam says as he heads towards the front door and sits in one of the cushy chairs. There's an older lady in the waiting area now. She isn't here for Dr. Epstein, so she must be seeing another therapist. Liam says hello to her cheerfully as he gets settled in his seat and pulls out his e-reader. She seems to be in good spirits. I guess you never know what kind of mood you're going to find people in around a place like this. I hear the two of them chatting about old-fashioned books going out of style as Dr. Epstein tells me to make myself at home and closes the door to the hypnotherapy room.

The only chair in the tiny room is a leather recliner. The space is small and cramped. I sit down and flip the footrest up, careful not to knock anything over as I do. The lights are dim and my eyes are still adjusting, so it's hard to see exactly what else is in the room. There's some sort of shelving to my left and a white noise machine is pumping a whooshing sound my way. I reach a hand over and locate it on the shelf just above my shoulder. The volume is okay, so I don't try to adjust it. There's a blanket folded neatly beside me in the chair. I figure I might as well loosen up and relax as much as possible, so I kick off my shoes and cover myself with the blanket. It smells like it's been freshly laundered. It reminds me of being at home with all the throw blankets Ali keeps around the house and of being a kid tucked securely under one of Mom's quilts. I close my eyes and breathe slowly and deeply. By the time I hear Dr. Epstein's voice, I'm so relaxed I could probably doze off and take a nap.

"George, can you hear me?" he says over the speaker system. It's odd hearing the doc's voice booming around me in this little cocoon-like room. Reminds me of the *Wizard of Oz* and the man behind the curtain. Or the voice of God depicted in movies. Or better yet, astronauts listening to commands from the control center while hurling through the heavens in tiny capsules. I've been to the U.S. Space and

Rocket Center in Huntsville, Alabama and have stepped inside replicas of the cramped capsules early astronauts traveled to space in. Talk about bravery.

"I do," I reply. "Loud and clear."

"Is the volume okay? Not too loud?" he says, clanking what sounds like a glass of water around on his desk and then taking a swallow.

"It's fine," I say.

"Did you find the blanket on the chair?" Dr. Epstein asks.

"I did," I reply. "I went ahead and took my shoes off and covered myself up. I could sleep in here. It's nice."

"Good," he returns. "Be sure to loosen anything that's too tight. Do whatever you need to in order to get really comfortable. The more relaxed you are, the more receptive you'll be to hypnosis."

A track of background music begins to play. I can't make out all the intricacies of the music because the whooshing is still louder, but it sounds like a low hum with some mid-range pulsing tones and higher, longer probing notes on top. It has a sci-fi vibe. It instantly makes me feel like I'm embarking on a journey. I like it. I notice myself relaxing even more. My thoughts again drift to my childhood and being covered up by one of Mom's quilts. I'm sure it's on my mind since we just talked about it and now here I am under a blanket with all of this soothing sound and darkness around me. It reminds me of the feeling of being a little kid and being completely safe and carefree. I could sleep deeply and peacefully then. My parents took care of everything and as long as I was with them, it was all I could ever need. I was loved completely. Through and through. I was cherished. All little kids should be so lucky.

"Please close your eyes if you haven't already, George. In a moment I'm going to count slowly backward from twenty to one in order to relax you more completely," Dr. Epstein says.

"Okay," I reply quietly. I wonder if he can hear me.

"Good, I heard you," he confirms, knowing what I was thinking. "When you hear me say the number twenty, allow your eyelids to remain closed. In your mind's eye, see yourself on the top floor of a tall building where you've just stepped into an elevator. Let any background distraction or thoughts fade away."

"Okay," I reply again.

"Good," he says. "You can just listen now as I give you instructions and help you deepen your level of relaxation. You don't have to respond verbally unless I ask you a question or you have something you want to tell me."

The whooshing and the pulsing and the long probing tones seem to be carrying me now. My limbs are beginning to feel heavy and if I don't consciously direct my attention towards them, it's like I don't feel them there at all. The sensation is odd, but soothing at the same time.

"The moment I say the number nineteen," Dr. Epstein continues. "And each number after that as we descend, you will simply move down in that elevator relaxing more completely. In your mind's eye, watch the numbers go lower one by one as the elevator sinks downward. At the base of the elevator is a large, soft bed, with a comfortable pillow. When I say the number one, you will sink into that bed, resting your head on that pillow. You will go so deep that your mind will no longer be limited by the usual barriers of time. So deep that you can remember everything you have ever experienced."

"Okay," I say, very quietly now, even though I know I don't have to answer out loud. My pulse has slowed. I think my heartbeat has synced up with the vibration of the low hum. I'm all in.

"Number twenty, eyes closed in that elevator, on the top floor of that building," he continues. "Twenty... Nineteen... You are safe. No harm can come to you here. Eighteen... Relaxing and letting go. Seventeen... Watching the numbers go lower as you descend. Sixteen... Lower. Fifteen... Sinking into a more comfortable, calm, peaceful position. Thirteen... Going down. Eleven... Moving down that elevator, relaxing more completely. Ten... Feeling good. Eight... Breathe in deeply. Six... Going way down. Five... Resting now. Four... Almost there, relaxing. Three... Deeper. A beautiful level of peace. Two... On the next number, number one, sink into that bed. And one... You're there. Sink into that soft bed. Let your muscles go limp and loose as you sink into a more calm, peaceful state of relaxation. You're very safe in this state of tranquility. This state of calm is healing and healthy for you."

I see the elevator in my mind's eye, just like Dr. Epstein tells me to. I watch as the numbers on the display near the roof tick lower and lower and lower. My limbs get even heavier, and the heavy feeling spreads around my whole body as the whoosh, pulse, and probe sounds carry me. I think I see what people mean about hypnosis. I'm present in my body and can wake up at any time if I choose to. But I'm not fully in my body either. I feel as if I've plugged my body in to charge or something. It's nice. I feel relaxed and completely at ease. I reach the bottom floor on the elevator and, as instructed, I sink down into the soft bed. As I do, I begin to feel like I'm outside of my body entirely. There's an overwhelming sense that my consciousness, what I consider to be me, can't be contained by my body. It's far too expansive. I feel like I can travel anywhere, unencumbered. Even in space, as nuts as that sounds. This must be what the meditation gurus talk about. I've never been a drug user either, but this might be similar to what people experience on drug trips. Native Americans and their peyote come to mind. I don't know, maybe I'm wrong about that. My brain is trying to pair what's happening now with something I have some frame of reference for. The closest I think I've come is a runner's high after endorphins kick in. Although, it reminds me of what I felt last weekend when I dreamed of Dad. And what Marjorie reported remembering of floating up and away from her body at the end of her Wild West life. You'd think all of this would freak me out at least a little, but it doesn't.

"We're going to do some exploring now, George, and I'm going to guide you through a series of memories from your childhood," Dr. Epstein explains. "If you feel uncomfortable with anything you experience, you can float above it like you're watching from a distance. Like you're watching a movie. Do you understand?"

"Yes," I say.

"Don't worry about analyzing what you see. There will be plenty of time for that later. Simply let yourself experience," he explains.

"Okay," I reply.

"When I count down from five to one, imagine that you're in a happy memory from your childhood. A time when you felt safe and loved. A place of perfect serenity and joy. You can remember everything. See this memory clearly as I reach the number one. Whatever comes into your mind is acceptable. Don't try to analyze. Five... Remembering a childhood memory. Four... Coming more and more into focus. You are perfectly safe and loved. Three... You can remember everything. Two... Breathing deeply and feeling good. One... a childhood memory. Be there with this memory. Where are you now? You may answer me out loud or simply answer in your mind and tell me about it later. It's up to you."

I feel myself sucked into a time and place. I let it happen. And suddenly, it's Brooklyn, early eighties. I'm very young. It's wintertime and it's snowing hard outside. I think we might even be snowed in. The snow is beautiful as it falls softly against the window panes. The entire borough is blanketed in white and is peaceful and still. No one is going anywhere this night. Animals are all huddled in their warm dens, tucked away from the weather. The air is warm inside our apartment. I'm in my parents' bed, snuggled tightly in between them. They're both sleeping. Dad is laying on his back and snoring lightly. I'm drowsy. I'm watching Dad's breath move a section of his jet-black hair around on his forehead every time he exhales. He looks strong and healthy and young. His skin is a vibrant pink. There's no sign of deterioration or disease in his body. His heartbeat is powerful. His steady pulse pounds reliably in his neck. I feel secure beside him.

Mom is rolled over away from me and towards the bedroom door. She is laying on her stomach with one of her blue and white patchwork quilts tucked carefully around her shoulders and under her chin. Her hair is a bright, vibrant red without any of the white strands I'm now used to seeing frame her face. Everything I see and feel and hear and smell is dynamic and present. It's entirely different than the shallow, highlights-only kind of memory most of us are accustomed to. I feel like I'm really there. Really in this memory. Not just referencing a snapshot.

"What are you becoming aware of?" Dr. Epstein prompts. "What do you look like?"

I follow his guidance and turn my attention towards my own appearance. I'm comfortable, dressed in pale yellow one-piece pajamas with snaps up and down the front and plastic soles built into the feet. A small, rudimentary outline of a teddy bear has been stitched onto the upper breast pocket area on one side of the front. I'm pretty sure Mom made this item of clothing for me. I can see a tag fixed onto the inside collar bearing her name. I'm wearing underpants instead of a diaper, so I must be old enough to be toilet trained. Ah, yes, I'm somewhere around three-years-old. When I need clarity on some part of the memory, I simply think of a question and focus my attention on it and the answer seems to come to me within a short time. My hair in this scene is lighter than I've ever remembered it before. It's almost dishwater blonde and it's cut into a bowl shape. Silky strands fall down across my forehead and land in a straight line just above my eyebrows. My hands are little and chubby. They're the hands of a toddler. My fingernails are clean. My little body, my clothing, and our home are all clean and well cared for. I can smell the lavender-scented lotion Mom slathered onto my back while getting me dressed for bed.

"What you become aware of may be more than just visual," Dr. Epstein says. "It may be hearing, or smelling, or tasting. Or even just a knowing. All of these senses are okay. The people you see may look younger to you. They were younger then."

"Yes," I say simply. Dr. Epstein must be curious about what I'm seeing, but I don't feel like articulating it all just yet. It's not that I want to withhold anything from him. I'm busy taking it in right now.

"If you have any discomfort, remember that you can detach and step back to watch from a distance," he reassures. "If you need more clarity or want to bring things into clearer focus, you can do that by taking a few slow breaths and going even deeper. You can go as deep as you like. You can remember everything."

I again follow his prompt and tell myself to go even deeper while taking a long, slow breath. When I do, more complex understandings wash over me. I feel Mom's frustration at Dad's long hours away from us while building his business, but I also feel her love for him and admiration for his work ethic. I feel Dad's pride at what he's building for his family. For Mom and me. I understand how meaningful what he's doing is. He has nothing but good intentions. His hopes and dreams are pure. He wants me to have every opportunity and to live comfortably and to pursue my every desire. He's literally building a world for me to thrive in, and Mom is supporting him in doing so. I've understood that intellectually, but I'm feeling and understanding it now in a different, more visceral way.

"The childhood memory you're experiencing may be connected to other memories," Dr. Epstein says. "It's okay to visit those as well. Let your subconscious mind take you where it wants you to go. Let it show you what it wants you to see and learn."

I float away from the winter bedroom scene and give myself permission to move on to other memories as the now familiar whoosh, pulse, and probing tones continue to lay the foundation for my journey and to push me onward. Floating in and out of memories is virtually effortless. I'm eager to find out what else my mind wants me to reconnect with. I rest peacefully in what looks like a dark hallway for a little while until a series of doors appear. I don't think Dr.Epstein mentioned doors, but for whatever reason, my mind has created them. Maybe it's continuing with the building theme due to my initial descent down the elevator. Each door is the hallway is closed tightly, but has brilliant, white light almost bursting out around the edges. I find myself curious about what's behind each door. I'm not frightened. Quite the opposite. I feel safe and good and deeply relaxed, so I decide to explore. As I move through the hallway, one particular door on the right pulls me towards it. I step close in front and place my hand on the knob, then open it wide and pass through the bright light as a new scene comes into view.

As I descend down towards a familiar land, I'm taken aback by the staggering beauty of steep, rugged cliffs and a surrounding blue-green sea. Something ancient within me is stirred and I feel the sides of my face getting wet with tears. This familiar yet foreign scene looks a lot like my hometown on Cayuga Lake, only the cliffs are more severe and the water is crystal clear with a million shades of blues and greens sparkling in the sunlight. Smooth, round pebbles frame the shoreline where swimmers frolic as they watch a boat coming into view on the horizon. This definitely isn't Cayuga Lake. It's an island. I attempt to orient myself as I near the ground within the scene my mind has presented. It feels very familiar, yet I don't remember having visited this place before. Maybe Mom and Dad brought me as a kid? Where in the world am I?

Before I can consider a childhood visit any further, I find myself standing on the stone floor of an outdoor arena amongst a group of soldiers clad in linen with metal armor plates and helmets topped with fiery red crests. In a flash, the recognition settles over me. I'm in Ancient Greece. And not just anywhere in Ancient Greece. I'm on the Island of Ithaca. What serendipity! There must be a bigger connection to my winding up in Ithaca, New York than I ever would have imagined. I don't care if anyone believes me when I tell them about this or whether or not there's scientific proof for what I'm experiencing. I know it in my bones as sure as I know I love my family: I'm in Ancient Greece. I lived in Ancient Greece! I remember.

I look down at my feet on the ground and am awestruck by the sensation that this is me. In Ancient Greece. It's exactly like Marjorie described when she told us about her past life memory from the Wild West. I'm the same. My consciousness is the same, only I'm here. I was here. I am here. My personality, my reactions to people and situations, and my thought processes are all the same. I'm certain of it. My mind whirls with a dizzying volume of questions and new understandings. And sweet little Ethan said it first. He must have remembered the same time and place. I didn't think he was wrong or making things up exactly, but I definitely don't doubt him now.

I examine my body more closely. I'm wearing shin guards and footwear that's sort of a mix between what I'd call boots and sandals. I'm tall. I'm about the same height as I am in this current life. I'm taller than many of the other soldiers. I'm strong, too, and muscular. A prime physical specimen, if I do say so myself. I can feel the latent energy in my muscles. They're agile, ready to move. My hands are rough and calloused from use. They have a strength the likes of which I've never known in my George Hartmann life. I feel like I could literally crush things with my bare hands. My hair is dark brownish-black, just like it is now and just like Ethan confirmed in his own memory. My skin has an olive tone. In a flash, I see my Greek face. It's very similar to my George Hartmann face. I have the same big, round eyes and long nose with a strong jawline and symmetrical features. I look different, for sure, but remarkably similar. I wonder if Marjorie looked similar to her present-day self in her Wild West life. Is that how this works? Or is it only a coincidence in my case?

The other soldiers and I are putting on an exhibition for the crowd. We're each holding a shield and a spear, and we have a short sword tucked into our belts. I assume it's for use in close combat. We're not a particularly aggressive army. We don't go out pillaging or trying to conquer other lands. Instead, we're proud protectors. Our focus is on keeping our city and our people safe.

I look to my right at the soldier standing beside me. His hair has been lightened from the sun and is a dusty brown. Same olive skin. He's younger. I'm in my mid-twenties and he's a teenager. About fourteen-years-old. I'm his mentor. I'm training him and teaching him the ropes. He's strong, too, but his body isn't as developed as mine. I still have to look out for him. He turns to face me and our eyes meet. When they do, I'm struck by the sudden recognition that he is Leo! It's my little Leo, here with me in Greece. He's the same in the eyes, just like Ethan described when talking to Marjorie about his own memories. This young soldier isn't my son here in Greece, but we're close. We spend a lot of time together and in many ways, we do have a relationship similar to a father and son. How amazing that he's now my actual son in New York. Apparently, relationships can switch around from one lifetime to another. It's all riveting. I'm enjoying this immensely. Still no fear or discomfort.

"George?" Dr. Epstein says over the speaker system. "Are you still exploring a memory? Do you feel comfortable?"

"Yes," I reply. "I'm happy."

I've been completely immersed. I wonder if Dr. E said something else when I wasn't paying attention. Hopefully, he'll stay quiet and give me more time. I don't want to leave this memory yet.

I look up at the crowd gathered to watch our exhibition. They're sitting on curved stone stadium-style seating in the arena. There must, of course, be Greek names for all of these things, but for whatever reason, they aren't coming to mind. I'll be sure to do some internet research soon in order to pair official names with what I'm observing. The architecture of the structure we're gathering in is beautiful. Even though it's made out of stone, it doesn't feel primitive at all. It feels refined and polished and very civilized. More information about our city and my life here washes over me. We're an educated and highly evolved people. We have delicious food and wine, fine items of clothing, and intellectual pastimes like theater and philosophical debates. We're governed by a body of wise individuals. For the most part, our laws are fair and just. Our land and surrounding waters are incredibly beautiful. Natural resources are plentiful. Life in the city is very good. Our powerful army provides protection. No harm comes to those of us living within the bounds of our city.

As I scan the group of people looking down on our exhibition, my eyes land on a stunning young woman seated in a special section of the arena. An older couple is seated nearby her and I get the idea they are King and Queen. Or members of our Senate. Those details are a little fuzzy. My focus is on the beautiful young woman. I know her. Her hair is long, reaching down to the middle of her back. It's dark like mine. And curly. She's dressed in the finest garments and jewels. It's obvious that great care has gone into her physical care and presentation. She's a little younger than me, in her early twenties. I don't know if she's a princess exactly, but she's someone important. She has special standing. She's in a designated separate section of the arena and is not mixed in with commoners. It's hard to tell from so far away, but I think she's looking at me. In a flash, I see myself with her. We're lovers. I care about this young woman deeply. We want nothing more than to be together and spend our lives together, but we have to sneak around because she's not supposed to be with me. As a soldier, I'm not of a high enough class to be with a princess. It would never be allowed. She kisses me passionately and while she does, she opens her eyes and I can see into her soul. Oh, my God. Is it? It's Alessandra! It's her. It's my Ali! We love each other just as completely as we do in this lifetime.

This realization is everything to me. No wonder Ali knew almost instantly that day in Patriot Park mall I was the Big George Hartmann Liam had been telling her about. No wonder he and Estella knew Ali and I belonged together. Thank God he was determined enough to keep mentioning me to her for more than two years. And no wonder Ali and I were engaged and married so quickly after we met. We had waited thousands of years across time and space to be together again. It was our destiny. I see that now. Our love is every bit as deep and true and everlasting as I always thought it was. She's mine and I'm hers. Fate brought us back together in this lifetime. Nothing can keep us apart.

My mind moves through a series of memories of Ali and me together in Ancient Greece. I see the two of us bathing together in the sea at night under twinkling stars. I feel her body pressed against mine as waves dance around us and blood rushes hot as lava to meet every sensual touch. I stroke her curly hair and tuck it gently behind her ear with my strong, calloused hands. She doesn't seem to mind their roughness. Next, the scene shifts and I see Ali and I laughing and making love on a hay-covered floor in a barn near an old farmer's animals. Then I see us running through a meadow full of the most beautiful flowers together, holding hands and smiling so much our cheeks feel like they might burst.

"George," Dr. Epstein interrupts. "I'm going to begin to bring you back now."

"Not yet," I mouth silently. I'm too immersed to say anything audible.

"I want you to begin to come back to this present moment, completely grounded in your body," Dr. Epstein continues. "I will bring you back to full waking consciousness by counting up from one to ten."

When I hear my time is running out, I set the intention to fast forward this memory and see some more of what happens. In response, I'm flooded with a rapid succession of scenes which show me highlights of major events as they unfold. I see Ali's belly distended and realize she's pregnant. I'm overjoyed! She's going to have my baby. My joy quickly turns to despair as I realize our secret is out and the powers that be are angry. They won't allow us to be together. Not only that, but a group of elders convenes and decides Ali must give up her status as a princess and be banished from the city. My heart breaks during this period of time and I can feel the pain in my chest now as I remember it. There's nothing either of us can do.

The rules about classes in our society are rigid and immutable. Ali is sent out of the city and finds refuge with an old medicine man who lives in a small village on the far side of the island. He doesn't have a wife or children of his own, so he takes Ali in and treats her like a daughter. I see the old man's face and look into his eyes to determine whether or not I recognize him from the here and now. As a matter of fact, I do. It's Roddy! Roderick Davies is the medicine man who took Ali in. Just as Ethan said. I don't think these soul recognition discoveries will ever get old. They are so powerful. So certain. I'm eager to piece together as many connections as I can. It's wonderful to know that Ali and Roddy had a father-daughter relationship in Greece even though they weren't father and daughter by blood. Like John Wendell told Sara last weekend at Yellow Cob, family is about much more than blood. Family finds each other all kinds of different ways and it always, always, always finds each other.

"With each number up, you'll be more and more awake and alert," Dr. Epstein says.

I tell myself to hurry. I want to know what else there is. What about our child? I see our infant being born in the little cottage Ali shares with Roddy the medicine man. My Greek self isn't there in person to welcome my child into the world. It's a boy. I have a son. He has dark hair like mine. He's beautiful. Sweet and innocent. I look into his eyes, and sure enough, it's our Ethan! Our Ethan is our baby boy in Greece. I'm so happy that it's him.

"One..." Dr. Epstein begins.

I'm filled with a mixture of love for my family and dread as I continue to remember. Ali and Ethan aren't safe in this little house outside of the city.

"Two…"

They don't have the protection of our army here. I stop in to see them as often as I can when my group travels this way, but it's usually months in between visits. I don't take another lover. I don't marry. Ali is my one true love. She and Ethan are my family. But I can't be with them.

"Three…"

A sinking feeling takes over as I recall what Ethan told Marjorie as we sat together the other day. It seemed so far-fetched then, but now I wish I didn't have to know it. Yet I already know it. I've always known it. Oh, how I wish it wasn't so.

"Four…" Dr. Epstein continues. "Becoming more and more awake and alert."

Ethan knew. He said the man who tried to take him from our house last weekend took him from his little house in Greece. And that we couldn't stop him then. He said he was scared and that he had to die.

"Five…"

Reluctantly, I set the intention to see exactly what happened. I see my son. He's somewhere around the age he is now at four or five-years-old. He's a handsome little guy, growing up strong. He and Ali and Roddy are as happy as they can be together. Ali misses the city terribly and longs to be with me. She feels cheated. Forgotten. Unfairly disgraced. She wishes our son could know and experience all that the city has to offer. She wishes she could be more carefree and rest easier within the safety of our walls. She makes the best of it though. She's raising Ethan to be a good boy.

"Six…" Dr. E says. "As you become fully alert, ask yourself if this memory is trying to tell you something. What is this memory's importance to you now?"

My heart aches as I watch the scene. I distance myself like Dr. Epstein said I could, partially because his counting is pulling me away from Greece and partially because it's too painful to watch up close. A group of men has come onto the shores of our island. I think they're pirates. Those details are fuzzy, too, so I don't know for sure why they're here. There are eight or ten of them. They're moving through the tiny villages on the part of the island where Ali, Ethan, and Roddy live and ransacking then burning down the houses. Screaming villagers are running around terrified.

"Seven…" the doc continues. "Is there any knowledge, wisdom or understanding that will help you in your current circumstances? What do you need to know?" He has no idea.

Two of the men approach my family's cottage carrying torches. They kick the door down and force their way inside. Roddy steps forward and tries to be a barrier for my wife and child. He's old and feeble and easily knocked to the side. The intruders make a beeline for Ethan, pushing Ali out of the way as she tries to protect him. They set fire to the little house, carelessly.

"Eight…"

One of the intruders takes the lead, grabbing Ethan and carrying him away while Ali and Roddy watch helplessly from their burning home.

"Nine… More and more awake and alert."

The fast forwarding accelerates further and I see Ethan's lifeless body, left in the woods alone for wild animals to consume. My God, he's dead. My son has been killed. I see Ali utterly devastated and inconsolable and without a proper shelter to live in. I see myself a few weeks later on the day I arrive for a visit when I instead find my family's house burned down and my son missing.

I didn't protect them. It's all my fault. This wouldn't have happened if they had been in the city. They were out here in the country because of me. I shouldn't have fallen in love with Ali and gotten her pregnant. She'd still be a princess right now. Ethan might have another father, but he'd be safe and alive. I'm a lowly soldier. I never deserved to be with a princess. What was I thinking? I've failed my family in the worst possible way. And I'm completely and totally helpless to do anything about it. My pain and my shame are overwhelming.

"Ten…" Dr. Epstein says. "Let your eyes open. Come all the way back to full waking consciousness."

I follow his instructions and open my eyes. When I do, I notice that the sides of my face and the back of my head and neck are saturated with tears. The recliner cushion below is so wet it looks like someone poured a bucket of water on it. I wasn't actively crying, but tears were flowing. It feels like the immense sadness of what happened has always been inside me. Today it was tapped, allowing the tears to flow freely.

"I'm coming to the hypnotherapy room to get you, George," Dr. Epstein says.

I hear what I assume is the water glass clinking again and then him taking a swallow. It strikes me as fundamentally wrong that life here and now goes on as if nothing happened when such an unspeakable tragedy occurred before. I feel terrible about my failures. Mostly though, I think about what Ethan said. The man who tried to take him from our house last weekend was the same one who took him and then killed him in Greece. I didn't have a chance to look into the eyes of that man in my memory to see if there was any soul recognition. I didn't have time to ask for more information. He was part of a pair. Was the other guy our getaway driver? Why in all of the heavens would they be after Ethan again? Why were they after him in the first place? They didn't rape or otherwise harm Ali, thank God. But why did they go right for Ethan like that? There must be more I don't know. I have to find out.

I'm deep in thought when I hear Dr. Epstein turn the door handle and enter the hypnotherapy room. He slowly raises the level of light with a dimmer switch and then audibly gasps when he sees the wetness from my tears and the puffiness of my eyes.

"My word, George," he says quietly, in the most serious tone I've heard from him yet. And that's saying a lot. "What happened? Did you remember something upsetting from your childhood?"

I don't know if I have the composure to converse like a reasonable person right now. I feel like a humongous scab has been ripped off of my very being. I believe what I just experienced was real, but I can't make sense of it all yet. I'm scared. Horrified. Ashamed. I want to run out of this building right now and find the getaway driver. I want to shake him until he gives me answers, then pummel him until he takes his last breath. I'll spend this life in prison. I don't care. If these creeps are chasing my son to do him harm across thousands of years, what's a prison sentence in order to protect Ethan for the rest of this lifetime? I'll gladly sign myself up. But I can't. I don't know where to find the guy. It's not like he's likely to remember Greece anyway, even if he is the second pillager. So many questions swirl through my mind. This is going to take a while to understand and unravel. To get justice and protect my family, I'm going to need to dedicate my energy to the endeavor. I'm overwhelmed by the task at hand. How am I ever going to accomplish this? And if I do, what's to stop the guys from coming back for Ethan in another lifetime? How does that even work? I take a long, deep breath and stand up from the recliner to face Dr. Epstein.

"I remembered a happy memory from my childhood," I say. "I was a toddler in bed with my parents in Brooklyn. They were sleeping and snow was falling outside. It was all good."

"I'm glad to hear that," Dr. Epstein says. "But there's clearly something else that's upsetting you. What else?"

I know I should think twice before telling Dr. Epstein I remembered a past life. I mean, most people would probably think that's bat-shit crazy. And Dr. Epstein doesn't strike me as the past life memory type. I need to get to Marjorie. And to the psychiatrists she mentioned who study this stuff.

"I remembered living in Ancient Greece with my family," I say, against my better judgment.

"What?" Dr. Epstein says, his face contorting into a look of disbelief.

"Yeah," I reply. "You said I could remember everything. I guess I took that to heart. I was very relaxed."

He crosses his arms against his chest again, then slowly raises one hand to cover his mouth. He begins to speak, not once, but twice, each time shifting his weight and adjusting his footing. He doesn't vocalize anything more than a mutter. He has no idea what to say right now. He's assessing me. He's probably combing through a list of mental disorders in his mind to try and figure out what's wrong with me. My concern for social niceties is gone and I don't give a damn what he thinks. I remain standing and we look at each other in silence for what feels like a long while. Finally, he finds words.

"George," he begins. "Have you ever had difficulty concentrating? Or a hard time remembering things?"

"What?" I ask. "No."

"Have you ever heard voices in your head?" he asks.

"I have not," I answer, although I must admit my dream about Dad and the scream no one else heard comes to mind.

"Do you sometimes have trouble figuring out what's real and what isn't?"

Now I'm becoming angry. "What are you getting at?" I ask. I'm not crazy. At least I don't think I am.

"I want to understand, George," Dr. Epstein says. "Whatever is going on, I'll help you work through it. I'll be sure you receive the appropriate treatment and medication if necessary. Let's go back to my office. I'd like to ask you a few more questions and add to my notes."

Before I have time to respond to that thinly veiled threat of being labeled certifiably insane, Liam appears and sticks his head into the hypnotherapy room.

"I'm sorry to interrupt," my uncle says. "George, your mom needs you right away."

I shake my head in an attempt to brace myself and absorb what he's saying. We were planning to head to her house when we left here anyway. Maybe she wants us to pick something up on the way. I take my mobile phone out of my pocket and see that I've missed eight calls from her. It's not like Mom to keep calling if she doesn't reach me on the first attempt.

"Linette says she tried your mobile phone. She called me when she couldn't get ahold of you," Liam continues.

"What's going on?" I ask. "Does she need us to swing by the store on our way to her house?" I know the answer to that question before I ask it, but I'm grasping for the possibility that nothing serious is going on.

"It's your grandpa, George. He fell trying to get out of bed and they think his hip is broken. You need to get to the hospital."

## 11

## GEORGE: RECOGNITION

The sky looks heavy and gray as we pull into the parking lot of the hospital emergency room. Snow clouds. Ithaca is due for more of the white stuff. I have a feeling it's going to come down hard and heavy once it begins. Liam's driving again. He offers to drop me off at the curb, but I'd rather wait on him so we can walk in together. He parks the Tesla and comes around to open my door when I don't get out right away.

I wonder if John Wendell arrived by ambulance. And I wonder if it will have been his last ride. Or his last time feeling the crisp, New York winter air on his face. He always loved the winter. I remember the January during my senior year in high school when it snowed so much the city came to a standstill. John Wendell didn't mind. He and Grandma still lived out on Ellis Hollow Road then, but when the snow started coming down they drove to our house to spend the night so John Wendell could get out on the sidewalks and walk around downtown the next morning. He was in his seventies at the time, but fit as a fiddle. He went up and down the block shoveling walkways and digging out vehicles alongside people half his age.

"Looks like your mom's car is parked right over there," Liam says, pointing to a nearby corner of the parking lot. "John Wendell rode in an ambulance and she drove herself over. I wish she would have called me before she got in the car. I would have driven her. I intend to be here for her as she moves through this. Alec would have wanted it that way."

"It's not your responsibility though," I mumble.

"Yeah, well, what kind of man would I be if I didn't take care of my brother's wife in her time of need?" Liam replies. "He'd be here to do it himself if he could. It's only right that I fill in. I know he'd do the same for me if the roles were reversed."

"You're a good brother," I say. "I hope my boys grow up to be half as good to each other as you and Dad were."

"They'll be better, George. They're growing up with the best family any kids could ask for. Those boys are going to make you prouder than you ever dreamed possible. Just wait and see," Liam says.

"That's what I'm hoping for," I say. "I wish John Wendell…" My voice trails off and I can't finish my sentence.

"I know, George," my uncle says, reaching over and wrapping an arm tightly around my shoulders as we walk towards the entrance.

No one likes hospitals. They're filled with scared people who are having some of the worst days of their lives. Not to mention that the buildings always smell funny. Disinfectant, disease, burning flesh, and God knows what else make for an assault on the olfactory organs. The scent of the hand soap alone has been seared into my memory and won't let go.

"Did anyone call Ali?" I ask.

"I don't think so, unless your Mom called her after she talked to me."

"Okay," I reply. "She won't be expecting us home for a while anyway, but I want to call her as soon as we see John Wendell and get a report from the doctor who is treating him. I hope Dr. Madera can be here since she knows his medical history and he's comfortable with her."

"Does Dr. Madera have hospital privileges?" Liam asks.

"I'm sure she does. She makes house calls from time to time, so I imagine she sees her patients all the way through."

"These days, a lot of hospitals utilize staff physicians to treat a patient while they're in the hospital so the primary care doctor doesn't have to," Liam explains.

"Yeah, well, call me old-fashioned, but I want him to have Dr. Madera. I guess we'll find out soon enough," I reply.

The emergency room is bustling with activity when we arrive. Liam leans down to ask a man at the reception desk where we should begin as I spot Mom sitting alone in a row of chairs towards the back of the waiting area. She looks so lonesome back there by herself. So vulnerable. She's been on her own for decades since Dad died, but until now, I think I've taken for granted what a support John Wendell has been for her. I won't soon forget what he said at Yellow Cob about me being in town and able to take care of her now.

"Breathe, George," Liam says, placing one hand on my back. I inhale deeply. I didn't realize I was holding my breath. "Let's go to her. I'm right behind you."

We weave our way around the rows of chairs and the sad visitors sitting in them, excusing ourselves as we go, until we get to the back section where Mom is waiting. She's fumbling with her phone. It looks like she's trying to compose a text message, but her hands are shaking too much. When she sees us, a look of relief washes over her face. She stands and hugs me tight. Mom has always been good in emergency situations with her patients, but she seems different now. Come to think of it, maybe she had already collected herself before I saw her after Dad died. She looks pretty shaken up right now.

"I just got word that he's in a room," she reports. "They went ahead and moved him up to the third floor where it's quieter. All the sounds from the E.R. were agitating him. He's in a lot of pain."

"Okay," I say. "Can we go up and be with him?"

"Yes, we can," she replies. "I was waiting on your guys to get here first, but let's go right away."

The three of us walk briskly past the nurse's desk, down the hall, and to the elevators in the center of the building. Mom, of course, knows her way around since she works here. Two separate staffers whizzing by in navy blue scrubs recognize her, but they must be able to tell from her demeanor she isn't up for chatting because neither one says anything. They sort of nod gently as she passes. She's too focused on getting upstairs to notice. When we reach John Wendell's room, the door is closed. I feel my knees weaken as I place my hand on the lever to open it and step inside. I take a few seconds to anchor myself. Liam is here. I know he'll support me. And Mom is here. She will take the lead with John Wendell. Together, we can do this.

"George, son, you're here just in time!" John Wendell exclaims. I'm surprised to see him awake and alert.

"In time for what, John Wendell?" I ask as I pull a chair close beside his bed and take his hand in mine. I give my grandfather the best smile I can muster. Liam positions himself out of the way near the heating unit while Mom looks over the medical equipment in the room to find out exactly how her dad is being treated.

"Your grandma was here. My Eleanor. She's taking me on a trip," he explains. I look at Mom and Liam and sigh heavily. We all know what kind of trip he's referring to.

"Oh?" I inquire. I figure I won't say much and will let him talk as long as he wants to. He's moving his hands around the bed a lot and fiddling with the covers. It seems like he's looking for something he thinks is on his lap.

"Do we have our tickets, son? I'll be leaving soon."

"Tickets?" I ask, tears forming in my already puffy eyes. "Where are you going, John Wendell?"

"Eleanor and I are going dancing. We're taking the train. I'll need those tickets. And my coat. Is my coat here? Snow is on the way."

"Your coat is here," I say even though I'm not sure if it actually is or not. We can always go and get one of his coats from Mom's house if necessary. It's more important to play along right now so John Wendell knows we're okay with what he's telling us.

"Good. Okay," he says. "Oh, and I need to check the train schedule. Where can I find the schedule?"

"I'll ask around and find out," I reply. "Don't worry, John Wendell. Everything will be ready when it's time to go."

I've never been present for the dying process before, but I've heard Mom discuss it enough to understand what's happening here. Many people talk in terms of traveling when they're preparing to leave this world. It's sad for those of us saying goodbye, but the dying are wrapped up in the busy preoccupation of preparing to embark on their next journey. In many cases, they're feeling hopeful. Making plans.

My grandfather sits up as much as he can in his hospital bed and leans in close to my face, wrapping one hand around the back of my head and leaning his forehead against mine. He's weak and frail. The bedding he's under now is much thinner than the quilt at Mom's was yesterday and I can tell he's lost weight. He hasn't been eating. "George, I'm ready," he says. "Are you, son?"

"Yes," I reply. "I'm ready. You go ahead on your trip. I'll look out for Linette while you're gone." I would normally refer to her as Mom in conversation with John Wendell, but I want to be absolutely sure he gets the message.

"Good," he says in return, sounding reassured and settling back down under the covers. "I think I'll take a little rest now until it's time to leave."

He smiles at me, then falls into a deep sleep. I hope Mom doesn't feel bad that John Wendell's lucid conversation was focused on me instead of her. He's her father and they're very close. I don't want to steal her thunder. She apparently sees the concern on my face, because she addresses what I'm thinking.

"I'm glad he was alert enough to talk to you like this, George," Mom says. "He and I had a similar conversation earlier today."

"Oh, good," I reply. "I was feeling a little bad about him talking to me without a word to you."

"No need to feel bad about that at all, dear," she reassures. "I think he's saying his goodbyes."

"Yeah, I got that," I reply, sadly.

Before we can go any further with our conversation, Dr. Madera walks in the door. Boy, am I glad to see her. Isabel Madera is originally from Puerto Rico. She came to the mainland U.S. for medical school and landed in Ithaca to do her residency. While here, she met and married a man who is a geneticist at Cornell. That marriage ended in divorce, but she liked the area and so decided to stay on. She's been taking care of both Mom and John Wendell in her family practice for years now. I'm really glad she's here because I want my grandfather to be around people who know and love him right now.

Ali and I met Isabel not long before Ethan was born during a visit home. It just so happened that John Wendell developed an ear infection after swimming in the lake and we took him to see Dr. Madera one day while Mom was at work. Ali and I stayed in the waiting room and didn't expect to actually be introduced to the doctor, but we were pleasantly surprised when she came bouncing out behind John Wendell, eager to meet more members of his family. Isabel is a stunning woman. Of course, no one can compare to my wife, but even Ali says she gorgeous. Her long, dark, wavy hair and her smooth, buttery skin set the stage for big, brown eyes, round cheeks, and full lips. Her body is near perfection with ample breasts and buttocks separated by a long, trim waist. Look, I wouldn't have noticed that level of detail about the woman if Ali hadn't pointed it out. I tend to be surrounded by beautiful women, but I don't think about them in a sexual way because Ali fulfills my sexual needs. Take Jen, for instance. I know she's beautiful, but she's like a sister to me. I only see her in the sister category. But something about Isabel Madera piqued Ali's interest and thus mine by extension. I feel like I've known Isabel a lot longer than I actually have for some reason. And I feel like Ali has known her longer, too. Ali talked about Isabel for weeks after meeting her for the first time. She still mentions her every once in a while, always with a comment about how beautiful and alluring Isabel is.

In fact, I think Isabel Madera might make my wife a little hot and bothered, if I'm being honest. I'm not sure how I feel about that, but the rush of warmth in my pants upon seeing Isabel again makes me think I might just be okay with it. I mean, Isabel wears curve-hugging clothes and bites her lip in a way that makes her hard to ignore. She's a couple of years younger than Ali, single, intelligent, and her strong-willed personality is definitely a turn on. Ali especially loved it when Isabel started speaking Spanish to another patient in the waiting room the day we met. Ali speaks Spanish, too. She learned it in order to converse with the Hispanic immigrants she works with. The thought of my hot wife and Isabel Madera speaking passionate Spanish to each other and then doing, well, let's just say other things is too much. My manhood is as hard as a rock now. I had better stay seated until it goes down. I tell myself to focus. We're here for John Wendell, after all.

"Linette, George, how are you, folks?" Isabel says warmly while getting a pump of sanitizer from the dispenser by the door and rubbing it onto her hands. She looks over at John Wendell and smiles a sad smile when she lays eyes on him. Her concern for him is evident. She's sincere. We can tell she hates to see him like this.

"We're doing as well as can be expected, Dr. Madera," Mom answers. "We're glad you're here."

I simply nod and smile.

"George, I hear you and Ali have another baby on the way," Isabel says as she looks in my direction. "I spoke with John Wendell briefly in the E.R. a little while ago and he told me the baby's coming."

"Well, yes, but he isn't due until next month," I reply. "I guess John Wendell is excited."

"Let me introduce you to my brother-in-law," Mom says, walking over towards where Liam is standing. "This is Alec's younger brother. He's in from D.C."

"Liam Hartmann," Uncle Liam says, reaching out to shake her hand then pulling it back when he remembers the wet sanitizer.

Isabel chuckles. "Wonderful to meet you, Liam," she replies. "I'm sure everyone here is glad you're in town right now. Good timing."

Liam agrees and doesn't offer any more information. I'm not sure if Isabel knows about the break-in at my house. She probably saw it in the news, but maybe not. I don't feel like explaining, so I'm relieved when she doesn't mention it.

"Will you be able to continue caring for my father while he's hospitalized?" Mom asks. John Wendell signed over power of attorney to Mom awhile back, so the medical providers already know she has permission to make decisions on his behalf.

"I do have hospital privileges, so yes," Isabel confirms. "There are a number of other doctors who will probably be involved though. Specialists, mainly. We're waiting on the x-rays they took downstairs to come back from radiology and then we'll need to consult with an orthopedic surgeon about repairing what we're assuming is a fracture of his right hip."

Isabel sits down in a chair next to Mom and rests quietly for a minute before saying anything else.

"Linette, is it okay to speak freely with George and Liam in the room?"

"Of course," Mom affirms.

"We have your dad's Do Not Resuscitate order on file," Isabel says. "He and I have talked about it on multiple occasions. Each time, he was clear that he wants to be allowed a natural death when the time comes."

"I understand," Mom replies quietly. She knows these ropes. She's seen this scene play out countless times as a nurse.

"We're faced with a pivotal decision here," Isabel continues. "Surgery is risky. Especially for a man John Wendell's age. Even under the best circumstances, electing to proceed with surgery on a ninety-five-year-old should not be taken lightly."

"I understand," Mom says again.

"In John Wendell's specific case, the fact that he hasn't been eating certainly gives me pause," she continues. "And you say he's been largely unresponsive for several days now, correct?"

"That's right," Mom confirms. "Ever since Sunday morning, he's spent most of his time asleep and he doesn't usually respond when I try to wake him."

"Did anything precipitate this sudden decline?" Isabel asks.

"We had a big night at Yellow Cob the evening before," Mom explains. "But otherwise, no. It came out of nowhere."

"How about his fluid intake?" Isabel asks.

"I've been able to get a little in him using a foam applicator on a stick. I wet it and then dab it onto his lips. That's all," Mom replies reluctantly.

"And urine output?"

"Not much," Mom answers.

Isabel reaches into the pocket of her lab coat and pulls out a little blue booklet. Mom must know exactly what it is because she begins to sob when she sees it. Isabel places her free hand on top on Mom's and pats it gently.

"I know, Linette," Isabel says. "I'm so sorry. This is not easy."

Mom nods as she tries to hold back tears.

"What is that?" I ask.

"It's the damn guide to understanding end-of-life signs and symptoms," Mom says angrily. I don't remember the last time I heard her curse. Or raise her voice, for that matter.

"Oh," I say solemnly. "So, Dr. Madera, you don't think we should bother with surgery?"

Isabel pauses before answering. She's choosing her words carefully.

"That's ultimately up to you folks to decide, based on what you think is best. However, we'd need an orthopedic surgeon to agree to perform the surgery, and that might be a challenge given John Wendell's general health right now. A palliative care doctor will have to be consulted."

Mom's face repeatedly balls up as she listens. Each time, she shakes it off and collects herself for a brief moment, only to be gripped by emotion again.

"No need," Mom finds the strength to say between waves. "No surgery."

It's one thing to know someone you love is nearing the end of the human lifespan. It's another to know they're declining steeply and seem to be ready to move on. And it's another yet to be the one making decisions which cement the end of this life as an immutable reality. To take the booklet. To say the words. I don't envy Mom right now.

"We can make him comfortable," Isabel says, continuing to pat Mom's hand gently as she speaks.

Mom nods her head in agreement.

"I'll order hospice care," Isabel confirms.

Again, Mom nods silently in agreement.

"There's a small residential facility on the outskirts of town which is outstanding," Isabel says, speaking slowly and softly and pausing before each new sentence. "It's located on a hill overlooking the countryside and each room has floor to ceiling windows on one exterior wall for enjoying the view. I've always thought it's prettiest in the winter. Their nursing staff is top notch. I took the liberty of inquiring before I came to speak with you and they do have a room available."

"Let's do it," Mom says without hesitation.

"Okay," Isabel affirms. "We'll have John Wendell transported there by ambulance, but once he arrives he won't have to deal with any medical procedures, or equipment, or hospital sounds. We'll turn on his favorite music and cover him with familiar bedding from home. He can wear his own pajamas or lounging-around clothes. You can bring in framed photos for the nightstand. Whatever he wants. It's warm and comfortable. There's a kitchen where volunteers usually cook for residents during mealtimes. He can eat a little if he feels like it, but no one will force anything on him."

"That sounds nice," I offer, looking at my grandfather as he snores lightly. "I want him to be comfortable and to feel loved and supported as he makes his transition out of this world."

"Then it's decided," Isabella says. "I'll coordinate with hospital staff, but I expect they'll be able to discharge John Wendell so he can be transported to the hospice residence this evening. The weather forecast is calling for a significant amount of snow. I want to get you folks settled in as quickly as possible so you're situated before the storm hits. I'll have the paperwork drawn up right away."

Isabel stands and pats John Wendell gently on the knee, then excuses herself and leaves the room to put the arrangements in motion. Liam moves from the corner he's standing in and walks around the end of the bed so he can put a hand on my shoulder. What would I do without him?

I'm still reeling from my experience at Dr.

Epstein's, not to mention this morning at the animal hospital and this entire screwball week. All I can do right now is try to compartmentalize. I lean my head back and close my eyes for a moment while I attempt to sort the multitude of things going through my brain into manageable bits. Mom is crying softly on the other side of the room as she strokes John Wendell's hair. It's hard to focus inward when I'm worried about what's happening with them. Turns out it doesn't matter anyway because my focus is interrupted when we hear a knock on the door.

"Come in," Liam says. He has more strength for pleasantries right now than the rest of us.

The door opens slowly, and to my surprise, it's Ali and Roddy. They're holding their coats under their arms as if they've been inside for at least a little while. Their cheeks aren't flush from the cold like they would be if they had just walked in.

"Ali, babe, what are you doing here?" I ask, standing to greet her with a hug and a kiss. Her lips are certainly warm. "I was going to call you, but I wanted to wait until I knew what was happening. Dr. Madera just left."

"We saw the Tesla in the parking lot, Georgie," my wife replies. "I tried to call your mobile, but didn't get an answer." I pull my phone out of my pocket and see the missed calls for the first time.

"Oh, babe, I'm sorry," I say. "I had the ringer off and I didn't feel it vibrate. I've been preoccupied."

"It's okay," she says. "Daddy has been taking care of me."

"Taking care of you?" I inquire. "What's going on? Wait. How did you know we were here at the hospital?"

"I didn't until we saw the Tesla. Tell me about John Wendell."

I briefly explain the situation with my grandfather, but at the moment, I'm more interested in what my wife is doing here.

"Come on, Ali," I plead. "What is it?"

"Probably just Braxton Hicks," she begins. "But I've been having some strong contractions and Mom and Dad thought I should get checked out. You know, just to be safe."

"Wow," I say. "Little Will isn't supposed to arrive until next month." I can't help but wonder how much the Universe can possibly pile on at once. Shouldn't there be some kind of quota? Like a point where you get a break and time to absorb what's happened?

"No big deal," Ali says. "We're old pros, remember?"

"You're right, babe," I reply. I raise my eyebrows and keep them raised as I look around the room at Roddy, Liam, and Mom to indicate my distress. Liam is still standing near me. He reaches a hand up and rests it on my shoulder again. He's here.

"Dad and I were talking about how to avoid the E.R. and I had the idea that maybe Dr. Madera could examine me," Ali explains. "Since I'm not officially established with the midwives yet, I'm sort of floating without anyone to turn without an appointment during business hours. I thought maybe Dr. Madera would help out since she knows us and already takes care of Linette and John Wendell. I called her office and they said she was here, so Dad drove me over on the chance I might be able to track her down and get checked out. I asked around a little, and we eventually found our way to you."

"Where are the boys?" I ask.

"They're home with Mom," Ali replies.

"Is Marjorie okay with having both boys and Lady there to manage by herself? Did Taye leave?"

"Taye left a couple of hours ago in order to be sure and make it to Massachusetts to pick Malcolm up before bedtime," Ali says. "He promises the security measures we have in place will actually keep us safe, so yes, Mom feels fine being there by herself with the boys and Lady. I also got in touch with Jen, so she and Duke are on standby to stop over if needed."

"Okay, that's good," I say. "Was the table delivered this afternoon?"

"It was," she confirms. "It's so pretty, Georgie. And huge. I love it. I can't wait to host big dinners around it. And to pick out some new table settings."

"Good, babe," I say. "I want you to love it and to be excited."

"Tell him what else," Roddy prompts.

"Oh, yeah," Ali says. "My office in D.C. called me to ask for guidance on a case. I only talked to them on the phone for a short time, but it felt so good to be needed and to be part of the professional world for a little while. You know what I mean?"

"I think I do," I reply. "That's great, babe. Excellent news."

"I think I know what you mean, too" Mom adds as she walks over and gives Ali a hug. "Good to see you, dear."

Ali takes a step away from me and turns to address Mom. It's getting crowded in this small space. I hope the rooms at the hospice house are bigger.

"How are you holding up?" Ali asks.

"Like I told Dr. Madera a little while ago, I guess I'm doing as well as can be expected," Mom answers.

"I understand," Ali reassures.

Mom looks like she's going to add something else, but her phone rings and she suddenly blushes when she sees who is calling. "Um, sorry, but... excuse me, I have to take this," she says as she walks quickly out of the room, fumbling with her phone and almost tripping on the door frame along the way. When the door is closed behind her, the rest of us look at each other inquisitively to see if anyone knows what that was all about.

"That was weird," I begin.

"She looked a little like a giddy teenager just now," Liam says. "Remember, I knew her back when she actually was a giddy teenager in love with Alec."

"You think that's what she's like in love?" Ali inquires as she smiles broadly. "She's awkward like my Georgie."

"I don't know," Liam answers. "But something about the look on her face definitely reminds me of the days when she and Alec were young, infatuated kids."

"Go, Linette," Roddy says with a chuckle. "Get 'em, tiger."

Ali laughs, but a contraction seizes her midway through and makes her gasp. She puts one hand on her lower belly and reaches out for me with the other as she breathes through it. The mood in the room suddenly gets more serious. Roddy takes the coat and bag off his daughter's arm and sets them down on a chair. John Wendell continues to sleep and snore and I wonder if we're bothering him. I have a hunch he kind of likes having us here and bustling around him though. They say people who aren't conscious still perceive what's happening around them. Based on the metaphysical experiences I've had lately, I'd tend to believe that's probably true. I'm glad to have John Wendell here and listening to what's going on with the family for as long as he wants to stay.

Liam offers to track down Dr. Isabel Madera and is on his way out of the room when we hear another knock on the door. It's her, thank goodness.

"I have those discharge and transfer orders," Isabel says proudly. "And in record time. They sympathized with my pleas to help get you folks settled before the storm."

"Excellent," I say. "We're grateful."

I hastily introduce Isabel to Roddy and then we get down to business regarding my wife's contractions. Liam and Roddy make note of the hospice house location and promise to meet us there if they have the opportunity to go along with Mom and John Wendell before Ali and I are finished. I'm glad. I want to see Mom and John Wendell have plenty of support. I'm appreciative of my family members stepping in to be there for them even though they aren't direct relatives. Now to focus on what my wife needs. I pick up her coat and bag to carry with me.

Ali and I explain our predicament and desire to avoid the E.R. to Isabel. We emphasize the fact that we're most likely dealing with run of the mill Braxton Hicks contractions. Isabel takes us to a private exam room and starts a chart by asking a lot of questions. Once she's satisfied that we probably don't belong in the E.R., she agrees to examine Ali. We'd been planning to use Isabel as our family physician anyway, so she's simply getting started a little early.

The exam room is dimly lit and not all that different from the hypnotherapy room at Dr. Epstein's office. We're in a part of the building which isn't typically utilized in the evening and it looks like most people have gone home for the weekend. I'm sure the incoming weather incentivized day shift employees to pack up and get out even earlier than usual. We don't mind. It's nice and quiet.

Ali knows the drill. This is her third pregnancy, after all. Before Isabel can even ask, Ali takes her jeans and panties off and positions herself on the exam table so Isabel can check her cervix.

"Oh," Isabel says when she sees my wife's positioning. "You don't have to lay flat on your back like that, Ali. It isn't the most comfortable position to be in when a contraction hits. How about you stand up at the end of the table and sort of squat a little while lifting one leg up? That will feel much better."

Ali agrees and moves into a standing position with one leg up like Isabel suggests. This is new, but Ali is open to it. It's not much different than the squatting the midwives in D.C. had her try during her previous labors and deliveries.

When I see my wife's naked bottom and glorious long legs standing exposed beside Isabel, the blood surges again and in an instant, I'm aroused. It's embarrassing, really. But I can't seem to help it. Isabel isn't wearing a lab coat or a name tag. Nothing that would distinguish her as a doctor if you didn't know who she was. She's clothed in a sheer pink blouse which clings to her round breasts and sits neatly against her trim, muscular back. Her long, wavy hair falls delicately around her shoulders and chest, dancing as she moves, and it's not difficult to imagine what her exposed torso must look like. In a flash, I image Ali unbuttoning Isabel's blouse and then her own as they press their supple breasts against each other. I try and tell myself to stop it.

I watch the exam begin in front of me as Isabel moves her hands lightly over Ali's forearms and guides her into position, then slowly reaches down and places her soft, delicate fingers on Ali's labia, which is engorged with blood thanks to pregnancy hormones. Isabel is wearing gloves, of course, but Ali arches her back and closes her eyes for a second at Isabel's touch. I'll bet her touch is soft and that it feels much different than a man's touch does. I wonder if Ali likes it. Ali shoots me a look to see how I'm feeling and I smile and nod to indicate my approval. My wife is apparently enjoying what's happening because she allows herself to close her eyes and bite her lip as Isabel explores her vagina and cervix. Isabel seems to be enjoying herself as well because she has stepped closer to my wife and has tilted her long, graceful neck to one side. She's breathing in deeply and seems to be sampling my wife's scent as she places her free hand on Ali's bare hip.

This is so incredibly hot. I'm liking this scene more than I can adequately express. I always thought I might be jealous at the sight of my wife being pleasured by someone other than myself— exam or not— but where Isabel Madera is concerned, I want to see more. My imagination is running wild now. I want to watch these two lovely ladies as they enjoy and explore each other's beautiful bodies. I imagine them both completely naked, Isabel leaning down and taking my wife's breast into her mouth just like I did last night. I want to see the bounce of Isabel's breasts and the grinding of her taut buttocks in the air as her soft, delicate mouth envelopes the entire area between my wife's legs while Ali screams out with unbridled pleasure. If we weren't in a hospital, I'd put my hand in my pants and pleasure myself right now just thinking about it. I need a release.

"Okay," Isabel says, removing her hands from Ali's body and snapping me back to reality. "You're three centimeters dilated and sixty percent effaced. That's not unusual for someone at this point in their third pregnancy." She pulls a pregnancy wheel out of her bag to calculate an exact gestational age.

"I checked my calendar this afternoon and it looks like I'll hit the thirty-seven-week mark tomorrow," Ali adds.

"That's right," Isabel says. "And thirty-seven weeks is considered full term."

"Wow," I say. "So much has been going on that I completely lost track of that fact."

"Me, too, Georgie," Ali says. "Ethan and Leo were both born right around their due dates. I guess that's what I expected with little Will as well."

"Makes sense," Isabel confirms. "You're not in active labor yet, but more than likely you won't go all the way to your due date. How far apart are your contractions?"

"Still pretty far apart," Ali says. "I haven't really been timing them because I think the closest two were something like six or seven minutes apart."

"Okay," Isabel confirms. "So, I think you're fine for now, Ali. Take it easy as much as possible this weekend, and call me if the contractions last thirty to sixty seconds each and occur every five minutes. You have an appointment at the birth center on Monday morning anyway, correct?"

"Correct," Ali replies.

"I know the midwives over there fairly well," Isabel adds. "If you should go into labor over the weekend, I'll personally call and talk to them about allowing you to deliver at the birth center instead of the hospital.

You meet all of their requirements for a low-risk pregnancy and you have a proven pelvis given your previous vaginal births with your older sons. And now I've examined you. I don't see any reason for them to turn you away."

"I appreciate that, Dr. Madera. Thank you," Ali says.

"To be clear," I inquire, "you think Ali could actually go into labor this weekend?"

"She could," Isabel replies.

"Wow," I say quietly as Ali and I look at each other in disbelief. It's hard to envision little Will arriving this early. And with everything going on. I keep saying the word everything as if it adequately explains the magnitude of what's happening in my life right now. It doesn't.

We thank Isabel Madera again and head back to John Wendell's room only to find out that he has already been transported to the hospice house. I check my phone and, sure enough, Liam has texted to let me know the rest of the gang is on their way over. They're following behind the ambulance. I really need to figure out why my phone isn't vibrating to alert me of calls and texts when I have the ringer turned off. I'll add it to my growing list of things to do. I reply back to say that Ali and I are finished and will meet them there.

I suggest walking through the desolate clinic section of the hospital on our way out to the car, and Ali agrees. We don't say it out loud, but we both have lovemaking in mind. We find a small unisex restroom with a single door. We enter the bathroom and lock the latch behind us without turning on the light. We peel each other's clothes off as much as necessary for me to enter my wife from behind and reach around to grip her perky breasts while I push. I thrust hard and fast. We climax quickly. When we're finished, we piece ourselves back together and walk out of the building holding hands. Neither of us mentions Isabel Madera. We don't have to.

## 12

## GEORGE: THE DAWN

When a baby is truly loved and when they're treated in every moment of their infancy and childhood like they're valuable beyond measure, they learn to treat themselves that way and they don't allow anyone into their adult lives who won't do the same. They'll find and make good friends who will have their backs through thick and thin. They'll marry loving partners who will honor and cherish them for decades. They'll raise kind children who will grow up to advocate for and protect them as they age. On their deathbeds one day, they'll lay still and solemn, ready to journey on the next invisible leg of this existence, and they'll know, deep down, how valuable they are. They'll know how valuable their precious life has been. They'll ask for and receive the kindest loving care. They'll believe they deserve it. Their loved ones will gather around and usher them into the unknown, and they'll go forth, knowing full well that they are wonderful, beautiful, valuable beings. And it all begins in the baby bed.

John Wendell was born in the nineteen twenties as part of the Greatest Generation. I never met his parents, but he says they were the ones who deserved to be known as the greatest. The love and affection they showed him provided a solid foundation which allowed him to find a great love in his Eleanor and to share that love with Mom. In turn, Mom found Dad and passed that love down to me, then I found Ali and together we are passing it on to our boys. It's awe-inspiring to think about how the loving environment which little Will is about to be born into has roots going all the way back to people I never met who cared for my precious John Wendell when he was a baby. He reminds me of an infant now, small and vulnerable in his bed. In a way, he's preparing to be born, the same as little Will is.

Heavy snow has begun to fall and it's blustery outside. Inside, the hospice house is warm and peaceful. We can't fully appreciate the scenery out the big windows in John Wendell's room yet because it's too dark, but I'm sure sunrise will be beautiful. The hospice nurse on duty, Gloria, brought in a couple of wireless speakers that work with electronic devices. Liam took charge of cueing up some of John Wendell's favorite songs and has *Dream a Little Dream* playing quietly in the background. The Bing Crosby version, of course. Roddy stopped by Mom's house on the way over from the hospital and picked some things up. Mom had already packed two bags which were waiting by the front door: one for herself and one for John Wendell. It looks odd to see my grandfather's clothing, shoes, and coat all stacked neatly on top of a dresser here in his room at the hospice house. He's clothed in his own pajamas now, but he won't be wearing any of the rest ever again. That realization sends a pang through my chest and puts a knot in my stomach. I hope I'm ready.

Gloria seems great. She's a Caucasian woman with what looks like naturally blonde hair cut neatly into a chin-length bob. White strands are interspersed with the blonde ones, but it doesn't seem like she's trying to hide them. I've always admired women who age gracefully and let their hair fade rather than hiding behind chemical color which they have to go into the salon and get touched up every two weeks. There are strength and a beauty in being willing to be yourself and being proud of your age. Women tend to think us guys like all of the fake color and adornment, but I know I, for one, prefer a more natural look. I hope Ali will let her hair fade rather than coloring it as she grows older. I'd guess that Gloria is somewhere in between mine and Liam's age. Probably closer to his age, but it's hard to tell with any degree of certainty. She has a midwestern accent and a kind smile. Sounds like Minnesota. I'll have to ask her where she's from when I have a chance.

It must take a special type of person to work with hospice patients on a day to day basis. I imagine tending to people as they die is an honor, but I'll bet it's emotionally and spiritually draining. The experience is such a vulnerable one for the patient. I knew a hospice worker years ago who told me people die as they live. Some have beautiful, peaceful deaths surrounded by loved ones, while others have fitful, jagged, fearful deaths. There are six bedrooms in this particular hospice house, so six is their max capacity at any given time. I wonder if the beds stay full or if they have lulls where there are fewer patients to care for. I'm guessing the former.

It's dinner time and we're hungry, so after a brief discussion about whether or not we should eat in front of John Wendell, we decide to order something in. Gloria assures us that John Wendell won't mind. She says if he's hungry, it's fine for him to eat. Besides, there's a big table in the common room we can eat at if we prefer. Most likely though, he won't be interested in our food or in eating. She explains how as part of the dying process, the body no longer needs to eat. She says it's hard on the family to see their loved one refusing food and drink, but that the patient truly doesn't feel hungry or thirsty and doesn't need the physical nourishment anymore. She asks if we received the blue booklet, then brings us a couple of extra copies upon hearing that we only have one.

We decide on delivery from Pepperoni Parlor. Maybe it's because they're new in town and want to build a base of loyal customers, but they're still delivering in the snow even though some other places have shut down for the night. We enjoyed the food when we were there last, so we're glad they're willing to take care of us. Mom hasn't tried them yet. Roddy coordinates our order like a pro and happily pays over the phone for a sumptuous spread of salad, mozzarella sticks, spinach and artichoke dip, meatballs in marinara, deep dish pizza, calzones, baked ziti, and chocolate cake for dessert. He calls Marjorie, who agrees to bring the boys and meet us at the hospice house for dinner. We want Ethan and Leo to have a chance to see John Wendell anyway. Marjorie has no problem driving in the snow. She kind of likes it, actually. Jen and Duke are going to spend the evening at our house to tend to Lady. I sure do appreciate all of the support. I know Mom is used to being by herself with John Wendell. I hope she isn't overwhelmed by my expansive crew. So far, she seems to be appreciating them, too.

Marjorie and the boys arrive first and I greet them in the common room. I want to make sure we aren't too rowdy so as not to disturb John Wendell, but I also want to prep the boys a little before they go in to see him. I kiss my mother-in-law on the cheek as both of my sons leap into my arms. You'd think I'd been gone for weeks as excited as they are to see me. The feeling is mutual. I adore these little guys. I'm especially glad to see Ethan safe and sound given what I remembered this afternoon at Dr. Epstein's and how it connects to the break-in. It's a surreal feeling to look into the eyes of my children and know we were all together previously, in Greece. I wonder if Leo remembers being a soldier with me. And I'm eager to tell Ethan that I remember what happened, too. Not to mention telling Marjorie. I'm extremely interested in the two psychiatrists she referenced. All of that will have to wait until another time though. We're here for John Wendell and we have no idea yet what's going to happen with Ali and little Will. I'm beginning to develop a hunch that little Will is ready to make his appearance. I'm thinking the comment John Wendell made to Isabel about us having a baby on the way might ought to be taken literally. Isn't it plausible that John Wendell and Will could communicate, I don't know— telepathically, since they both have one foot in another dimension right now? Maybe they've known each other before, in another time and place. I suspect we're all connected.

Dinner arrives right behind my family. Ethan and Leo cheer as Marjorie and I take the food from the delivery lady and begin to open it up on the big table. These two are easily entertained. We should all move through life with their level of enthusiasm. And to think, Ethan suffered horrible trauma in Greece and a damn scary incident last weekend, yet he is somehow resilient enough to find joy in dinner being delivered. Are we all that resilient in the grand scheme of things? Or do some of us hang on to hurts and trauma more perilously than others, crossing time and space to settle scores and right wrongs? I have so many questions about life and the Universe. So much to learn. And I'd venture a guess that no human being will ever have all the answers. I think it's beyond us to comprehend.

Roddy, Liam, and Mom come out to join us for dinner. Mom wants to stay beside John Wendell, but Gloria encourages her to take care of herself by getting a good meal and talking about something else, even if only for a few minutes. John Wendell's tired from all the hubbub at the hospital anyway and Gloria expects him to sleep soundly for a while. She promises to let us know if he wakes up.

We eat and we talk, mostly about John Wendell and the fun times we've had together. Roddy, Marjorie, and Liam do more listening than talking since they haven't known him as well as the rest of us, but even they have stories to share. I guess that's a testament to the kind of man my grandfather is. He touches every single person he meets. He has a good-natured demeanor about him that draws people in. He never met a stranger, as the saying goes. Roddy tells us how much he's inspired by John Wendell and Grandma's dancing and how he was serious when he said he would have written them into one of his plays. He says maybe he still will somehow, posthumously. We all agree John Wendell would love that. Ethan and Leo clap zealously at the idea after they see how happy it makes us adults. We're finishing dinner when Ali gets up and heads toward the bathroom without saying a word. She's walking kind of funny. Roddy, Marjorie, and I glance at each other and take a collective deep breath. Marjorie gestures for me to follow my wife and see what's happening.

"Ali, babe," I say as I knock lightly on the bathroom door. It's a small unisex restroom with a single door just like the one we enjoyed a couple of hours ago, only this time I suspect something much different is happening inside.

"Georgie," Ali whines in response. I can tell she's in pain.

"Babe, open the door," I say. "Let me help you."

"I think my water broke," she adds. "And I just had a mean contraction…"

"Everything's alright," I say while motioning to Marjorie and Roddy to come here. "Ali, open up the door. I'm here and so are your parents."

"I'm trying, Georgie," my wife mews. "I'm sitting on the floor and it's a mess in here. It hurts to try and stand up. I'm having another…." Her voice trails off as it turns into a groan.

"Roddy," I say as he and Marjorie reach me. "Please call Dr. Madera. Her number is saved on my phone. Tell her Ali's water broke and that she's having strong contractions."

"Got it," Roddy says, stepping outdoors onto the front walkway in order to talk as loud as needed without being disruptive in the hospice house.

"And Marjorie," I begin.

"I know," she inserts. "Let's take care of our girl. We're right here, George. We're ready." Tears bubble up in my eyes. I'm so grateful for our extended family. They truly are the best. These are the moments we'll remember all of our lives. My heart is full.

Ali manages to stand up and open the door just as the rest of our crew gets the idea that something is going on and begins to gather around us. I wrap my arms around my wife and help support her weight. I can see that her belly looks different. Little Will looks almost shrink-wrapped in there now that the amniotic fluid has drained out. This didn't happen with Ethan or Leo. With each of those guys, Ali's water broke sometime after she was already in labor and drained out more slowly. It wasn't such a sudden change.

"Daddy, is baby Will coming out now?" Ethan asks.

"Yes, son, he is on his way," I answer. "He'll be here very soon."

The entire family breaks out into enthusiastic cheering and clapping at the good news. I wonder if the walls of this hospice house have ever seen such a celebration. Ethan and Leo clasp hands and jump up and down gleefully.

"Leo," Ethan says proudly. "Now you'll be a big brother, like me!"

"Yay!" Leo says happily, prancing around the room.

"We have to get Mommy to someone who can help her deliver him," I add, as Roddy's walks back in the front door with a big smile on his face. "What's the word?" I ask.

"Dr. Madera had a feeling Ali would go into labor soon," Roddy explains. "So she went ahead and called the midwives after seeing you at the hospital. Ali is cleared to deliver at the birth center. They're expecting her now."

"Thank goodness," Ali says between heavy breaths. I can tell she's as excited as the rest of us, but she has hard work ahead of her and has to focus inward.

"That's such great news," I say. "Looks like we're

having a baby tonight!" Tears of happiness fill my eyes and stream down my cheeks. I love my family. I can't wait to hold little Will in my arms and smell his sweet newborn scent. And to look into his wise eyes. He's probably been with us before. What a joy it will be to welcome him home again.

"You go, dear," Mom says as she comes over to hug my neck. "Don't worry about us here. I'm going to spend the night in John Wendell's room."

"Ok, Mom," I say. "I had hoped to spend the night with you…"

"No need," she inserts. "Go welcome my littlest grandson into the world. And take the very best care of our Ali." I nod as I kiss the top of her head and give her shoulder a squeeze.

"I'm staying here," Liam adds. "Gloria says there's a guest room I can stay in. I'll be out of Linette and John Wendell's way, but here in case they need me."

"Thank you, dear brother-in-law," Mom says.

"Yes, Liam," I add. "I appreciate you more than you'll ever know."

"The feeling is mutual, buddy," my uncle replies as an extra burst of tears wells up in my eyes.

"The mess?" Ali manages to ask.

"I'll take care of that, too," Liam says. "I'm sure Gloria will help me out. Don't you worry about it."

"Okay, how are we going to do this?" I say as I look at Roddy and Marjorie. "The boys?"

"We've got them," Roddy says. "We'll drive you and Ali to the birth center and bring the boys along."

"Yay!" Ethan and Leo cheer. We had planned all

along to have them at the birth center when Will is born. We don't have anything prepared for tonight, really, but with Roddy and Marjorie's help, we should be able to manage. There's no time for them to see John Wendell now, which saddens me. Hopefully tomorrow.

"Then it's settled," I say. "Let's get to the car, and we'll be on our way."

Roddy guides Ali out to the Tesla and buckles her up while I step away for a minute to tell my grandfather goodbye. My steps are quick as I walk down the hall and I can't help but feel out of place. I doubt anyone walks this quickly here. I've got to hurry though. I slow my pace a little as I reach John Wendell's room and the gravity of his situation hits me like a lead weight. I wonder if he'll be here when I get back. The birth centers usually let you go home within a few hours, assuming no complications. I'd like to bring Will to meet his great-grandfather.

"John Wendell," I say quietly as I take my grandfather's hand. He stirs and opens his eyes to look at me, but doesn't respond verbally. "Little Will is on the way," I continue. "Ali is in labor. I have to leave for a while to go to the birth center." It takes him a minute to register the information, but when he does he smiles broadly and nods his head emphatically, then pushes my hand away as if to tell me to go ahead. "I'll be back here as soon as I can," I say as I kiss his forehead. "Mom and Liam are staying with you." He nods again, clearly understanding what's happening. For some reason, it doesn't seem like he can speak though. I'll have to check the blue booklet to find out if that's a normal part of the dying process. I hug Mom and Liam again and rush out of the room and down the hall, waving to Gloria as I hurry past. She'll take good care of my grandfather, I know it.

I allow myself to leave the heaviness of the hospice house behind as I jog to the Tesla and jump in the backseat behind Ali. Roddy is driving so that I can reach forward and help comfort Ali on the ride. Her contractions are coming hard and heavy now, keeping pace with the snow falling around us. The scene is ethereal. Marjorie has the boys all buckled into their car seats in the third row and she's seated beside me. Our excitement is building and I almost feel bad for being so animated when Ali's in pain. But, little Will is coming. Our son. Another member of our circle. And he has quite a crowd here to welcome him. The happiness is so full and round and palpable that it feels like it's bursting right out of me. I love my family so very much.

The birth center is relatively close to the hospice house. I guess in a way that makes sense. They're both portals, for coming and going into and out of this life. From a spiritual perspective, they should be in close proximity, right? Birth centers are required to be located very near hospitals in case of complications during delivery. Maybe hospice houses are, too, for transport in and out? At any rate, the ride down the hill is smooth and easy. Very few cars are on the roads. When we arrive, Isabel Madera is waiting for us. Roddy pulls right up to the curb and Isabel greets Ali,

Marjorie, and I as we get out of the SUV and walk into the building. Roddy will bring the boys in and keep them occupied until we're ready for them to join us in the birthing suite.

"I had a feeling I'd be hearing from you two again soon," Isabel says.

"You were right," Ali says between groans. Contractions are gripping her almost constantly now. Her labor has intensified rapidly.

"Let's get you inside," Isabel says, waving us in. "I'll introduce you to Mama, the midwife on call tonight, and Sahima, her assistant."

"Mama?" I ask. "Is that her name?"

"It is," Isabel confirms. "She's from Ghana and Mama is a name given to baby girls born on a Saturday. You're going to love her. Everyone does."

"Nice," I say.

"It looks like your baby will be born on a Saturday, too. If he waits until after midnight, that is," Isabel says. "He and Mama may have something in common already."

The inside of the birth center strikes me as remarkably similar to the hospice house. There's a common room, four birthing suites, a nurse's desk, an office, and a kitchen where families can make meals if they like. No other patients of the birth center are in labor tonight, so we get the run of the place. Isabel ushers us into a large birthing suite closest to the back door and nurse's desk. It's a huge room with sliding glass doors that look out over the countryside, very similar to the ones in John Wendell's room. I'll bet the sunrise will be beautiful.

Our room has a large tub for water birth, which Ali is elated to learn. She wanted a water birth with Leo, but the tub in the room he was born in ended up too narrow. She labored in the tub and wanted to stay there for delivery. She ultimately had to get out of the tub and walk to the bed to deliver though, and it was extremely uncomfortable to shift positions at that point. I think she was in the hardest phase of labor called transition when they moved her. It looked miserable. Hopefully, she can labor and deliver in the tub tonight. This tub is huge. Ali makes a beeline for the tub the minute she lays eyes on it as if it's calling to her. Sahima comes in and introduces herself, then proceeds to fill the tub as Marjorie helps Ali get undressed. Ali's wearing a maternity bra that looks a lot like a sports bra today anyway. She seems fine with stripping down to bra-only in front of everyone. I learned back when Ethan was born that a pregnant woman in labor loses all concern about modesty. It's just not the time or place to be embarrassed. She has work to do.

Ali labors and delivers her babies without the aid of drugs. Of course, something could go wrong which would necessitate medical intervention, but so far so good. Ethan and Leo were delivered vaginally and without drugs, so we have solid reason to believe the same will happen now as she delivers little Will. It's impressive to see Ali go through the labor and delivery process like a gladiator, strong and determined to do the hard work all on her own. Not to slight any woman who needs intervention, because I realize it usually can't be avoided if that's the way things play out, but watching Ali do what she does is extraordinary. I have that wife.

Sahima is a twenty-something graduate student from India doing an internship in nurse-midwifery. She's pretty, cheerful, and she seems eager to participate. Some student interns are hesitant and tentative, but not Sahima. She's jumping in confidently. Maybe she's been around awhile and is nearing the end of her training. We instantly know she's going to take good care of Ali and Will. When we compliment her bedside manner, she tells us that midwifery and natural childbirth are standard practice in her country. She explains how she has had an interest in assisting laboring mothers since she was a young girl and how she has attended hundreds of births already. She came to the U.S. to get American credentials and cement her career. Her big, brown eyes and sweet smile exude warmth. We can trust her. We're in capable hands.

Mama comes in to introduce herself and we can instantly tell why someone as gifted as Sahima would want to study under her. Like Gloria, she's somewhere between mine and Liam's ages. Probably closer to his. She has a calm, powerful presence which fills up the room. I get the feeling she tends her end of the life-giving portal with the utmost dedication. She speaks slowly and deliberately. She walks with such smooth, fluid motions that it almost looks like she's floating.

Her skin is a rich, dark ebony color and her limbs are long and graceful. She's stunning. I wasn't kidding when I said I tend to be surrounded by beautiful women. I think we're in the very best hands here. What are the odds that we'd get Gloria, Sahima, and Mama to take care of our family on this special, snowy night? I can't imagine any alternatives being as phenomenal. The certainty of finding ourselves in the right place at the right time washes over me. I'm grateful.

I hear Roddy and the boys out in the common area now. They have their toy bags and they adore their Papa Roddy. It may end up being a late night for them, but I know they'll be fine while Marjorie and I tend to Ali. We'll bring them in the suite when it's time for Will to be born if they're still awake. In the meantime, though, they'll play out there and will go to sleep when they're ready.

In the birthing suite, it's time to get down to business. We dim the overhead lights and place candles near the tub where Ali lays laboring. The room is warm and the water is hot enough to help ease her contractions. We can see the snow still coming down hard out the back windows. It's lovely.

"Can I put on any music for you?" Sahima asks.

Ali is too preoccupied to answer, so we do it for her.

"Cello," Marjorie and I say at the same time. Ali opens her eyes long enough to look at each of us and smile.

"Ali plays the cello," I say. "Do you have any cello music?"

"How about the Unaccompanied Cello Suites by Bach?" Marjorie asks. "If you have Yo-Yo Ma, that would be amazing," she adds with a smile. She doesn't tell Sahima she knows the man or that she plays viola in the New York Philharmonic.

"We can arrange it," Sahima says as she reaches for her mobile phone which is already connected to the speaker system. She smiles as she cues up suite number one with Yo-Yo Ma beginning his intrepid rise and fall. Ali's entire body relaxes when she hears the music.

"That hits the spot," Ali says.

"Thank you, Sahima," Marjorie says. "What exquisite sounds for birthing and being born on this magical night."

"I couldn't agree more," I say. "Everything is perfect."

Mama comes over and uses a doppler on Ali's belly between contractions to monitor Will's heartbeat. She asks us some questions to confirm what Isabel notated in Ali's new chart, then goes over a few key details in the records our D.C. midwives shared. Once everything checks out to her satisfaction, she gives Ali the go-ahead to let her body progress as it wishes.

In a quick turn I'd find almost hard to believe if I wasn't seeing it with my own eyes, Ali reacts immediately to Mama's permission to progress. She begins to instinctively move and stretch as if she's performing an intricate dance only she knows the steps to. The pace quickens to a fever pitch as she shakes and twists and moans a primal moan. My wife looks like the most beautiful, the most powerful, and the most awe-inspiring creature in this entire world right now. She's taking part in an ancient ritual, bringing forth life itself. Nothing is more miraculous. When she's ready to push, she asks Mama if it's okay. Mama does a quick check of her cervix and gives the go-ahead. Ali is fully dilated and effaced. Little Will is ready to join us and we have the approval to stay in the birthing tub for the duration.

"Roddy," I call out as I stand and step near the closed door of the suite. "Come on in and bring the boys if they're awake! It's time."

Marjorie positions herself on the far side of the tub and strokes Ali's arm as she whispers encouraging words in her daughter's ear. I walk back towards the tub, unsure of where I should be.

"You want to get in?" Mama asks.

"In the tub?" I clarify.

"Yes, Georgie, get in," Ali says emphatically. "Hold me."

"Do as she asks, George," Mama says.

"Of course, babe," I say to my wife. "I'm coming in right now."

Ali continues to heave and groan as I strip down to my underwear and climb into the tub behind her. I'm not concerned about modesty right now either. I want to be with my wife and fully present for this visceral experience. I wrap my arms tight around her chest and provide a steady frame for her to hold onto.

Mama lowers her hand to check Will's progress as Roddy, Ethan, and Leo burst in the door like a crowd at a surprise party. Their excitement is surging out of them and cannot be contained. They take a spot near the bottom end of the tub with a good view of what's happening and cling to each other with pure glee.

It doesn't take long for Will to make his way down the birth canal. Before we know it, Mama announces that his head is crowning. Ali waits as instructed while Mama makes sure it's okay for her to keep bearing down with the contraction. When she gets the all clear to journey the final leg, Ali pushes with every ounce of her might. I reach my hand down and feel my son's little head as it emerges from my wife's body. This is amazing. What a gift to be right here, right now. Mama eases little Will gently up and out of the water then places him in Ali's arms. He's beautiful! He has red hair like Mom and Marjorie. I already love him so very much. Sahima moves to Mama's side and places a stack of towels and a stethoscope on a table beside the tub. Then she suctions his nose and mouth gently using a bulb syringe. The water we're sitting in is a bloody mess, but we don't care. Marjorie kisses her daughter on the head and congratulates her for on a job well done, then moves to jump up and down at the end of the tub with Roddy, Ethan, and Leo. Yo-Yo Ma is still emoting on the cello. The joy in this birthing suite is off the charts.

"He waited until just after midnight," Mama says with a smile. "Sahima, what time did you record?"

"12:02 am," Sahima answers. "January 30th."

"He's born on a Saturday, just like me," Mama adds, sounding proud.

"Thank you so much, Mama," Ali says through tears of happiness. "You and Sahima have been so good to us."

"It's what we do, child," Mama says.

"What's his full name?" Sahima asks. "For the birth certificate."

Oddly enough, we've been so distracted that we haven't talked about a middle name for little Will yet. Without so much as glancing at me, Ali answers: "John William Hartmann. After our beloved John Wendell. We'll call him Will, but John will be his proper name."

Upon hearing this, I begin to cry big, ugly tears. I'm overcome with emotion. The good, the bad, and everything in between encircle me as I sob. "Perfect," I manage. Little Will looks up at us and seems to approve. I can see the depth and wisdom in his eyes. Ali brings him to her breast and he begins to nurse. He's strong. And healthy. We are blessed.

When you deliver with midwives at a birth center you can go home a few hours afterward, assuming no complications for mom or baby. That's one of the benefits of having a natural birth without drugs. Marjorie educated us while Ali was pregnant with Ethan. The mom is exhausted after a natural birth, but well enough to leave. Tonight, I'm especially glad for this particular perk because I need to get back to my grandfather at the hospice house. Once Ali has had some time to gather her strength, she and I shower while Mama and Sahima do a complete exam on little Will. Mama has an infant car seat she lets us borrow until we see her at our follow-up appointment Monday morning. She also gives us diapers, a couple of onesies, a hat, and several warm blankets. We ask her if she thinks it's okay to take Will to the hospice house to meet John Wendell, given the urgency of the situation. She runs down a list of precautions to take with germs and emphasizes her recommendation that we don't let strangers anywhere near our newborn. No passing the baby around, regardless of how eager people are to touch and hold him. We completely agree. We wouldn't let that happen anyway. Once we promise to be extra vigilant, Mama gives her okay. We say our grateful goodbyes and bundle up, then pile into the Tesla.

Snow continues to fall as we make our way back up the hill to the hospice house. We haven't called Mom or Liam yet to tell them little Will is here. Normally, we would have, but under these circumstances, we figure we'll introduce them to our baby boy in person. It's late into the night and there are even fewer people than before out on the roads. The sun will be coming up soon. For now, though, Ithaca is an untouched winter wonderland. We go slowly and carefully. Roddy drives while Marjorie rides in the passenger seat. Ali and I fill the middle seats with little Will in Mama's car seat in between us. Ethan and Leo reclaim their spots in the back. They slept briefly while we showered, but they're awake again. There's a stillness amongst us. No one makes a sound. It's as if we all know what's going to happen when we arrive.

Gloria welcomes us in with a warm smile. She's nearly at the end of a twelve-hour shift and she's looking tired.

"Well, I must say," she begins when she sees little Will in Ali's arms, "this is a first. Look at that beautiful baby" She doesn't get too close or try to touch him. She's a nurse. She knows better. "Come on in. Linette and John Wendell will be glad you're back. Liam is asleep in the guest room."

"Thanks, Gloria," I say with a smile. I wonder if she knows Mama and Sahima. Shouldn't all the portal-tenders know each other?

I head towards John Wendell's room to see how he is. The rest of my family waits in the common area. They'll come to the room once I tell them it's alright to do so. Gloria walks with me.

"Things have progressed quite a bit since you've been gone," she tells me. "He's having some trouble breathing. Truth be told, I think he's been waiting on you to get back here."

My heart sinks as I reach the door to my grandfather's room. I hope I'm ready. I open the door and step inside to see Mom dozing lightly in the chair beside the bed. John Wendell's there, but he looks somehow worse than he did just a few hours ago. I find myself watching his chest to see if he's breathing.

"George, dear," Mom says as she jerks awake. "I'm glad you're back."

"He looks rough," I say before I've had time to

consider whether or not I should be talking like that right here in front of John Wendell.

"I know," she says. "We're close."

"And to think we were talking about hip surgery, what, fourteen hours ago?" I muse.

"I was in denial," Mom replies. "But I've known ever since last Sunday. I just didn't want it to be true."

"I get it," I say as I walk around the bed to embrace my mom. John Wendell is sleeping hard and looks completely out of it. Smooth jazz is playing quietly in the background, but I'm not sure he's hearing it.

"Did my newest grandson arrive?" Mom asks.

"He sure did," I answer. "He's a big boy. Eight pounds, six ounces. And he has red hair like yours."

Upon hearing the news, John Wendell opens his eyes and smiles at me, then points to himself insistently. He wants me to bring Will in to see him. "I'll be right back, grandfather," I say as I walk quickly out of the room to get the rest of my family. I don't usually call John Wendell grandfather. For some reason, it feels right this time.

I return hurriedly with the gang following behind. Liam has emerged from the guest room and he joins in, too. We pile in the room and fill every available space as the first hints of sunrise begin to show themselves. It's almost time for shift change, so Gloria and her replacement, Angela, pack in as well. I think they want to see John Wendell meet his great-grandson.

"A baker's dozen," John Wendell says, clear as day,

while pointing to the group of us. We laugh and he seems to be glad to lighten the mood. That's John Wendell for you. He will find the positive and a way to enjoy the present moment no matter what's happening.

"Just like last Saturday at Yellow Cob," I confirm. "You're exactly right."

I bring Ethan and Leo to see him first. Ethan climbs right onto the side of John Wendell's bed without hesitation. I hold Leo in my arms and lean down so he can get close as well.

"Daddy?" Ethan begins while gazing intently into his great-grandfather's eyes.

"Yes, son," I say. "What is it?"

"He's all done with his body," Ethan says, matter-of-factly. Leave it to the four-year-old to lay it all out there. John Wendell doesn't mind though. He nods his head yes, then leans his forehead against Ethan's like he did mine last night. They stay like that for a minute. It's one of the most touching things I've ever witnessed. It's like they understand each other completely. They're communicating without words. "He'll get a new one when he's ready," Ethan continues. "He's not scared." Again, John Wendell nods in agreement. Leo lurches forward and gently kisses his great-grandfather on the cheek, then both boys climb down from the bed and walk over to Roddy to sit on his lap.

When John Wendell sees Ali walking towards him with little Will in her arms, his entire face lights up. He turns toward Mom and they share a happy, knowing look. She reaches for her father's hand and he grips hers back tightly as he beams at our beautiful addition to the family.

"Meet your newest great-grandson," Ali says as she lowers Will down on top of John Wendell's arms. He can't support Will's weight himself, but Ali positions the baby as if my grandfather is holding him on his own. Will looks deeply into John Wendell's eyes.

"Grandfather," I say through tears which are forcing themselves insistently down my cheeks. "His name is John William Hartmann, after the best man I know."

I don't think there's a dry eye in the room when John Wendell's eyebrows raise as he registers the significance of our baby's name. He points to himself again.

"That's right," I say. "The best man I know."

John Wendell looks at Mom again, then at me, then at Ali and the others in the room while wearing the biggest, most sincere smile I think I've ever seen on him. And that's saying a lot. Suddenly, he pushes Ali's arm lightly as his eyes begin to close. She lifts Will back up against her chest and steps back with the others. The sun peeks it's pink lines above the horizon to expose the snow-covered countryside as my grandfather takes one long, deep breath. And then nothing.

Life and death are profound. There's so much meaning in it all. Far more than what lies on the surface. I don't know what the rest of this life will bring. It's a hell of a ride. I don't know how I'll handle things as they come up or how I'll respond to the inevitable sadness that is a part of it all. I hope I'll remain willing to dig in and face any challenge when given an opportunity to find out what I'm made of.

What I do know, for sure, is that I'll continue this journey with my people by my side. We'll stand beside each other, fight for each other, and love each other fiercely. We'll go forward from here with love and hope and a commitment to savor every single thing that's beautiful in this precious, precious life. My grandfather would have wanted it that way.

## WHAT DID YOU THINK OF ITHACA'S SOLDIER?

Thank you for purchasing Ithaca's Soldier, Book One in the Love and Transience series. We hope you've enjoyed it.

Please **provide feedback for the author** by writing a review on Amazon and Goodreads. Your review is very important. It will help Kelly Utt-Grubb hone her craft and make future books even better.

Please **share this book with your friends and family** by posting a photo to Facebook, Twitter, or Instagram along with the hashtags #ithacassoldier and #loveandtransience.

# ACKNOWLEDGMENTS

My most sincere gratitude to my editor, Rebecca Raskin; to my talented cover artist, Ivan Kurylenko; to my friends and patrons, Jerry Stifelman, Sami Grover, Judy McKinley, Justin Noble, and Anne Marie Kempf; to my enthusiastic beta readers, Christy, Andrea, Jennifer, Natalie, Jim, Robin, Nichole, John, Emily, Laura, Angela, Libby, Rick, Priscilla, Christian, Judy, Vernawn, Whitney, Ronni, and Shavika; to my brother, Dan Utt, who helped with graphics, formatting, and emotional support; to my life-long friend and honorary sister, Crystal Palone, who has been a sounding board and cheerleader since we met in first grade; to my strong and tenacious long-time friend, Elizabeth Moise, for her love and encouragement over the years; to my adventurous friend, Susan Easter, for her warmth and willingness to journey with me; to my husband, Sam Utt-Grubb, my sons, Andrew Utt-Grubb and Christopher Utt-

Grubb, my father, David Utt, my grandfathers, Harold Francis and Cecil Staley, my uncles, Clinton Utt, Allen Utt, David Francis, and Dick Franco, my godfather, Anthony Serluco, and my father-in-law, Bruce Grubb, who have each shown me what being loved by good men is like in order that I could write about it; to my mom, Lucy Utt, my honorary grandmother, Evelynn DuBois, and the rest of my family and friends for the love and happiness they bring; and to my loyal animal companions, Ellie, the golden retriever, Pepper, the Llewellin setter, and Jack, the cat, who all sit at my feet as I write and remind me how beautiful it is to live in the moment, simply being in each other's presence.